the
spawning
grounds

the spawning grounds

GAIL ANDERSON-DARGATZ

Alfred A. Knopf Canada

PUBLISHED BY ALFRED A. KNOPF CANADA

Copyright © 2016 Gail Anderson-Dargatz

www.penguinrandomhouse.ca

Alfred A. Knopf Canada and colophon are registered trademarks.

Grateful acknowledgment is made for permission to reprint an excerpt from the foreword "The River Spirit" by Alan Haig-Brown in *Adam's River: The Mystery of the Adams River Sockeye* by Mark Hume (New Star Press, 1994). Reprinted by permission of the author, Alan Haig-Brown.

LIBRARY AND ARCHIVES CANADA CATALOGUING IN PUBLICATION

Anderson-Dargatz, Gail, 1963– , author
The spawning grounds / Gail Anderson-Dargatz.

Issued in print and electronic formats.

ISBN 978-0-345-81081-6
eBook ISBN 978-0-345-81083-0

I. Title.
PS8551.N3574S63 2016   C813'.54   C2016-902494-6

Book design by Kelly Hill
Cover images: (trees) © Seamartini Graphics, (wolf) © eva_mask, (antlers) © diana pryadieva, (salmon) © Ivan Kotliar, (background) © wawritto, all Shutterstock.com

Printed and bound in the United States of America

2   4   6   8   9   7   5   3   1

Penguin
Random House
KNOPF CANADA

For Hadarah,
Graham,
Jasper
and Lydia

Without the salmon, the land and the rivers
would only survive as a corpse survives
the death of the nervous system and
the departure of the spirit.

ALAN HAIG-BROWN

the
spawning
grounds

Advent

September 1857

EUGENE ROBERTSON WOKE in his tethered dugout to a thunderous rush, as if the river had let loose a flash flood upon the narrow valley floor. But the furor travelled upriver, not down, and the wave that lifted and pounded his boat was not made of water.

He sat up and peered into the current, then immediately recoiled: multitudes of dark forms swam under him. For a dream-laden moment, these strange spectres were the "water mysteries" the Indians had warned him of. Like the water sprites of his homeland, these spirits would drag a man down into their world, a land that in many ways mirrored this one but was home to creatures that were neither man nor beast, but both, as in the beginning. Pictographs of these spirits covered the cliff face upriver, above the narrows. Lichen and the roots of trees growing, incredibly, off the cliff surface, covered many of the images. One was still clearly visible, though, even to Eugene sitting in his dugout this far downriver: a huge zigzag painted on the cliff face, a red lightning bolt. A creature sprang from the lightning, part fish, part man, surrounded by sketches of the bones of salmon. On Eugene's arrival that summer, one of the Indians had warned him to stay out of these waters or he would be taken by the spirit that haunted the river at this place.

Eugene thrust a hand into the dark water—into his irrational fear—and felt them there, sliding against his fingers, these terrible phantoms with their gold eyes, fang-filled jaws and monstrous humps on brilliant red backs. The sockeye salmon had returned. Flying overhead or perched on scrags that lined the river, hundreds of eagles had arrived to feed on them.

The river was thick with salmon, red with them, from shore to shore. Here was the biblical plague, Eugene thought, the river of blood. The noise the fish made as they fought their way upstream was the rumble of an oncoming squall, the collective splash and slap of thousands upon thousands of bodies upon bodies, tails beating water, as they thrashed in their struggle to the spawning grounds. When the throng of fish reached the white water at the narrows, the rapids slowed their advance upriver. Unable to breathe in the waters now starved of oxygen by the smothering number of fish, the sockeye panicked and rushed back downriver, where they met the fish travelling upriver behind them. Eugene fell backwards in his boat as it heaved up on the mass of undulating fish, a red tide of sockeye, their bodies spilling out of the riverbed and onto shore.

Eugene Robertson wasn't the first white man to fish this river—the fur traders had been coming for decades—but this past summer, the summer of 1857, he was the first to stake a claim along its rocky shore; the first to muddy its waters with a gold rocker in his hunt for riches; and the first of the many miners who followed within the next five years, eating the salmon and stirring the silt of this river so that it blanketed and suffocated the sockeye eggs as they slept in their gravel nests. The miners would all but wipe out the salmon run; the fish would never return in such numbers. When the other miners had taken what little gold they found and moved on, Eugene became the first of the homesteaders to call the shores along the Lightning River home; the first to take down trees on the thin strip of river plain; the first to put up fences; the first to water his livestock from this river and pollute its waters. Each future generation of Robertsons would take more from this river and this land. And Eugene was the last white man to witness this miracle on the river, the mass return of the sockeye.

He righted himself in the pitching boat, then removed his suspenders, jack shirt and pants, his long underwear, and sat for a time watching the fish writhing around him. In the milky morning light, his ginger hair glowed and his muscular body shone white. A drift of freckles ran along his shoulders and down his arms and legs. Already, dragonflies hovered over the shallows where his boat rocked, flitting like winged folk, the capricious woodland faeries—the old gods—of his grandfather's stories. They darted away as he slid from the dugout into the water, into a river made almost entirely of fish.

The salmon's skin was slippery and cold and yet Eugene grew erect from their jostling against him. The water, like the air above it, was charged, electric, permeated with the over-powering smell of salmon, of ocean, of sex. In the sky over his head, two eagles shrieked and flew together, grappling with their talons. They fell, cartwheeling, and only pulled apart as they were about to hit water. As the eagles flew back into the air, Eugene saw a boy ascend naked from the river, as if lifted by the eagles, to stand on the surface of the water. The panic that had gripped Eugene on the sockeye's arrival returned. Surely this was no human boy, though he appeared to be. He was perhaps fifteen or sixteen, no lon-ger a child, not yet a man. The salmon leapt all around him, frenzied, as if rejoicing in his presence. Yet it was Eugene the boy watched intently and not the fish. Eugene wiped the water from his eyes as he struggled to keep the strange boy in view, but the countless salmon spun him and carried him around the river's bend. For a moment, Eugene's soul was adrift. He was water. He was fin. He was fish.

Initiation

September, present day

THE SOCKEYE ARE, by nature, transformers. They change in appearance throughout their lives, protecting themselves in this way. As fry, their skin is striped and spotted to conceal them within the vegetation of the lake as they grow. As they make themselves ready for their journey to the sea, their skin becomes reflection, becomes ocean.

Then, four years after their lives began in gravel, they come out of hiding to reveal their warrior natures. As they return home, their skin reddens, a hump appears on their backs, and their faces flush green. The sockeye paint themselves for battle as battle they must: they fight every inch of their way home, upriver, upriver, upstream. By these vestments, they know their own generation—who they can wrestle for territory and who they can take as a mate—once they reach the spawning grounds.

White settlers thought the story of the sockeye's return was incredible, impossible. But the *Secwepemc*—in English, the Shuswap—knew the sockeye followed the faint scent of home all the way from the Pacific up the Fraser, through Hells Gate, and then up the Thompson to their home river and spawning grounds, and even to the marriage bed in which their parents had conceived them.

The sockeye Hannah Robertson picked up this day was at the end of this long journey, exhausted from it. She carried it up the middle of Lightning River, a river that was no longer difficult to traverse, at least not here, at the shallows near the lake. To her right, equipment sat idle by the unfinished houses of the new lakeshore development as protestors had blocked the construction crew's passage at the bridge. To her left, her grandfather's fields and pastures bordered the river from the lake all the way up to the road. Here, the river widened, dispersing into shoals and sandbars as it spilled into Shuswap Lake. The water was so muddied and shallow, the few sockeye that had returned couldn't swim in it. Silt, sand and gravel, washed downriver from farms in the lower end of the valley and from the logged hills along the upper river, had collected here, blocking the salmon's entrance to their spawning grounds. The river grew narrower and the water progressively deeper as Hannah headed upriver towards Dead Man's Bend, but it was still far shallower than it should have been.

A line of her grandfather's fence posts dangled from barbed wire over the section of eroded bank at Dead Man's Bend, where the bodies of the drowned were often located. Shortly before her father was born, her grandfather had straightened the river there, attempting to add the fertile soil to his hayfield. With no bush to hold the soil in place, the reclaimed land had simply washed away from under the fence, clogging the estuary with silt.

To make matters worse, trees from the logging upriver had formed a dam under the bridge over the narrows, lowering water levels below it. The many farmers and landowners who lived along these shores also drew water for their crops and lawns from here. After three years of hot, dry summers, water levels were so low that the sockeye attempting to swim from the lake to the spawning grounds couldn't navigate the lower part of the river. A few made it, but most beached on sand or got hung up on snags deposited by spring freshets and died.

Hannah had arranged to miss the coming week of classes in her environmental studies program to save the fish, to carry them upriver alongside a handful of other volunteers from the reserve. Her instructors understood. Every living thing around them depended on the return of the salmon. The rotting fish would nourish the water this fall and again in early spring when the sun warmed what was left of the sockeye's frozen bodies. Their flesh would feed the tiny creatures that in turn fed the sockeye fry when they burst from their stone nests come spring. In this way, the sockeye fed their young with their own bodies and were resurrected within their children's flesh. If not enough sockeye returned during this run, if not enough died here, the river would starve, the sockeye fry would starve, the lake would starve, the eagles and bears and the land around them would starve.

Hannah carried the fish around Dead Man's Bend and released it into the spawning grounds. Then she squatted to rinse her hands, reminding herself not to touch her mouth. Along with the rotting bodies of the few salmon that had made it this far to spawn, the water was also fetid with leaks from septic fields and the feces of cattle from farms up and down the river, and poisoned by pesticides and herbicides sprayed on riverside fields and lawns.

On shore, her brother, Brandon, waited for her on Eugene's Rock, the name etched into the boulder by an ancestor she knew little about: *Eugene Robertson, September 1857*. Eugene had also chiselled a crude representation of a fish, a symbol of his faith, Hannah had assumed as a child when she still had a faith of her own. Now, at eighteen, she wondered if Eugene had simply loved fishing as much as her grandfather did.

"Finally decided to help, did you?" Hannah asked her younger brother. Brandon *was* supposed to help her this weekend, as the other volunteers were at the protest on the bridge, but he had quickly grown tired of the chore. He had complained that his hands ached from carrying the heavy fish and his feet had lost feeling from walking through the cold water.

Brandon shook his head. "I figured you'd want to know Grandpa's protesting the protest."

Hannah shaded her eyes to look to where Bran pointed. The protestors had nailed signs to the bridge railings: *They Disturbed a Secwepemc Burial Site!*; *This Is Unceded Secwepemc Territory*; and *O Canada, Your Home on Native Land*. And from the white environmentalists: *Stop Overdevelopment on Our River! Save Our Fish!* Indians from the reserve on the far bank had started the protest after a construction crew widening the road to the development had dug up the shallow grave of a toddler, an Indian kid, old bones from the gold-rush era. White environmentalists had jumped on board for this day's protest rally, hoping to bring attention to the damage the new lakefront development would inflict on the river and the spawning grounds.

Just below the bridge, their grandfather, Stew, had ridden his horse into the water as he could barely stand on his own, to fish the deep pool below the rapids, thumbing his nose at the protestors on the bridge above. He knew he couldn't fish the river anymore. The band had posted a sign on the far shore that read: *This river is closed to all fishing. By order of Lightning Bay Indian Band Council.*

"Shit," Hannah said.

"You want me to handle it this time?"

"No, I'll deal with it." She started towards shore, but then a shadow passed over them both and Hannah looked up. "Bran, look!" She pointed to the sky.

Brandon squinted as they watched two eagles lock talons and spiral down together. They disengaged and flew off, only to meet again in the sky. "Are the eagles fighting over territory?" Brandon asked. "The salmon?"

"Sometimes that's what it's about," she said, "but that's a male and a female courting. They cartwheel like that in spring, for hours."

"So why are they cartwheeling now?"

"I don't know. Sometimes their talons lock and they'll fall to the ground and starve to death. Remember those eagle skeletons Grandpa showed us in the bush over there?" She pointed to the reserve land above the new lakeside development, one of the few places where trees still grew along the river shore.

Brandon nodded. It had been strange to see the eagle claws still clutching each other. The bones had been ancient and moss covered. He expected they were still there, hidden beneath snowberry bushes and kinnikinnick.

He shielded his eyes to watch as the cartwheeling eagles once again fell from the sky. The huge birds separated just before hitting water. It was then he saw the boy about his own age standing naked in the middle of the river.

"Hey, do you see that?" Brandon asked his sister.

"See what?" she said.

The boy sank under the surface before Brandon could explain. He stepped into the water, wading upriver, as he scanned the depths for the boy. A sockeye salmon, startled by his intrusion into the spawning grounds, flicked out of his way, its snout and teeth terrifying, an image from a nightmare. Brandon saw something coming towards him from behind the fish, something that moved like a swimming snake. The thing was transparent, not quite there, made from water, like a wave.

Brandon panicked, fell backwards into the river, attempted to take a breath and took in water instead.

Hannah ran to him and helped him onto a shore churned into gumbo by the stinking hooves of their grandfather's cattle. "You okay?" she asked, as he coughed.

"There was something in the water," he said, when he was able. He could still see the thing, rippling just beneath the surface, heading back to the narrows.

Hannah looked back at the river. "What, the salmon?"

"A water mystery, I think," Brandon said.

"A *water mystery*?" Hannah laughed. "You don't actually believe Alex's stories, do you?" Alex was one of their friends from the reserve. Hannah had known him for as long as she could remember, but she rarely sat through his storytelling sessions. Bran did, though. It was Alex's accounts of his people's initiation rituals that interested Bran most. In the old days, Shuswap kids had gone out alone into the bush to hone their survival skills and seek visions of their guardian spirits. That appealed to Brandon. He craved some ritual to mark his entrance into manhood.

Brandon didn't bother to answer. Instead he grabbed his cell from the jean jacket he'd dumped on shore and texted Alex about what he had just seen. He turned to look upriver at the bridge over the narrows where Alex sat with other young men from the reserve, and as he did so, he saw the naked boy rise from the river to once again stand on water. The boy watched him as intently as Brandon watched him.

"What is it?" Hannah asked her brother.

But as soon as she spoke the boy was gone again. He didn't sink into the water this time. He simply vanished.

"Bran, what's going on?"

"Nothing," Brandon said. He watched the river for a time, searching for ripples in the water, for the boy to resurface. Above them, the eagle pair circled and cried *eye-EYE*, as Alex's ancestors had, to urge a storyteller on. *Eye-EYE!*

— 2 —

Unmooring

STEW'S BORDER COLLIE, Abby, stood on alert, staring at something in the water. His mare watched the river with the dog, her ears cocked forward, and it was then, as Stew looked to see what had caught his animals' attention, that he saw the boy standing on the water. A naked Indian kid in his teens. In recent years, as this world loosened its grip on Stew, he often saw this boy watching him from the river. He glanced at the bridge to see if any of the protestors had noticed the boy. When he looked back at the river, the boy was gone.

Stew sat on Spice, a strawberry roan who stood up to her chest in rushing water. This horse's legs were his now. His hips and knees were so far gone that he was lame without her, and couldn't stand upright in the river to fish. Here, at the deep pool below the rapids, the water boiled as it did nowhere else on this river, and could pull a man under. The water appeared thick, the consistency of glycerine, and was jade green, reflecting the algae clinging to the rocks beneath the surface; tiny bubbles rose up from below as if from a submerged creature. As he cast, he kept a firm grip on his glass rod, his old friend. The line arched over water and caught light, like spiders' silk floating on the breeze. The protestors on the bridge upriver booed at him. Stew cast and cast again, just to taunt them.

In the past, before those logs had dammed the flow above the bridge, sockeye had grouped here like pilgrims paying reverence at a holy place. They had waited for some signal, some change in light, some clue in the smell of the water that only they could discern, before leaping the rapids to spawn in the clean gravel of the upper river. Rainbow trout had often waited with them to eat the orange-red eggs. The trout, following the salmon up this river, were the fish Stew cast for, but now there were only a handful in the water beneath him and they weren't biting.

Abby barked from shore and Stew turned to see a woman walking up the river path. As the dog bounded towards her, Stew squinted at her in the way a lost hiker searches the forest for human trails. A wave of relief passed over him as he recognized her as his own granddaughter. "Hannah," he said.

"What are you doing, Grandpa?" she called.

"What does it look like? I'm fishing."

She pointed at the rifle in his scabbard as she reached him. "With a gun?"

"Gun's for trespassers. Those protestors left my gates open. Cows got onto the road, into Gina's yard." He nodded at their neighbour's small acreage across from his own front gate. "I had a bugger of a time getting them back in."

As Hannah attempted to get as close to her grandfather as she could, she stepped onto a rock outcropping over the river that had been rounded into a bowl of stone by swirling eddies. River breezes carried the smell of the horse to her, along with the smell of rum from her grandfather. The red feather in the brim of his cowboy hat fluttered in the breeze. Over the summer his face had taken on the gaunt look of the terminally ill.

"Grandpa, you know you're not allowed to fish here anymore."

"And that asshole's not allowed on my property."

Hannah turned to follow her grandfather's gaze to Alex, who was heading towards them from the bridge, following the river path that ran the length of her grandfather's land. He looked so different from the boy she'd known in her childhood. He had grown muscular and was almost too well groomed, like an actor on a movie set, purposefully setting himself apart from both the rez community where he lived and the valley at large with his expensive jeans and leather jacket, this urban identity he had assumed. Hannah felt intimidated by him now in a way she never had before he went to university, when he was still that gangly teen.

Stew tucked his fishing rod between his thigh and saddle, pulled his rifle from the scabbard, and tipped back his cowboy hat as he aimed the gun at Alex. Alex stopped in mid-step and gave Hannah a look that said, *Here we go again.*

"Grandpa, put the gun down."

Stew ignored her, peering at Alex through the scope on his gun. "What the hell do you want?" Stew yelled. "What are you doing on my land?"

Alex held out both hands as if to offer himself up. "If you're looking for something to fill your freezer, I'll take you moose hunting on my uncle's hunting ground," he called to Stew. "Nothing but tough meat on these bones."

"So you *are* off the reserve, then? You look Indian, though it's hard to tell these days. All these red-haired, blue-eyed Indians. My granddaughter here says she's going to college with a blonde who claims she's Cree. Says she's got status and everything."

Hannah felt the heat rise to her face. She realized her grandfather didn't recognize Alex, even though he had been to the farmhouse many times over the years. To him, Alex was just another trespasser, another protestor, another Indian.

"Grandpa, this is Alex. You remember, *Coyote*."

Alex made a face at hearing the nickname. His aunt Sara had given it to him, not because she thought Alex was the archetypal trickster of many of the stories he told, but because his aunt felt he—like Coyote—spent too much of his energy on getting laid. Or at least that used to be the case, before he went to university, when he seemed to have a new girlfriend every week. Hannah should have been too young at the time to be jealous, but she had been.

"Alex is Dennis Moses's grandson, his great-grandson," Hannah told her grandfather. "He comes over to our place, remember?"

Recognition crossed Stew's face, and he lowered his gun. Alex took that as his cue to continue walking towards them. He joined Hannah on the outcropping over the river.

"Grandpa's pissed because the protestors left the far gate open," Hannah told him. "The cows got out."

"What the hell are you protesting anyway?" Stew asked Alex. "You people are always getting worked up about your bones. What does it matter? The kid is dead, isn't he?"

"How would you feel if I dug up old Eugene's bones?"

"You don't even know who that kid is."

Alex licked his thumb and rubbed a smudge from Hannah's cheek before responding. She wiped her face with her sleeve, embarrassed both by his touch and her grubby appearance.

"He's family," Alex said to Stew. "I'll tell the others to shut the gates if they go through the pastures. Most of them will be gone in a couple of hours anyway. But you've got to stop fishing. Zach is threatening to call Fish and Wildlife." He waved and his cousin Zach waved back from the bridge. Zach was in his early thirties, several years older than Alex. He was more political than Alex, and bitter. Hannah did her best to avoid him.

"Nobody's going to tell me I can't fish in this river," Stew said. "I've been taking fish out of these waters all my life, just like my father and his father before him." Stew lifted his chin towards Eugene's Rock. "Every generation of my family—going all the way back to Eugene Robertson—fished here. And goddammit, my grandson is going to fish here too." Bran biked towards them now down a path so slender it was hard to believe Stew's cattle had created it. One cow had followed the steps of the next, their hooves slipping neatly into the hoof prints of the one before them, much like his own family had.

"Oh, I know all about it," said Alex. "My family fished here for thousands of years before you guys turned up and trashed the place. Keep it up and there won't be any fish here to catch."

"When are you Indians going to get over the fact that this land belongs to us now," Stew said.

"You remember what my grandpa Dennis told you every time you asked him that?"

Stew looked away. He did remember. Dennis Moses had said white men were like infants in their baths who tried to grab the water their mothers poured over them, thinking the water was a thing they could possess. But, Dennis said, they would never own this river or this land. The waters, the soil, would run through the cracks between their fingers, the way bathwater runs through a child's fist.

Nevertheless, Stew tapped his chest and repeated himself, defiant. "It's ours now."

Alex shook his head but didn't respond. Brandon skidded his bike to a stop next to him, as Abby leapt and barked around him. He petted the dog to calm her as he looked at the gun in Stew's hands.

"Where the hell have you been?" Stew asked him.

"Had to change my clothes," he said. "I fell in the river."

"I told you, never swim in that water. You know how many have died here? Christ, your own mother."

"You don't need to remind him," Hannah said.

"I said I fell in," Brandon told his grandfather. "And I was just in the shallows."

"So you saw your first water mystery, did you?" Alex asked Brandon, grinning.

"What was that?" At last Stew tucked his rifle back in his scabbard.

"I saw something in the water when I fell in," Brandon said.

"Something like what?" Stew asked.

"I don't know. It was see-through. But it *was* there, you know?"

"Like a ghost swimming through water," Alex said.

Brandon turned to look at him. "You've seen it?"

Alex paused, glancing at Stew. "Many people have seen it."

"I thought I saw a boy, too, standing on the river," Brandon said. "I mean he was standing right on the water, like he was Jesus or something. Then he sank and I saw that ghost thing swimming towards me."

Alex nodded. "That's the water mystery. The boy and the river ghost are one and the same."

Stew asked, "Your head wasn't underwater, was it? You didn't drink that thing in?" His grandfather's expression was so grim, Brandon laughed a little in confusion.

"No. Hannah pulled me up."

"Seriously," said Alex. "That ghost in the water didn't get inside you, did it?"

Brandon shook his head. "No, I saw it on the river after."

"What's this all about?" Hannah asked.

"Nothing," Stew said, cutting off Alex's answer. Then he eyed Brandon. "Your imagination," he said. He settled himself on his horse to face the river. Hannah raised an eyebrow at Alex, but he held up a hand as if to say, *Later*.

As Stew cast his line, Hannah said, "For god's sake, Grandpa, put the rod down. You don't want to get yourself in trouble."

Stew reeled in his line and cast again. The fly hovered in the air until a swallow swooped down and nabbed it, flitting off with the fly in its mouth as it would a mosquito. Stew swore, cranked his line and the swallow fluttered towards him. "My own granddaughter thinks she can tell me what to do. Says I got to fence the river so my cattle can't get themselves a drink when they want it. Then all of them environmentalist assholes at that meeting last week told me I can't sell my own land."

"They don't care if you sell," Alex told him. "They just don't want you to sell to this developer."

Stew grabbed the swallow and, tucking the glass rod under his arm, plucked the hook from the bird's mouth. "The lot of you can go to hell," he said as he opened his fist to let the bird go. The swallow flapped, confused, then darted away to skim the surface of the water.

"You know, you're the only local who supports that housing development," Alex told Stew.

"I don't give a rat's ass about that hellhole," Stew said. "I can barely walk even with my canes. Won't be long before I can't get on the tractor. What am I going to do? Feed the cattle from a wheelchair? What kind of life is that? I want a few years of comfort before I'm gone. Is that asking too much?"

"You're always going on about how this farm has been passed on one generation to the next," Brandon told him.

Stew turned in his saddle to face his grandson. "Are you going to take it over? You up to running a cow-calf operation?"

Brandon had nothing to say to that.

"Your father sure as hell isn't."

"You didn't ask me if I wanted the farm," Hannah said. "I suppose because I'm a woman."

"You're a woman now, are you?" Alex asked her, and grinned. And Hannah realized that Alex still saw her as that girl he had left behind. Hannah had only been fourteen when he went to university.

"I won't hand you the farm because you're a goddamned environmentalist," Stew told her. "You'd sell off the cows and let these fields go to bush."

"And what's that developer going to do?" She waited for him to respond, but he only cast again. "You're right," she said. "I would let the land along the river recover. The spawning grounds are on our land and they need protection. We're losing the salmon."

"No way I'm backing out of the deal now. That developer's got his offer on the table, as long as the zoning change

goes through. All that's in the way now are those assholes."
Stew pointed his fishing rod at the protestors. "You tell your
friends over there to get their cars the hell out of my field.
They're frickin' trespassers. That goes for you too," he told
Alex. "Go on, get out of here."

Stew leaned to poke Alex with his fishing rod and when
Alex stepped back the old glass rod slipped from his grasp
and fell into the water. As it circled on an eddy, Stew bent to
save it but the rod disappeared as if something had yanked
it down. Stew made one last attempt to retrieve it, lost his
balance and slid from his saddle into the river.

"Shit," Hannah cried. She jumped in after her grandfather, weighed down by her waders, and Brandon leapt in
after her. Cold river water filled Hannah's boots, grabbed
her legs, lit up her scalp, and tried to pull her below.

Brandon strained to keep his head above water as he
reached for his grandfather, but they were all drawn under
the surface by the boiling eddies. For a split second before
he was submerged, Brandon glimpsed the naked boy
standing in the middle of the river, as if on solid ground.
Underwater, Brandon kicked and kicked and kicked, and
then, his energy spent, he sank, drifting like a dying salmon.
He was aware of the water that enveloped him, but he no
longer attempted to remove himself from it. He opened his
eyes as something brushed past his arm and saw a sockeye
dart away. Then he saw the thing snaking through water
towards him, this energy in the water, this ghost; it pushed
into him, filling his mouth, travelling down his throat and
through the streams of his body. He felt the thrashing in his

mind, a disturbance of black waters. He exhaled the last of his breath and bubbles leapt from his mouth, and with them his soul expanded: he was rushing water; he was blinding reflection; he was air, and robin's egg sky.

— 3 —

Surfacing

AN EXPLOSION OF bubbles burst in front of Hannah as Alex jumped in: his legs in jeans, the rippled muscles of his stomach, his billowing T-shirt, his face made strange by water, his black hair adrift above him. She felt the warmth of his arms around her as he kicked towards the surface and then swam with her to shore.

Abby greeted them, barking and shaking with anxiety. Alex helped Hannah lie back into the roots of the lone, ancient cottonwood that Eugene Robertson had left standing on this shore. "You okay?" he asked her, pushing her hair out of her eyes.

She coughed as she spoke. "Go! Help Bran and Grandpa."

Brandon had already crawled onto shore, pulling himself on his elbows like a lungfish making its clumsy journey onto land. He rolled onto his back, wheezing as his chest rose and fell unevenly, as if breath itself was something foreign to him. Alex sprinted to Dead Man's Bend, where he found Stew face down, his jacket snagged on the barbed-wire fence hanging low over the river. Alex charged into the muddy water and flipped the old man over, untangled him from the fence, then hauled him back to shore. There he started CPR, pinching his nose as he forced breath into his mouth, and pressing, pressing, pressing his chest.

Hannah stumbled over river rock to her brother and took his hand to haul him up so they could go to their grandfather, but he wouldn't, or couldn't, get up. She knelt beside him. "Bran, look at me," she said, and when he didn't respond she turned his face towards her. He seemed only half-aware of her presence. He was shivering; Hannah was too. "Brandon! Are you all right?" His pupils were unnaturally large in this bright daylight. "Jesus, did you hit your head?" Hannah ran her fingers over Brandon's scalp, searching through his ginger hair for bumps or gashes. She didn't find any, yet Brandon was clearly disoriented. When Abby nosed him, looking for reassurance, Brandon shifted away, seeming to be afraid of the dog.

Hannah felt in her pocket for her cell, to call an ambulance, but it was gone. Panicked, she looked around for help. People spread down from the bridge, on the way towards them, but their neighbour Gina, one of her father's old flames, was first to arrive. She took Spice's reins and walked the mare out of the water as if she were family, which even in crisis annoyed Hannah. "Phone 911," she called to her.

"An ambulance is already on the way," Gina told her. She held up her cell as she led the horse towards them.

"Grandpa," Hannah cried.

"Alex knows what to do," said Gina, her voice steady, with only an echo of the Shuswap inflection. She tied the mare to the cottonwood, wrapping the reins around a sprout growing up from the base of the dying tree, and then came to squat beside Brandon. "Is he hurt?"

"I don't know. There's no blood or swelling, but he seems confused."

Gina studied his eyes in the way Hannah's mother once had after a childhood tumble. "Brandon," she said. "How you doing? Talk to me, buddy." Brandon only looked bewildered. Gina patted his face as she repeatedly said his name, and the confusion slowly drained. He pushed away from the water's edge. "The water mystery," he said. "It was coming for me." Then he saw Stew. "Is Grandpa dead?"

Alex looked up briefly at them and shook his head, but then Stew coughed and began breathing on his own. "Oh, thank god," said Hannah.

Gina helped Brandon stand and she and Hannah walked him down to Stew. Brandon behaved as if his legs were new to him.

One of the protestors had retrieved Stew's hat. Another had brought a grey wool blanket and Alex had draped it over Stew. His skin was pasty white and he had lost his glasses to the river. He looked around blindly as Abby licked his face. "Brandon!" he cried, pointing not at his grandson, but at the water.

"Bran is right here," Hannah said. She took her brother's hand and tugged Brandon to his knees beside him. As soon as Stew saw his grandson, he closed his eyes and seemed to lose consciousness, then mumbled for a time. There was mud on his scalp and one wayward, wiry hair stood at attention at his brow. "Wunks got him!"

"The what?" Gina asked. "He's not making sense."

"It's something from a poem," Hannah said. A poem called 'The Raggedy Man.'"

> *He showed me the hole 'at the Wunks is got,*
> *'At lives 'way deep in the ground ...*

When Hannah was little, Stew had read that poem to her over and again until her father, Jesse, put a stop to it. Stew had told her the Wunks were real, that they lived in the rushing waters beneath the bridge and could turn into him, or Jesse, or anyone. His story had scared the crap out of her. Hannah imagined that was her grandfather's intention. He didn't want her swimming in the dangerous river.

Gina wiped the mud from Stew's scalp, looking for blood, but there wasn't any. "He may have suffered some brain damage."

"He was out too long," said Alex. "Maybe if I got to him sooner."

"Hey," said Gina, putting a hand on his shoulder. "Don't go blaming yourself. You did good. You're the hero here today."

Brandon said, "Grandpa won't come home from the hospital, will he?" He glanced at Hannah as they both remembered when their father had revived their mother from drowning but she died in intensive care.

"I think the time has come for long-term care," said Gina. "You'll have to phone your dad and let him know he's got to come home and deal with things."

Jesse lived in the lower mainland and hadn't been home in years. "I can deal with things," Hannah said.

Alex wrapped an arm around Hannah, the gesture so natural she found herself settling into it as easily as she had once relaxed into her father's hug. Even though Alex's clothes were as wet as hers, his body radiated heat and his warmth moved into her.

"The farm is Jesse's responsibility now," Alex said. "You can't sort out all this alone." Alex was right, of course. She would have to cancel her first semester's classes even if her father did come home to help out. If the past was any guide, she knew Jesse wouldn't stay long. Since their mother died, he couldn't stand to be around. If their grandpa didn't come home, Jesse would sell off the animals, arrange the sale of the farm and disappear again. She and Brandon were on their own.

Stew tried to sit up but failed. Then he reached to tug on Brandon's arm, pulling his grandson closer. "I saw you on the river," Stew whispered. "You were there, in the water with me, at the same time you were on shore with Hannah."

"You were drowning," said Hannah.

"No, I saw his ghost, his—what's the word?"

"Doppelgänger," said Alex.

"Did you drink that thing in?" Stew asked Brandon. "You know what I'm talking about. That thing you saw in the water."

"I guess," Brandon told Stew. "There was a boy . . ." He touched his throat, his temple. "Then I felt something, inside."

"Shit," said Alex.

Hannah took Alex's arm to get him to look at her, willing him to explain.

He briefly scanned the small crowd around them, then lowered his voice. "If that water mystery has him, if Brandon's soul is out walking, he could die."

"What do you mean 'out walking'?"

Alex didn't answer. He clawed a hand through his hair and turned to the zigzag of lightning on the cliff face of Little Mountain, to the ghostly figure—both fish and man— that emerged from it. The siren of an ambulance blared as it rushed down the road towards them.

— 4 —

First Light

THE WATER HAD two surfaces, one above and one below, worlds that mirrored each other, with the depths between. Swimming from one surface to the other took effort, stamina. The boy had struggled up through water and to that distant shore with great difficulty. When he finally arrived, he was exhausted and blinded by the sunlight that shifted and flared off everything around him. Objects had shape and colour but little meaning, as if he was an infant.

The boy followed a blue wall with his hands and came to a pool of water hanging on it. He attempted to slide his hand into the water but his fingertips wouldn't penetrate. In the hard surface of the frozen water, he saw the face of a stranger.

He had travelled into this stranger's mind in the way salmon fry swim the tiniest underground tributaries through rock, to appear as if by some enchantment within household wells. The day before, on the river shore, the boy had surfaced briefly, but it would be some time before he was strong enough to wrangle full control.

"Bran," a girl called. "Get dressed. We'll feed the animals, then go straight in to see Grandpa. You'll have to hurry. I've got to move salmon up the river this morning." She paused. "You hear me?"

The boy remembered hearing that name at the river. He was this boy now, Bran. He pressed a hand to the face reflected in the magic pool and saw this hand reflected there as well. Two hands meeting. He remembered, then. These people had found a way to capture a still pond and hang it on the wall. He pressed his nose to it and tried to see to the pool's pebbled bottom.

"Are you awake?" When the girl opened the door, he turned to her, but he could take in only pieces: a mouth, a long, slender nose, a tangle of reddish-brown curls, one hazel eye that appeared both green and golden in the early morning light. With effort, he pulled together the parts of her face and saw that she was strikingly handsome, though she carried herself with the uncertainty of a girl who didn't yet know herself. He had heard her name called along the river shore. She was this boy's sister, Hannah.

"Bran, for Christ's sake, put on some underwear."

He remembered few words of her language, but nodded.

Then she took a step forward and she was in pieces again. "Are you stoned?" She sniffed the air around him. "Are you drunk?" Beside her, the bare, pale blue walls took shape, along with an unmade bed and clothes scattered across the floor. There was a bureau here he recognized from an earlier journey to this place. At that time, the house had smelled of freshly cut pine. Now that smell was overpowered by the human scent of a young man coming of age.

Behind Hannah, a shadow wavered and lingered, a woman spirit that followed her. He knew this woman. He knew her intimately. When she was alive, in this world, she had carried him within herself for a time. He knew her name. "Elaine," he said, pointing at her.

Hannah laughed, confused, afraid.

"Elaine," he said again, but Hannah couldn't see her mother.

She picked up an armful of clothes from the floor and threw them at him. "Get yourself dressed."

He caught the underwear and T-shirt, this body acting on instinct. Hardness was everywhere here—under his feet, in the walls of this building—so unlike the floors and walls of a *kekuli*, the winter home of his past forays into this world, a house built into the ground, with walls made of earth. Within this white man's house, even the light above him was hard, captured within an upturned bowl fixed to the ceiling. He stared up at it, captivated.

Hannah snapped her fingers. "Brandon! What's the matter with you this morning?"

He rubbed his eyes to show his fatigue, hoping this would calm her. And he was tired. He sank back down on the bed, back into that dark river. He hung there for a time, neither in this world nor his own, but in the waters between. Here he would rest and gain strength in the way his brothers' and sisters' children grew over the winter within their stone nests before bursting up into the river water as fry come spring.

"What's going on?" Hannah asked.

He turned away from the girl, from her chaotic form and gibberish, to the window. There he saw the soul of the boy Brandon banging against the glass, displaced, a refugee from his own body.

— 5 —

A Hummingbird's Flight

GINA LEFT THE door open as she entered the kitchen with a basketful of tomatoes, the last of the year. She lined them up, one by one, on the windowsill over the sink. Some were still green, but most were overripe. She would have to use them this week. So, a salad for lunch, cubes of tomatoes tossed over lettuce bathed in olive oil and balsamic vinegar, garlic and basil. Later, a tomato sauce over spaghetti for supper. She'd make fresh salsa and maybe use that as an excuse to invite a few friends over and fill the kitchen with the warmth and conversation she craved. The house had seemed so lonely lately. But what friends? She couldn't think of anyone she really wanted to invite. Certainly none of Grant's buddies from work, other cops. Or her own coworkers from family services, women she saw too much of as it was. She had let her other friendships slide away. And few relatives from the reserve felt comfortable here, in Grant's home, a cop's home.

She paused after placing the last tomato on the sill to look over at the old Robertson place. It had been a week since Stew's fall in the river, and Hannah and Bran were alone in that house. Bran hadn't been catching the bus to school, but then Hannah had been missing her classes as well. Gina had seen them both in the pasture and barn, feeding the animals, cleaning the stalls. She imagined school was more than either of them could handle right now.

She had expected Jesse to return after she phoned him, and after Hannah had called too. Jesse had said he would try to head up into the interior within a day or two. But she still didn't see his truck in the yard. She thought of phoning him again, but she would have to wait until Grant was at work. She should take something over for the kids, a lasagne maybe.

Gina felt Grant's footsteps reverberate through the kitchen floorboards and she turned away from the window.

"Looking for someone?" Grant asked. "Jesse, maybe?"

"Just lost in thought." She lifted a ripe tomato to her nose to breathe in its fragrance, as this smell had always calmed her. "You ready for lunch?"

"Always."

He poured himself coffee and reached into the cupboard beside her for sugar, whitener. She felt petite beside her husband, though she was a tall woman herself. Today Grant was dressed in jeans and a T-shirt and his feet were bare, but he still wore his authority. He was clean-cut and broad-shouldered, one of those cops who could not have gone undercover and got away with it. Early in their marriage Grant's demeanour had made her feel safe, protected. Now she so often felt on edge in his presence.

Gina picked up a knife and started cutting up the tomato, praying Grant wouldn't bring up Jesse again. There was a hum, a buzzing, and they both turned to see a hummingbird fly into the house through the open door. It darted around the kitchen, then hovered in front of Gina, right at eye level, as if eliciting her attention. Such a beautiful, unexpected thing. Its body was grey and olive; its head and throat a glistening red.

"What the hell?" Grant asked. "Hummingbirds should be long gone by now."

"This is an Anna's hummingbird," said Gina. "They've started overwintering on the coast in the last decade. I saw in the newspaper that one hung around all winter in Vernon last year. There was a picture of it at a feeder covered in snow. A bonus of global warming, I suppose. I'll fill up my hummingbird feeder; I might just keep this one around."

The bird left her and flew to the window over the sink, banging into the pane above the tomatoes.

Gina said, "We need to get it out of here before it injures itself."

The bird stopped to rest on the windowsill, the rapid beat of its heart visible in its tiny chest, and Gina dropped a mug over it, then slipped her hand quickly beneath the bird so it could not escape. It was so unbelievably tiny, smaller even than it appeared in flight, no bigger than her thumb, its wings beating madly against her hand. Gina tentatively lifted a finger from the cup, to take a last look before releasing it, and the bird shot upward, then zipped through the open door. It flew directly across the road to the Robertson house, where it buzzed against the upstairs window to Bran's room.

Gina stood on the kitchen stoop for a time, watching the hummingbird's relentless attempt to get into the window, into the mountain landscape it saw reflected there, or, perhaps, it fought its mirrored image.

"Lunch?" Grant called.

"I'll be right there," she said, but stayed exactly where she was. She looked back at the Robertson house but the hummingbird was gone. She searched a countryside shining brightly in the yellow and orange leaves of a sunny Shuswap fall, hoping to spot the tiny bird again. The ferns along the road had turned brown and the rosehips a vivid, glossy red, yet chicory still bloomed indigo. Autumn was here now, but warm, warmer than she remembered from her childhood. Still, she wrapped her sweater around herself as a wind picked up, scattering leaves and signalling a change in the weather.

— 6 —

Homecoming

JESSE ROBERTSON RATTLED along the highway in the baby blue '57 Chevy pickup that had once belonged to his father, Stew, a truck that Jesse had intended to restore for as long as he owned it, which was almost a decade. He carried his equipment in the truck bed: his welder and tanks, his toolbox and grinders, torches, hoses, rods. The one bumper sticker read, *Welding Ain't for Wimps*.

He had put off this trip back home for a full week, telling his daughter he had a welding job to complete, which was not the truth. But now, as he drove through the arid country past Kamloops, he felt the emotion start to rise: *home*. Bunchgrass, sagebrush, ponderosa pine. At Little Shuswap Lake the landscape shrugged off its austerity and grew lush: the small green farms and acreages of Chase, the emerald hills that surrounded the town.

The GPS unit stuck to his front windshield told him where to go, as if he didn't know. *In two hundred metres, turn right*. He turned off the highway at the Squilax Bridge, then followed the slow, winding road along Shuswap Lake, over the bridge at Adams River and then at Scotch Creek, heading for the home in which his parents had conceived him, where his father had been conceived, and his grandfather too.

The road diverted from the lake and rose over Lightning Hill. At the summit, Jesse pulled into the community hall parking lot to smoke a joint before facing his family. He stared at what was left of the forest, pines in the red attack stage of pine beetle infestation, still alive but dying. A sign read, *Mountain Beetle Salvage Harvesting*. The pines looked like an army of rusted tin soldiers standing at attention, interspersed with the dead, propped corpses, grey hair hanging. At their feet yearling pines no more than a foot or so high were also red, also dying.

Below him, Lightning River snaked through the narrow strip of river plain. Above the bridge at the narrows, the valley was still dominated by small farms of one kind or another. Holsteins lounged in pastures outside dairies, Herefords munched on dry grass, and he could even spot llamas out to pasture.

Stew's cow-calf operation stretched from the bridge to the lake. He could see the farmhouse nestled in an orchard close to the shore, the barns and outbuildings scattered around it, the beef cows—Herefords—drinking from the river. The snaking wooden rail fences that bordered the Robertson homestead had been built by Eugene a hundred and fifty years earlier. He had constructed them without nails and they still stood, hugging the curves of what had once been a wagon road, and before that an Indian trail. On the opposite side of the river, the reserve houses were tucked between the shore and the benchland. The cliff face of Little Mountain towered over the community, monolithic.

Jesse breathed in a last toke as his gaze settled inevitably on Gina's property just across the road from his father's. Smoke curled from the chimney, so she was home. He felt a tug in his gut at the thought of seeing her again. He had talked to her on the phone a few times in the years since he left, most recently about Stew's health and his plans for the sale of the property, but they hadn't spoken face-to-face since Elaine's funeral, and even then Gina had only whispered a few guarded sympathies under her husband's watchful eye. Jesse hadn't been sure Grant knew about them until that moment. But conjecture had obviously spread after Elaine took her life. Grant had not offered his hand or his condolences to Jesse. He had stood behind Gina in his tailored suit and kept his eye on the crowd, standing guard as if he was on duty.

Jesse pinched out his roach and pocketed it, to roll into another joint later. He rubbed his face as he prepared himself for the difficult afternoon ahead, then he slipped back into his truck and headed downhill.

A big yellow "community watch" sign welcomed Jesse to Lightning River Valley. *The Details of Your Vehicle Will Be Recorded*, it cheerfully warned. Jesse crossed a Texas gate, a cattle guard, past another sign telling him to *Watch for Livestock* and then drove through a patch of swampy wetland. The foliage and bulrushes were a wash of fall colour, but even so, on this cloudy September day, the swamp was dreary and forbidding, covered in a haze of fog. On a day like this one many years before, when Jesse had noted how haunted the swamp looked, Stew, seated in the passenger seat beside him, nodded and said, "Good place to hide a body."

Turn right, the voice on his GPS told him. The contraption was wrong: he wasn't yet at the farm gate. He slapped the side of the unit in the way he attempted to fix most of his electrical gadgets.

It was then Jesse spotted a figure standing in the mist on the shoulder. A teen, a boy. Was he naked? He *was* naked. As Jesse passed him, he recognized him with a start: it was Brandon, his own son. Jesse hit the brakes and looked in his rear-view mirror, but Brandon was gone, just *gone*, as if he'd never been there in the first place.

A sockeye salmon thumped on the truck windshield, cracking it, and rolled down the hood of Jesse's truck.

"Shit."

Turn right, the voice said.

Jesse jerked the Chevy to the shoulder using both hands; the steering was stiff as molasses. He turned off the ignition and, shaking, grabbed the leg bone of one of his father's long-dead cows from the front dash and got out to place it under the front tire as an emergency brake. He left the door open as he peered at the salmon in the middle of the road, a salmon that had dropped from the sky. A passing Dodge pickup flattened it, leaving a streak of blood and flesh down the road. Jesse searched, but the naked boy—his son—was gone. Above Jesse, the eagle that had dropped the fish on his truck circled and laughed, *eye-EYE!*

Jesse sat on Eugene's Rock scratching Stew's dog behind the ears as he waited on Hannah. Behind him, the yellow leaves of a lone poplar rattled with a sound like falling rain.

His daughter sloshed upriver towards him, cradling a salmon against her chest as if it were a child. The fish was big, and already the fungi that would consume its body had taken hold: white around its snout, its eyes, in spots on its back. Turbulent river breezes lifted the curls that escaped Hannah's ponytail. From this distance, Hannah could have been Elaine, dressed in her waders as she and Jesse fished in this river in the years before her drowning, before her illness, before they had children. She looked so much like her mother that Jesse felt momentarily disoriented.

Beyond Hannah a row of other volunteers—all women, all from the reserve, and all related by the looks of them—formed a relay up the river, handing the sockeye one to the other before the last released the fish to the spawning grounds. On the shore behind them a handful of eagles waited on the rocks for the women to leave so they could scavenge the carcasses. When Jesse was a kid, dozens of eagles had lined these spawning grounds to gorge themselves on salmon flesh over the spawning season. Stew had told him that when he was a child, he had counted nearly five hundred along the river. Now so few salmon returned, the eagles were forced to hunt for other food sources. They ate the afterbirth of Stew's cattle, the entrails of sheep slaughtered behind the Wilkinsons' barns, and plucked Gina's chickens from her fence posts.

"You're taller," Jesse called across the water to his daughter as she moved closer. He paused, lowering his voice so she wouldn't hear him. "You're a woman now."

Hannah stopped and looked him over. "You don't look so different."

She was being kind, he knew. He had much more grey in his ginger curls, and many more lines around his hazel eyes. He had acquired that rumpled look men get when they don't have a woman around. The lines of his palms were black with grease, his fingers gashed and covered in burns. His jeans and T-shirt were shot through with holes and his workboots were burned in spots from the fiery spray of his welding torch.

Hannah released the sockeye into the water at her father's feet and together they watched as it slid away to the spawning grounds.

"Is Bran around?" Jesse asked her.

"He's in the house."

"Are you sure?"

Hannah cocked her head. "Yeah, why?"

The naked boy he'd thought was his son. The fish that fell from the sky. "Nothing," he said. When she raised an eyebrow to him, he said, "I knocked and no one answered."

"He was sleeping when I got back from the hospital a couple of hours ago."

"Sleeping?" Jesse checked his watch. "It's nearly one o'clock."

Hannah shrugged. "He had a late night." She shook river water from her hands as she stood. "I've got something to show you."

"I thought we'd head straight into town to see Dad."

"I was already at the hospital, this morning."

"It would be nice for Dad, don't you think, for all three of us to visit?"

Hannah crossed her arms. "You just don't want to face Grandpa alone."

Jesse scratched the dog's head as he looked back to the house, to the yard, to his truck. She was right. He didn't want to face his father's judgment of him, another recounting of his many failures.

"I'd like you and Bran to come with me," he said finally.

Hannah turned her back to him. "This won't take long." She set off downstream, clearly expecting him to follow. Abby abandoned him to trot behind her.

Jesse jogged to catch up with his daughter. "Where are you taking me?"

"You'll see."

Along the shore, there was a path worn first by coyote, deer and bears, then by the ancestors to the modern

Shuswap, and then by white fur traders, miners, settlers
and their cattle, and finally by tourists walking to and from
the beach at the lake. The remains of the dead fish that
bears had dragged from the river, along with the occasional
mound of bear excrement, were scattered along the trail.

Hannah led Jesse across the sandbars over to the new
development, then up the river path to reserve land.

"Here we are," she said and waved her hand at the
shore. The riverbank in this area was shored up with boulders and logs and planted in young willow.

"So what am I looking at exactly?" Jesse asked.

Hannah pointed to one of the many willow saplings
along the bank, its leaves now yellow, and launched into the
same presentation she had given the elementary school kids
during their field trip at the beginning of September, at the
start of the three-week sockeye run. "I planted this willow
last summer," she said. "The roots of the tree swim through
dirt, seeking water, holding the soil in place. In two or three
years, this bank will be bush again. The trees will provide
cover for the river and fish, keep the water cool and stop the
soil from washing away and suffocating the salmon eggs."

"This is what you want to do on our side?"

"We're losing the salmon," Hannah told her father. "And
Grandpa is losing his land."

Jesse turned to survey a line of Stew's fence posts dangling from barbed wire over the section of eroded bank at
Dead Man's Bend, nothing holding them in place.

Hannah said, "The flow of water will continue to eat
away the bank until we deal with the problem."

Abby trotted towards them and Jesse threw her a stick to fetch. "So what's involved?" he asked as he watched the dog run off. "What were you asking Dad to do?"

"The first step is to keep the cattle away from the water. We have government funding for fencing materials and volunteers to help put up new fences along the river. Next summer, after the salmon fry are in the lake, we can shore up the banks with boulders and logs and plant willows to hold the soil in place."

"Next *summer*?"

"We'd have to do the work then. If we do it at any other time, we risk disturbing the spawning salmon or their eggs or the fry."

"I hope the place sells by then. And even if it doesn't, I don't see the point of doing all that work if we *are* going to sell." Jesse saw the look on Hannah's face and immediately realized his mistake. She had been asking him to keep the farm. She had been asking him to stay.

Abby bounded up the river path towards them with the stick in her mouth and Jesse threw it again, welcoming the brief distraction. He hadn't expected to have this discussion with Hannah so soon. "From what Gina has told me, I'd be silly to turn down that developer's offer."

"Gina? You've been talking to her?"

"She phoned me a few weeks back, and again this past week after Dad ended up in hospital. She was worried about Dad's behaviour, about the load you were carrying because of it."

Hannah kicked at an empty bottle to dislodge it from the sand and river rock and then picked it up: Jägermeister, no doubt left by a teenager hiking the trails. "So you knew about Grandpa weeks ago," she said. "You knew and you didn't come back to help."

Here it comes, Jesse thought. "Look," he said. "I'm sorry about Dad, about leaving everything in your hands."

"You say you're sorry, and yet you left me to take care of Grandpa all by myself. And now you're just going to sell the place and leave."

"There's that facility in town. Bastion Place, is it? Gina says there's a waiting list, but I'll arrange for Dad to go there. I thought you and Brandon would come live with me."

"I won't leave Grandpa. I'll get a job and find a place of my own. Bran can live with me until he graduates."

"He's a minor. I'll have to support him until he's out of school."

"He won't want to leave his friends." Her tone made it clear that if Jesse had been around, if he was a father to his son, he would know this. "You should have been supporting us all along."

Jesse turned to the bridge to avoid his daughter's eyes. Jesse had heard about the protest on the news. The handful of protestors sitting there now were all from the reserve, elders and young men and women who didn't have to work that day. Aside from the backhoe and the plywood signs of protest, the gathering resembled a family reunion. One of the elders gestured theatrically as he told some story. Jesse felt a jolt of adrenaline as it occurred to him that the young woman he had known from the mill office might be there. He struggled to remember her name. How old would she be now? She might have a family by now, a kid in preschool, a child that, in his carelessness, might have been his.

A pickup truck edged by the protestors and honked, in approval or annoyance Jesse wasn't sure. Probably annoyance. The driver was white, likely one of the millworkers on his way to his afternoon shift at the mill. After the truck passed, an Indian kid in his early twenties left the bridge to walk down the reserve road. When he spotted Hannah, he raised a hand and Hannah waved back.

"You remember Alex?" she asked her father.

"Alex?"

"He used to come over with Dennis Moses, when you were still around. We sometimes called him Coyote."

"*That's* Dennis Moses's grandson?" Jesse asked.

Hannah nodded. "His great-grandson."

Jesse recalled the skinny kid Dennis brought with him when he came over to visit Stew, and who ate the oatmeal cookies Jesse had bought for himself. Alex was older than Hannah and Brandon but he'd entertained them with games and stories while Dennis and Stew jawed away the afternoon. Jesse had no idea who his children hung out with now. Maybe this Alex she watched so intently was her boyfriend.

"Alex organized that protest," Hannah said. "I wish he'd shut it down."

"You're not involved?"

"I don't like the development any more than he docs. But the protest has only managed to piss off most of the landowners and millworkers who use that bridge, and that's making our job that much more difficult."

"*Your* job?"

"Getting the landowners onside to help restore the river." She paused as she watched Alex head to his house. "I expect the protest will be over soon in any case."

"How so?"

"Alex announced the protest on Facebook, so the developer knew exactly what he was up to ahead of time. The developer got an injunction to remove the blockade *before* the protest even started. He had the court order in hand by the time Alex had the backhoe in place. The blockade is still there only because Grant has held off enforcing the court order."

"Grant?"

"Gina's husband."

Jesse's stomach tightened. "He can do that?"

"I guess it's up to the RCMP as to when the injunction is enforced. Grant must have persuaded his bosses that things needed to cool down before they waded into this one. Both sides are pretty emotional. You should have seen the construction workers when they left, all of them spitting nails."

Jesse smiled at Hannah's use of *spitting nails*, one of Stew's sayings.

"Alex expects the police will shut the protest down once the archaeologist gets here. Listen, Dad, to save the spawning grounds we've got to restore these riverbanks. If we don't, we'll lose the fish altogether."

"I take it your grandfather didn't care for the idea."

"Grandpa doesn't like anyone telling him what to do with his land."

Jesse laughed. "That would be an understatement."

"Will you at least consider it?"

Jesse threw a stone that skipped across the shallow water. "I just want to sell the place and get on with my life."

Hannah tucked a strand of hair behind her ear and nodded, tight-lipped. Then she pointed at Abby. "Stay with Jesse," she said, and strode away from him down the path to the river, where she picked up a salmon from the murky waters and doggedly walked back up through river water, past the line of Shuswap volunteers, evidently determined to carry the fish all the way to the spawning grounds on her own. Jesse watched her, uncertain how to reopen this door he'd just slammed shut between them. Then he jogged after her.

Hannah finally stopped and let the fish go. Abby barked and barked again as she would on seeing a bear, and Jesse turned to see his son walking unsteadily down the narrow cattle path through the pasture in nothing but his underwear. Jesse went to meet him, but Brandon wandered right past without seeming to recognize his dad.

"What the fuck?" Jesse said to the boy's back.

Brandon waded into the cold water up to his shins and stood there, staring up at the cliff face of Little Mountain, at the huge painted fishtailed figure rising from the zigzag of lightning. Jesse had once overheard Dennis Moses instruct Hannah and Brandon not to look too long at this pictograph or the wind would start to blow, clouds would gather, lightning would flicker across the sky, thunder would boom and rain would fall and fall and fall. Dennis had said that if a person knew what he was doing, he could use the pictograph to bring on a storm that could wipe out everything in the valley.

Hannah pushed through water to reach her brother. "Bran, what's going on?"

Her question seemed to rouse him. "I've got to talk to Grandpa," he said. He left the water and headed back to the house, once again walking right by his father. His shins and the soles of his feet were blue from the cold.

"You want to tell me what he's using?" Jesse asked his daughter.

Hannah stared at him long enough that he became uncomfortable. Elaine had done the same when she was upset with him. "Nothing worse than you," she said at last.

Jesse, aware of the smell of weed on his jean jacket, decided to drop the issue for now. "Are you coming up to the hospital with Bran and me?" he asked. When Hannah didn't immediately answer, Jesse tried again, softening his voice. "I'd like you to come."

"I've got to get changed first," she said, then called the dog. Together they walked through the pasture back to the house. Jesse said he would wait for her and Brandon in his truck. He wasn't ready to face the demons waiting for him inside the house.

Hannah heard Brandon rustling in his room as she washed the fish from her hands in the bathroom, and then again as she changed into fresh jeans and a T-shirt. Then she heard him thump down the stairs and the kitchen door close, and she peered out her window to see her brother join Jesse in the truck, fully dressed now, except for socks: the pale bone of his bare ankle showed above his runner as he climbed in. Hannah stole the moment to sneak into Brandon's room to see if she could find his stash, but when she opened his bedroom door, she was confronted with images scrawled in pencil and charcoal across the whole of the opposite wall. Every one of the drawings was of a half man, half animal: a figure with the head of a coyote; a bear with the head of a man, standing on his hind legs; a crow with the oversized eyes of a human woman. The pictures were layered one over the other in a manner so like the cave paintings of Lascaux that it chilled her. More chilling was the fact that these could have been the images Hannah had found scattered around the house on scraps of paper when she was a girl—pictures that her mother had drawn, evidence of Elaine's obsession at the onset of her illness. Elaine had drawn picture after picture of transforming animals, and then later of a teenaged native boy, his face drawn again and again, so one image overlapped the other.

Hannah backed out of Brandon's room and closed the door, standing for a time with her hand on the knob. When she joined Jesse and her brother in the Chevy, she didn't say a word about the drawings. The dream catcher she had made for her father back in elementary school, during some lame social studies lesson on aboriginal peoples, dangled from Jesse's rear-view mirror as they pulled out of the yard.

Ties That Bind

STEW SAT IN a wheelchair facing the window, trying to yank off the clear plastic tray affixed to it. His lunch was still on that tray, untouched, bland mounds of potato and meat. His black cowboy hat, with the red feather in its brim, sat on the table beside his bed. If he hadn't spotted the hat there, Jesse wasn't sure he would have recognized his father. The old man had been sturdy the last time Jesse had seen him, his face full, his hands and arms well muscled, but now his hands were bony, his eyes deep-set, and the skin of his cheeks sunken. There was a little yellow sign above his bed, a person in a swing, representing the lift Stew needed to get to the toilet.

"Dad," Jesse said, and he was struck by the wild confusion on Stew's face as he looked up at him. "It's me, Jesse." He watched recognition rise in his father's face, swiftly followed by anger.

"Where the hell have you been?"

"At work," Jesse said, thinking the old man's sense of time had eroded with his memory.

"You've been at work for five frickin' years? You couldn't take a weekend off to visit your kids? It's some woman, isn't it?"

"No," Jesse said. "No woman."

"It's always some woman." Stew squinted at Brandon's bare feet. "Where are your shoes?" Jesse looked down to see that Brandon had slipped off his runners at the door to the hospital room, as if he were entering a friend's home.

"Jesus, Bran, put your shoes back on," Hannah said. "Think about what's been on that floor, what you could catch in this place."

"They bug me," Bran said. "They don't feel right." He fiddled with the tag on the back of his blue T-shirt as if that didn't feel right either.

"Elaine did that when she got sick, remember?" Stew asked Jesse. "She went barefoot, even this time of year, even in winter."

Jesse felt a shot of heat in his gut as he recalled his wife's bare footprints making a trail through snow to the bridge.

Stew took his grandson's arm. "Look at me," he said, and grasped Brandon by the T-shirt, pulling him close to inspect the boy's face. "That thing got you, didn't it?" he said, and let go.

Jesse leaned into his daughter. "What the hell is he talking about?"

Hannah took a step away from her father, but it was clear from the worried expression on her face that she harboured the same doubts about her grandfather's mental state.

"You said you saw me in the river," Brandon told Stew. "When you drowned."

"I did. We both stepped out of our own skins and into that river." Stew held out his hands. "I saw my body dead on shore, but then I looked down and saw myself in the river. My hands were young. I was young."

Brandon nodded as if he, too, remembered.

"I was dead," Stew told Brandon. "But you weren't. Your body was still alive. That thing took hold of it."

Stew sat back in the wheelchair. "I never believed the stories my grandfather and Dennis Moses told about that ghost in the river. Even after it took Elaine, I wasn't sure. Then I fell in the water Saturday, saw things for myself." He pointed a finger at Hannah as if defending himself against an unfair accusation. "I always told you two not to swim there, and chased off any tourist foolish enough to try. At least the Indians know enough not to go in."

Stew had told Jesse the same thing, too many times.

"Your mother never listened, not to me, not to Dennis, not to your father."

Jesse understood what Stew was referring to. On one hot Indian summer afternoon, Elaine had taken Jesse by the hand and pulled him to the river to witness the return of the sockeye and they had both marvelled at the salmon's frustrated attempts to leap the new logjam. Logging upriver had exposed the soil on the steep slopes. When spring rains had hit that year, a slide cascaded down one of the hills, washing mud and the remaining trees into the river. The current carried the mass of logs to the narrows where the logs became trapped in the trestles under the bridge, blocking the flow to the lower part of the river and creating a reservoir above. The salmon could no longer leap the rapids to reach the place where they had once spawned. From then on, the fish could only spawn in the waters that bordered Stew's land.

Watching the salmon that day, Elaine got it in her head to swim with them. When Jesse refused to join her, she stripped down to her bra and underwear and leapt into the pool below the rapids with her arms wide, embracing the danger as she would a lover. There had always been a reckless quality in her that both fascinated and repelled him. Elaine had constantly goaded him past his fears, but he wouldn't follow her into that river. She let out a whoop as she hit cold water. When she popped back up to the surface she quacked like a duck, willing Jesse to laugh with her. Then her expression changed, first to one of awe and wonder, and then to alarm, as her attention was caught by something in the river. Then Elaine was gone, suddenly pulled under by the currents. Panicked, Jesse stumbled down after her along the bank and found her minutes later at Dead Man's Bend, curled into herself like a newborn. She was dazed, barely breathing, terrified.

In the weeks that followed, Elaine slid into madness. Jesse became convinced that some part of her had died in the river. One time he saw his wife standing out in the middle of the river, even as he knew she was sitting in the living room. He checked to make sure he was right and, sure enough, Elaine was seated at the window as she had been for days, staring out. When he turned back to the river, the ghost of his wife was gone.

"That ghost, that Indian boy, has been watching, waiting for another fool to jump in that river," said Stew. He pointed his finger at his grandson's chest. His yellowed nails were clean for the first time Jesse could remember. "Now that thing's inside you."

Jesse glanced at Brandon, expecting him to tell his granddad that the old man had really lost it now. Instead Brandon avoided eye contact as he bit his thumbnail. "What's inside me?" he asked Stew. "What is it, exactly?"

"The Wunks," Stew said, then grinned. He knew how foolish he sounded, how old, how far gone.

"But what *are* the Wunks?" Brandon asked his grandfather.

"You ask Dennis about that," Stew said. "He knows. He'll tell you stories."

"Dennis Moses, you mean?" asked Hannah. "Alex's grandfather? Grandpa, he died several years ago."

Confusion spread across Stew's face, quickly followed by a flush of new grief. "Yes, yes, of course," he said. Then he rattled the plastic tray on his wheelchair. "Let me out! I've got to get back home!"

Jesse put a hand on Stew's arm. "You can't go home, Dad."

Stew made an animal cry of frustration and swept the plate of food from the tray. Brandon jumped back as mashed potatoes flew across the floor and the plastic plate clattered and spun away.

A nurse rushed in, her scrubs printed with penguins. "He's certainly keeping us busy," she said with the patience and cheerfulness of a well-trained daycare worker. She patted Stew's tray. "This has to stay on," she told him. "Do you understand? *On*. So you don't fall out." Then she knelt to clean up the food from the floor.

She looked up briefly at Hannah, at Brandon, at Jesse. "Jesse, isn't it?" she asked him. "Your daughter said you'd likely be here today. I'm Annette." She scraped Stew's lunch back onto the plate with the butter knife. "Stew gets restless, throws things around. I know it's hard to believe, but that's a good sign. He's got fight."

Jesse picked up Stew's cowboy hat from the night table. The scent of his father was bonded to the inner band of the hat: wood shavings and the needles of lodgepole pine, as if, born to this place, Stew had taken the forests into himself.

"I meant to tell Hannah you should take his wallet and keys home too," Annette said. "Things go missing here. They're in that locker." She stood, plate in hand. "Do you have to use the washroom?" she asked Stew. When the old man ignored her, she said, "He's due for potty time. We'll give it a try and see if that calms him down."

"He's not a child," Hannah said.

"No, of course not." Annette patted Hannah's arm as if she was, then left the room, carrying Stew's plate.

Jesse opened the locker door and picked up Stew's thin, cracked wallet. He had bought that wallet for his father one

Christmas, what, twenty-five years earlier? Under the wallet Stew's clothes were neatly folded: muddied work pants and a wrinkled white T-shirt with a spawning sockeye salmon on the front.

"This isn't his T-shirt, is it?" Jesse asked his daughter. Stew rarely wore a T-shirt with an image on it. His standard outfit was jeans or green work pants and a plaid shirt, summer or winter.

"I bought that for him," Hannah said. She looked away as she added, "For Father's Day." Hannah and Brandon had given Jesse nothing for Father's Day, not even a card. They hadn't phoned Jesse and Jesse hadn't called them.

Annette came back with a male nurse and the hoist to lift Stew. Brandon faced the door, his face reddening, as the two nurses fitted the sling under his grandfather. Annette switched on the contraption and Stew rose into the air. His ridiculous blue gown opened, exposing his bony bare arse in the sling.

"Feel like Peter Pan?" the male nurse said and Stew turned his face away, his eyes watering.

"We should go," Hannah said. "Grandpa doesn't want us watching."

"Let's wait in the hall," Jesse said. He ushered his son and daughter past the hoist. They sat in the orange plastic chairs in the hallway. Staff had propped up a few elderly patients in the waiting area at the end of the hall, their wheelchairs facing the television. One or two watched a football game. Others sat with their heads back, staring at the ceiling, but most slept with their chins on their chests.

Jesse could hear Annette in the bathroom, congratulating Stew. "Great! That's two successes today!" The old man mumbled in response. The stink of shit. What milestone was this in his father's life when a bowel movement had become something to celebrate? Jesse thought of Hannah and then Brandon when they were toddlers and the poop discussions he'd have with Elaine on returning home from work. *Brandon went potty twice today!* Hannah had jumped in excitement around him, her little pigtails bobbing, as he'd clapped his hands.

"Grandpa would rather be shot than end up like this," Brandon said. "He wants to die at home."

"I know," Jesse said.

Hannah shifted in her seat. "I could help take care of him. I already pulled out of my classes this semester."

"You didn't need to do that."

"Didn't I?"

"I'm here now."

"Then let's bring Grandpa home."

Jesse said, "We couldn't even get him to the toilet, for Christ's sake."

"You just don't want to deal with him," Hannah said.

Jesse didn't reply. There was no point in arguing. He knew this to be true as much as she did. He turned to Brandon. "Gina says you've been skipping school too."

"I can't think," he said. "I can't read. Nothing makes sense."

"It's just stress," said Hannah. Then, to her father she added, "I needed Bran's help on the farm."

"What was all that crap about the Wunks?" Jesse asked Brandon. "You think you're possessed or something?" Brandon wouldn't look at his father. Jesse eyed him and sat back in his chair.

Through the space between the doorway and the curtain Annette had closed for privacy, Jesse saw the male nurse help Stew to the bed, then fasten a diaper around his hips. He looked away, anywhere but at his father: at the man who slept, open-mouthed, in the room beside Stew's; at the old woman shuffling her wheelchair down the hall towards them, calling for help.

When she reached them, she stopped and took Hannah's hand in hers. "Help me," she said. Her voice was old and shaky and flat. "Help me."

Hannah removed the old woman's hand from hers, setting it gently back on the handle of her wheelchair, and the woman carried on down the hall as if she hadn't stopped, still calling for help. From one of the rooms an elderly man took up her cry. "Help me, help me, help me," he mumbled in a monotone, as if he had long ago given up hope that help would arrive.

— 8 —

The Red Door

THE WEATHERED WOODEN sign that greeted them at the gate when they got home from the hospital read, simply, *Robertson*, a sign that had served the family for three generations. Pink flamingos perched on the fence posts on either side of the gate, and a hodgepodge of garden gnomes, birdbaths and lawn ornaments covered the lawn, a patch of grass Stew never mowed anymore. The ornaments were Stew's idea of a joke: elaborate decorations on his junky, decaying estate.

Abby ran up to greet them as Jesse parked the truck, and then barked and leapt up to gain his attention as he got out. As Jesse scratched the dog behind the ears, Brandon disappeared into the house without saying a word. Hannah headed towards the pasture.

Jesse called after her, "Hey, I thought we'd have a bite to eat." He hauled the cooler out of the back of his truck.

"I picked up a bucket of KFC in Kamloops." When Hannah didn't respond he called, "Where you going?"

She kept her back to him. "To see a man about a fish."

He glanced at Gina's house, where he saw a figure watching them from the kitchen window. Gina, undoubtedly, though Grant's truck was also in the driveway. Jesse raised a hand, but the figure moved away from the window.

Abby whined and Jesse shifted the cooler as he turned to confront his past, this farm that had been his home, not just in his childhood but also throughout his married life. Along with the cattle, the past summer's plague of grasshoppers had eaten the pastures down to a brown ragged matt. Then the insects had turned to the orchard that surrounded the house, eating the leaves from the apple trees. Small, scarred apples dangled from the bare branches.

The willow by the kitchen door had grown. He had planted the tree the week Hannah was born, assuming that he and Elaine would raise their daughter together here on this farm, his inheritance. Planting that willow had been foolish, he thought now. The roots of the tree had pushed under the house, cracking the foundation on that side. They had likely crept into the septic field as well, fingering their way into the pipes.

The house was as Jesse had left it, the work on the exterior still undone. A stack of cedar siding sat on the front deck; tarpaper flapped by the back door that led into the kitchen. He'd gotten that far putting up the new siding before Elaine got sick; it was a job he could have finished in a weekend if he'd put his mind to it.

The kitchen door was red, and in need of paint, as it had been when Jesse was a child. His father had always referred to this red door as the servants' entrance, the one he used himself. Stew had told him that his ancestor, Eugene Robertson, the first homesteader in the valley, had indulged his Shuswap wife by allowing her family to enter through this door to visit her in the kitchen. Eugene would not permit them to enter through the front door, nor would he let his wife entertain her kin in the small room that served as a parlour, though she had sat there with Eugene in the evenings. Together, at night, Eugene and his Shuswap wife read the Bible by lamplight, both for her spiritual illumination and so she could practise her reading. Eugene had attempted to exorcise what he viewed as her pagan beliefs from the house so they would not infect the children he had hoped they would have together.

Jesse turned the knob of this ancient door with its peeling red paint but then hesitated before stepping across the worn wood of the threshold. The dark kitchen cupboards and the stove were the same ones he'd known in his teens and young adulthood. But so much else had changed. His wife had been dead eight years, yet he felt the same anxiety and guilt he'd experienced the last night he had come home smelling of another woman, that sweet girl from the reserve who wasn't yet out of her teens, the new receptionist at the mill where he worked, a girl who hid behind giggles as a child might hide behind bubbles she dispensed from a wand. Her name once again escaped him. It was something young, green. *Fern.* The girl had had a scar on her shoulder, made by human teeth, he'd discovered that evening. Fern had been bitten by a

white man, she told him, when he'd touched the pale crescent.
A *white* man, she had said with emphasis, perhaps acknowledging that Jesse had been accepted at least somewhat by
his Shuswap co-workers at the mill. That's all she had said
after he'd moved Brandon's backpack to the front seat and
folded down the back of the minivan to accommodate their
lovemaking. He had tried to please her, in his way—it had
been important to him to please her. He'd circled her small
breasts, hid his fingers in the cleavage between her legs until
her unresponsiveness told him that she was deriving no pleasure from it, and then he took his own.

He had come home that night and sat in the van for a
time, looking through the side window of the living room,
watching his wife and his father. Stew had been drinking a
glass of rum and Coke and reading in his scruffy armchair.
Elaine, as usual, sat on a wooden captain's chair facing the
front window, one that overlooked the river.

Stew had waited up for Jesse that night with her and,
as it turned out, had phoned around trying to find him too.
Jesse hadn't called to say he'd be late, that he would miss
dinner. Why hadn't he just phoned that night to say he was
pulling a double shift?

When Jesse finally entered the house through the back
door, he'd found his father at the kitchen sink, rinsing his
glass. His shoulders had curved with age. He had become
an old man.

"What is it with you and these Indian women?" he'd
asked Jesse, without turning to him. "Do you really believe
they'll ask less of you?"

Jesse took off his jacket and hung it on a hook by the door. "Does Elaine know? Did you tell her?" Elaine was just around the corner, in the living room, likely still staring at the dark glass of the window as she had for weeks now.

"Of course Elaine knows. A wife always knows." Stew paused. "Some part of her knows." In that moment Jesse realized how naïve he'd been—no, foolish—in his pursuit of other women, even before Elaine took ill. He had been the boy who stole from his mother's box of chocolates while she was in the kitchen, thinking she wouldn't hear his footfalls over the clatter of dishes, that she wouldn't notice the missing nougat, her favourite.

"I didn't tell Elaine nothing," Stew said. "I didn't worry the kids either. They're in bed. I told them you were at work."

Later, as Elaine died in that intensive care bed, Hannah would tell Jesse she had heard this conversation between her father and grandfather through the heat vent in her bedroom floor. She knew about his affairs in the same way Jesse knew about his father's drinking, when Stew was still trying to hide it, the bottles he kept in the barn. Children always knew more about their parents' lives than their parents suspected.

"Who did you phone?" Jesse asked his father. "Did you phone Gina?"

"No! I'm not stupid. I see you and Gina slipping off together. It's a wonder Grant hasn't come pounding on this door already." Stew pointed a finger at Jesse, his nails blackened with grease. "Gina will hear about this soon enough. Those Indians are as thick as thieves. But you already know that. I expect that's why you disappeared with that other Indian girl tonight."

Jesse tried to come up with a defence, but he had none. He had made a decision to end things with Gina. She had begun to talk of a future together, of leaving Grant. She would find out about Fern, eventually, though, as it turned out, not as quickly as Stew imagined. Aside from her work, Gina kept her distance from her home reserve. It was only after Elaine's funeral that Gina phoned to confront Jesse about Fern. And by then his affair with Gina was already over. It had not survived Elaine's suicide.

"Your place is here, with your sick wife," Stew said. "Not out there, chasing skirts."

Jesse and Stew had fallen silent as Elaine entered the kitchen. Her medication and illness left her drowsy and vacant and she walked unsteadily. She hadn't showered or combed her hair in nearly a week and had stopped wearing a bra, her breasts shifting under the cotton of her blue T-shirt. She walked up to Jesse slowly, and when he tried to turn away to mumble his apology at being late, she took his face in both her hands and held him there while she looked him over carefully, her eyes wild as a feral cat's. Then she'd let him go. Later Jesse found her huddled in the bathtub, in the dark, and led her to their bed. He went back to the living room to sleep on the couch.

As Jesse came through the door, Brandon wandered into the kitchen, eating vegetable soup straight from the can. He stopped when he saw his father and turned a little as if he was about to go back upstairs to his bedroom. His hair was dishevelled and his shirt was stained with bits of food. Nevertheless, Jesse was struck by Bran's youthful beauty, his colouring, so like his own: Brandon's ginger hair, his smooth, freckled face; his pale, sinewy arms and thin wrists; the white anklebone beneath his sweats. At this cusp between childhood and adulthood, he appeared unfinished, a thought half-spoken.

"I've got a bucket of chicken in the cooler," Jesse said, pointing to the container on the table. "You're welcome to it."

Brandon held up the soup can, as if unheated soup was a better option than what Jesse had to offer.

"These yours?" Jesse asked Brandon, lifting one of several honour roll certificates hanging by magnets on the front of Stew's fridge. Both Brandon and Hannah had evidently made the honour roll at their school, year after year. "You're smart, eh?"

Brandon shrugged.

That had been one of Stew's many complaints about Jesse, that he was too damn smart. Stew had always said Jesse never had to work for anything so he had never learned to finish what he started.

"What's your best subject?"

"I don't know. Art, I guess."

"You drew these?" Jesse pointed at the pictures on the side of the fridge. *Star Wars* characters, various bipedal beasts dressed as men.

"When I was a kid." Brandon tossed the soup can in the garbage and wiped his hand on his sweats, then turned and headed to the stairs that led to his room. Jesse heard him climb the stairs, then close his door behind him.

Jesse stared at the magnetic school photos of his daughter and son on the fridge door. There used to be other family pictures on the kitchen walls, of Jesse and Elaine seated with Hannah and Brandon; of Stew, Jesse and his mother, Amanda, taken when Jesse was a toddler, shortly before his mother died of breast cancer. He remembered little of his mother, only a drift of sensations, emotions: a longing for her presence; her absence like a stone in his mouth. Stew had mounted that photo of the three of them over the kitchen table where, throughout most of his childhood, only Stew and Jesse had eaten their meals. In it, his mother held Jesse on her lap, while Stew stood behind. Amanda's face was stressed and drawn—she was already ill—and her eyes looked through the camera rather than at it. He could see the distance between his mother and father, and even between mother and son: her hold on him was loose and formal. She had already begun to leave him. Where had that photo gone? Where had the photos of Jesse and Elaine and the kids gone?

The only photograph that remained was of his ancestor Eugene Robertson, a shot taken in the late-Victorian era: a careful, freckled man, sitting beside his petite, proper British wife, their children encircling them. Like so many of his countrymen, Eugene had sought out the wilderness but then forced his British civilities upon it.

Jesse recalled a scrap of story Stew had told him about this first Robertson, who had crossed an ocean and a continent to reach British Columbia in his hunt for gold, leaving a young wife behind in the old country, and who had stayed on in this new world even though he had never found the treasure he sought. There was no bridge over the river at the time Eugene made his decision to stay. He had not yet built this house and he slept outside on a fragrant mattress of balsam boughs. Perhaps his decision was thrust upon him— he had lost everything and couldn't afford to go home—or maybe he had found something here, in the Shuswap, that he could not leave behind: these blue, forested mountains, this hidden valley, this river that was so full of life then. Eugene sent for his wife almost a decade after finding this place, having spent those intervening years with a Shuswap woman.

As the salmon ran the river, Eugene had untied his cottonwood dugout from a riverside willow and took up paddles to cross the water with the express purpose of finding himself a woman in the Shuswap village. As he stepped out onto the far shore, he looked up and saw a pair of eagles, talons locked, cartwheeling down from above in a mating display. Directly below the courting birds, a girl prepared salmon for drying on racks. She looked up first at the eagles, and then at Eugene watching her. The eagles didn't separate on the wing as Eugene expected, but fell from the sky and crashed into the bush close to the girl, their talons still locked together. They flapped and hopped through boxwood and salal as they tried, unsuccessfully, to untangle themselves one from the other.

Here was divine providence, Eugene thought: his choice had been made for him. He and the girl would join as the eagles had. What the girl thought had not been passed down in this family story. She was much younger than Eugene, less than half his age. Eugene ferried her back across the river in his canoe, and took her as his wife that day, without a priest to formalize the marriage, and without a roof to hide their lovemaking from God and the angels. Their first union could not have been what the girl had hoped for.

Jesse had no idea how that relationship between Eugene and the Indian girl had ended or if children were born from that union. Maybe he had distant cousins across the river. A great many of the current surnames on the reserve originated with white fur traders or miners who had taken Indian wives and had children, then deserted their Shuswap families when they moved on or went home with whatever fortunes they had accumulated. It struck Jesse that he was as irresponsible as those men. More so. He didn't have the cultural ignorance—the arrogance—of that past era to hide behind.

The kitchen phone rang but he didn't answer it. He leaned against the fridge, listening as the answering machine recorded the message.

"Jesse, it's Gina."

As if he wouldn't recognize the weight and texture of her voice.

"If you're there, pick up. I see your truck in the yard."

She was nearly whispering. She didn't want Grant to hear. When Jesse didn't pick up the receiver, Gina said, "We need to talk about Brandon. I saw him walk into the river today. His behaviour recently has been . . ." She paused. "I'm worried about him. Call me."

Jesse waited for a goodbye, but there wasn't one. The message light blinked after Gina hung up. He hit play and listened again to the rise and fall of Gina's voice, the only thing that seemed familiar in this moment. Not this decaying house. Not this farm settling, sinking back into the earth. Not his own son and daughter. They were all strangers to him now.

He pressed the message button a second time, searching for some hint of that old affection for him that he had always found so comforting. But Gina wore what he had jokingly called her shrink voice, one that kept the native teens she counselled at once placated, orderly and at a distance. He listened to her message a last time, nevertheless.

We need to talk about Brandon.

Jesse took Brandon's school photo from the fridge and held it a moment before placing it back beneath a magnet. Then he climbed the stairs to his son's door and knocked. "I thought we could spend a little time together tonight," he told his son, through the door.

"What?"

"Maybe we could hang together?" Jesse opened the door as he spoke. "It's been a while—" He stopped when he saw the state of his son's room. The same light blue paint on the walls; the same bowl light fixture on the ceiling; the same orange, green and brown bedspread, a 1980s castoff from his father's bed; the same mirror on the wall. Brandon had even left the *Back to the Future Part III* poster up in the corner, one

Jesse had duct-taped there. Brandon had turned the antique bureau—a relic from Eugene Robertson's time—into a desk for his laptop. He had littered both it and the floor with books, dirty clothes and a mountain of junk food wrappers. A pile of his dirty socks and underwear sat in the corner. But Jesse was stopped in his tracks, struck with nausea, not by this disorder, but by the images Brandon had drawn on the walls. His wife, Elaine, had sketched these same creatures, over and over, in the months before she had taken her own life. Brandon was at work on one now, squatting in the corner of the room to complete a sketch of a fox with human feet.

"Jesus, Bran."

Brandon stood to face his father, charcoal in hand, his blank look unreadable. Behind him, on the wall, the drawing of a crow with the eyes of a woman stared at Jesse.

"What the hell is going on?" Jesse asked, though he feared he already knew.

Bran searched his circling thoughts for some explanation that his father would accept. These weren't all his own thoughts, he knew. Many belonged to another. For a fleeting moment Brandon understood what this other was telling him, but then his awareness fell away, as dreams do once the sleeper wakes.

"I don't know," he said. "Not yet."

Then his attention was caught by a flash of water on the wall, a reflection, this pretty thing, catching light. He reached out to touch the mirror, and as one thought skipped across his mind another took its place, one overlapping the other like concentric circles in the water.

— 9 —

Skipping Stones

ALEX HAD WALKED so quietly through grass and mud to where Hannah waited on Eugene's Rock that she hadn't heard him, just felt the warmth that radiated from him as he stood beside her, the shelter his body provided from the cool, late-afternoon breeze. Below her in the water, a sockeye pair prepared to mate in the gravel of the riverbed. The female sockeye had swept the rocks, flicking her body to clear away the algae and silt that might suffocate the eggs she would lay here. The male hovered by the female, stroking her with his whole body, waiting. When she was ready and released her eggs, he quivered, letting loose his milt to swirl within the water, to cover the eggs. He would soon swim away to die, but the female would stay as long as her tail beat, to protect her nest of stone.

Alex sat down beside Hannah with the old familiarity, close enough that the hairs of his forearms raised goose bumps on the skin of hers. He smelled, faintly, of cigarettes and of the orange he must have just eaten.

"Got your smoke signal," he said. When Hannah raised an eyebrow at him, he tapped the cellphone in his jacket pocket.

Hannah wasn't sure what to think of these small jokes Alex made. Had the Shuswap even used smoke signals? She figured he was making fun of her, poking holes in the preconceptions he assumed she carried from her white world. Then again, maybe not. He had, after all, reinvented himself during his time away at university; he had distanced himself from his roots, even as he returned to them.

"So what's up?" he asked.

"Jesse finally got back. I was just in town with him and Bran, visiting Grandpa. Christ, Alex, I think Grandpa's losing it. He says Bran is possessed or something." She rubbed her knees. "Thing is, Bran seems to think he is too. He's drawing on his walls. Crazy shit. Animals that are part human."

"Like what your mom drew."

Hannah glanced away and nodded. "That day we fell in the river, you talked about a water mystery. I thought maybe if I knew what you told Bran I could make him understand it isn't real. Or maybe you could?"

Alex shook his head. "I can't do that. Only he knows what he's dealing with."

Hannah shifted away from him. "What *did* you tell him?"

"Stew must have told you about Eugene Robertson."

"No, not much. Sounds like he was an asshole. He was married to some woman back in England when he took a

Shuswap wife. Grandpa said he would only let her family visit through the back door."

"Libby," Alex said. "Her name was Elizabeth, but everyone called her Libby."

"You know her name?"

"Interesting that you don't, given Eugene was *your* ancestor."

She shrugged. "I don't know much about our family history."

"I don't suppose I would either if Grandpa Dennis hadn't forced me to sit and listen to his stories."

Alex pointed across the river, to the tent over the toddler's grave that the construction crew had exposed as they widened the road. "Have you been to the site?"

"No, I didn't feel—" Hannah stopped there. She hadn't felt she had the right to visit that grave, a white girl intruding on sacred space.

She didn't need to finish her sentence. Alex understood. "We're not telling most people this, of course," he told her, "but the boy in that grave was buried—or reburied—with a nugget of gold. When I saw that, I knew who that boy was." Alex didn't say that he was also convinced the timing of the child's unearthing was no accident. It was an announcement of a kind, for the few who had heard Dennis's stories and were willing to believe them. Within that grave, the remains were arranged crudely in the foetal position and the thin bones of the boy's hand gripped the gold as a cherished possession, even in death. Some of the bones were missing and others were out of order, which meant, from what Dennis had told him, that this child had been of special importance. The Shuswap, the *Secwepemc,* had once removed the bones of their honoured dead from their graves, cleaned them and reburied them in fresh garments every so often until there was no one left to remember. This grave, however, wasn't all that old, dating from around the time of the gold rush. The *Secwepemc* had already been forced to give up the old ways, and buried their dead—and after the arrival of the traders and the miners there were so many dead, struck down by disease and starvation—in the ground under simple white crosses, the graves enclosed by tiny white picket fences.

"That boy in the grave, his name was Samuel," Alex told Hannah. "Samuel Robertson. He drowned in the river."

"Samuel Robertson was my great-great-grandfather, I think," she said. "Stew's great-grandfather."

Alex nodded. "I suspect Eugene named him after his first child, the one he'd had with Libby. The son he lost. Libby was one of my ancestors."

"Shit. You're not going to tell me we're related."

Hannah appeared genuinely panicked by the thought and Alex grinned. "No, not directly, not by blood," he said, although he knew their family stories were painfully inter-twined. "Samuel found the nugget of gold he was buried with right here, in these spawning grounds. He was just a little kid, not quite four years old. He gave it to his mother, to Libby, as a gift." In the way any small child might offer a river-polished stone or ragged bunch of wildflowers to his mother, his first love.

The gold within the gravel of the river bottom had caught Samuel's eye, a reflection within reflection underwater. He'd plucked the nugget from the shallows and ran up shore crying, "Mama!"

Just upriver, Libby squatted by the boulder Eugene had marked with his name, shortly before he had asked her to be his wife. Here, by this boulder, she scrubbed her husband's shirt on river rock with the soap she had made herself from tallow and ashes. There weren't many salmon here to hamper her task. The run hadn't returned in anything close to their usual numbers and Libby knew why. In 1857, Eugene Robertson had been the first miner to arrive on this river, but when word spread that he had found a little gold here, other whites had followed. By the fall of 1862, the river was filled with miners. Up and down these shores, white men had staked their claims and now mined for gold in the shallows. They didn't wash, these miners, and their stench carried on the river breeze. They wore the same long underwear, the same wool pants and shirts, day in and day out, sleeping and eating in their clothes. They smelled of pork and the pissy scent of ground coffee, of unwashed skin, of armpit stink and of the semen crusted on their underclothes. They dumped bucketfuls of rocks, sand, mud, and the red eggs of the sockeye into the screen at the top of the box, then rocked and rocked the contraption by its broomstick handle, sifting the mess into the stepped riffles below so that only the larger rocks remained on the screen. Then the miners picked through the rocks, hunting for gold. Hundreds, thousands of white men, running from the Pacific up the rivers into the interior and then to this river, like the sockeye.

"No, not like the salmon," Alex told Hannah. "Like an army, or like a sickness, a plague. They did carry a plague."

Hannah waved a hand in impatience. "You were going to tell me what's going on with Bran."

"I am," said Alex.

Libby stood as her son called her name a second time. "Mama!" This girl who wasn't yet twenty, wearing the string of trade beads her mother had given her. She had embroidered the bodice of her dress herself, using thread Eugene had brought her from the Kamloops trading post as a Christmas gift.

Samuel offered her the shining stone he had found. "What do you have here?" she asked in the secret language they spoke when Eugene wasn't around. Libby turned the rock over in the palm of her hand. She glanced upriver and then down, to the white men sullying the river in their hunt for gold. "Do you know what this is?" she asked her son. "Your father came here to find this. These other men have come from great distances to find this. They are churning up the rivers and killing our fish to find this."

"What is it?" Samuel asked.

"The English call it *gold*," she said. "We won't tell any-one—especially your father—you found it."

"Why?"

"This gold makes some men foolish," she said. "Your father is foolish enough as it is. So, no telling, all right?"

"All right."

"In any case, it belongs in the river. Shall we send it back?"

Samuel nodded.

"The rock will try to escape by running across the water," she said, "but the river will swallow it." Libby skipped the nugget across the shallows, hitting one, two, three, four, five, six times and then the river swallowed the rock, just as she said it would.

"She threw it back?" Hannah asked Alex. "But you said Samuel was buried with that nugget."

"Libby talked big," Alex said. He grinned. "But even she couldn't resist that gold. She went back later and searched the river until she found it."

In the moment she skipped the gold across the river, she was content to let it go in the way she had once released a bob-cat from one of Eugene's snares. Libby turned back to her washing, but Samuel patted her breast. "Mama," he said.

Libby wiped her hands on her skirt and, glancing at the men busy on the river, opened her blouse and sat on Eugene's Rock. Samuel stood beside her and suckled, kneading her breast, and they both closed their eyes as they were enveloped in the sweet scent of her milk letting down.

"What are you doing?" Eugene cried.

Libby startled to find her husband standing on the riverbank beside her. Samuel detached from her breast to look up at him, exposing her nipple. Libby quickly covered herself as the miners were all now watching.

"For god's sake, Libby. The boy is nearly four years old."

Libby buttoned her bodice. "A child knows what he needs," she told Eugene, in English.

"How in hell will you conceive another child if you're still suckling him? Don't you want more children?"

She squatted to wash Eugene's shirt, her back to him. "How will I conceive another child if you never touch me?" she said.

Libby felt the waiting in the air, like the seconds following a lightning flash, before the boom and roll of thunder. Eugene grabbed her arm and raised a hand as if to strike her, but instead let her go. "Why would I want you?" he said. "You stink of old milk."

Eugene marched away from her, back into the forest he was cutting, tree by tree, bush by bush, making way for fields. He had long ago given up on finding gold in the river, even as the other men searched on. Instead he had succeeded in bringing down enough of the forest that the wind now helped him do the job, ripping trees from their roots during summer storms.

Libby sat back upon Eugene's Rock with his wet shirt in her lap.

"Mama." Samuel patted her breast, to reassure her, to reassure himself. But she didn't open her blouse to him. Instead she picked up the wedge of soap from the river shore and walked into the river fully clothed to wash the stink of milk from her person.

The next day, Libby left the cabin at first light while both Eugene and Samuel were still in bed. Samuel heard the door close and got up to peer through the window. His mother was heading towards the shallows. Samuel ran after her, leaving the door open.

"Go back to your father," she called.

But still he followed. She ran faster, to escape him, her skirts billowing. She ran until she was far ahead of him and still Samuel followed, crying and calling for his mother as he ran through the field of stumps, the bush along the river, stumbling and climbing over windfall. He fell, bloodying his hands and knees, and when he stood again he couldn't see her. He searched and searched until he heard his father calling them both and he returned to the cabin alone.

The sun was low in the sky when Libby finally came home.

Samuel listened from his small room as his father demanded to know where she had gone, but Libby wouldn't tell him.

"You want Samuel weaned," she told him. "Then we shall wean him."

The following morning, Libby jumped on her horse and once again left Samuel with his father. She rode bareback, her skirts hiked up to expose her legs, her long black hair flowing like her mare's mane behind her. Eugene tried to stop her from leaving with almost as much force as Samuel, both of them running after her. She wouldn't tell Eugene or her son where she was going. Libby had secrets from them both now.

Samuel followed her to the shallows, where the river spilled into the lake. There, from a distance, he saw his mother dismount, wrap the reins of the horse around a young cotton-wood, and lift her skirts to wade through the estuary, to meet a man waiting for her on the other side of the river. Samuel hid himself in the bush to watch them. He saw his mother look back and then upriver to make sure neither his father nor the miners could see them.

The man she met was dressed like his father, in denim trousers and a cowboy hat, but he looked nothing like Eugene. Where his father's hair was ginger, this man's was black, like his mother's. Where his father's skin was white and freckled, this man's skin was brown and smooth, like his mother's. The stranger was young, as young as his mother.

"I didn't think you were coming," the man said as Libby reached him, his voice skipping like a stone towards Samuel across the shallows. The stranger used his mother's secret words to talk to her. So, they were not so secret. The man pointed at her breasts, to the stain of milk on her blouse. "You're wet."

Libby crossed her arms to cover herself. "I've weaned Samuel," she said.

"Don't hide. I want to look at you." He walked around her, smiling, and ran his hand down her cheek, to her neck, to her collarbone, to her breast. He squeezed it, kneading it as Samuel had when he suckled. But Libby withdrew. "It hurts," she said. "My milk. I'm so full."

"I could relieve you."

She laughed.

He took her hand. "Come lie with me."

She shook her head but allowed him to undo the buttons of her blouse. When she was naked, he suckled her.

"There's nothing there," he said.

"I'm shy. My milk won't come when I'm shy."

"Then don't be shy." He drew her down to lie in the long grasses along the river shore and suckled her breast again and then went on suckling, taking Libby's milk, Samuel's milk. She reached down and undid the buttons of his trousers, but he took her hand in his and laced their fingers together. "Let me help you," he said.

When he had emptied each breast he moved up to kiss her, an open-mouthed kiss, to give her a taste of her own milk. Then he rolled her over and entered her as Eugene's bull entered a cow, pushing at her from behind. This man who had taken Samuel's milk. This man who had taken his mother from him.

Samuel ran to tell his father. When the boy reached him, Eugene stopped to look at him, then bent back to his chore, felling yet another tree. The saw, saw, saw of the blade teeth through wood. He had not left his work to find his son. "Where in hell were you?"

"The man drank Mama's milk," Samuel told him.

Eugene's face took on the colour of blood, but he didn't stop or run to find Libby and punish her and the man as Samuel hoped he would. So Samuel took it upon himself to bring his mother home. He ran back to the river, took off his clothes and folded them neatly as he had seen his father do when Eugene took his Saturday bath in the river. Then Samuel walked naked into the water as his father always did. He felt, first, his bare feet on river stone, then the frigid water engulfing his tiny body as the current dragged him beneath the black surface.

When he sloshed his way out of that river onto the far shore, he followed his own body as he would follow his mother, observing himself from without: his own small figure seen from behind, walking first on river gravel, then on white mud, then on wet grass. A storm gathered over Little Mountain, conjuring mosquitoes from the moist air. They bit his face, his shoulders, his back, his thighs, but he didn't—couldn't—slap them away. The insects followed the trail of his breath backwards, until they reached his mouth, the exhalation of breath that both his mother's and father's ancestors believed was the intangible soul, whether called mystery or *spiritus*. But even the mosquitoes knew breath— spirit—led to flesh and blood.

As Hannah mulled over Alex's story, she reached down into the water to stroke the hump of one of the sockeye bucks, this old man who was too exhausted to take flight. She knew by the slowing of the fish's tail he would soon die. The tail beat as the heart beat, continuously and without thought, until life ended. A smaller sockeye buck waited to the side, hoping for a chance to mate with the female once this bigger male was gone. Other males, already spent, rocked in the shallows, their tails flicking from time to time as their lives unravelled.

"So the mystery took Samuel," Hannah said. "Like you think it took Bran."

Alex paused before responding. "Like it took your mother."

"My *mother*." Hannah looked to the far shore as she considered what he'd said.

In that moment Alex thought he might bring her to some genuine understanding, but then she swung her scepticism around herself like a cloak. "You do understand how fucked all this sounds," she said.

"You know something's going on," Alex told her, "or you wouldn't be here asking me about it. And hey, if you don't believe me, go ask your grandfather. Stew knows more than he's been telling you."

"Grandpa says the Wunks got Bran."

"The Wunks? Is that what Stew calls the mysteries?"

Hannah tilted her head to appraise him. "Trying to get other people to believe Dennis's stories isn't going to make you believe them yourself, you know," she said.

Alex raised both hands, exasperated. He wouldn't try to convince her, not now. She would see things for herself or she wouldn't. Dennis had taught him that it was an elder's job, a teacher's job, to guide a kid into discovering things for himself, rather than cutting the lesson into little pieces and feeding it to him, as the teachers did in the white school system. When Alex had asked Dennis to teach him how to drive a car, Dennis threw him the keys to his Buick and said, "Go to it." Since Alex had watched him drive, Dennis figured that was enough. Dennis was more or less right, Alex thought, though on his second day out he ran the car into a tree.

"When you're ready to hear me out," Alex told her, "I'll tell you the rest of the story."

"Tell me now."

Alex stood to skip a stone across the water. "You're not ready."

Hannah found a rock and made a sullen attempt to skip it, but the stone plopped sadly into the river.

"How could you grow up around this much water and not know how to skip stones?"

Hannah shrugged. "I don't know. Dad left. Grandpa never got around to teaching me."

"Come on." Alex waved her downriver.

"Where are we going?"

"To the lake. You've got to learn how to skip stones and I don't want to scare the fish."

He led Hannah past Dead Man's Bend to the lakeshore. There, he picked up a stone and took her hand in both of his to position the rock in her palm. "Now throw with your whole arm, like this," he said, and he showed her.

Hannah flicked her wrist, holding the image of his throw in her mind. The rock landed with a splash.

"No, don't flick your wrist. Throw with your whole arm. Whip it!"

She watched the way his grip simply let go in the last instant. Then she tried again, and the stone skipped once.

"Here," he said, and he picked up another rock. "You want a flat stone," he said, "but one that's rounded on the bottom, like a dinner plate."

One of the miniature plates from the tea set she had as a child, she thought. He sent it skimming across the water, three, four, five, six times, the circles spreading out, meeting each other.

"And you want one with a bit of weight," he said, bending to search for another. "Not so light that the wind will catch it. I like them just a little pointed on one end, something I can set my finger on." He held just such a rock between index finger and thumb, his middle finger supporting the stone from beneath, then sent the rock blazing across the water. A dozen concentric circles melting one into the other.

Hannah chose and threw a rock, but again it only skipped once before sinking into the river. She took a moment to remove a gumboot and stood on one foot to dump the water from it. Her sock was wet and as she removed it, Alex took her hand to help her balance, and she kept on holding it as she stepped, barefoot, back into her boot even though she no longer needed the steadying. She was both surprised and thrilled by the warmth of his hand.

"Wet socks make me crazy," she said, to explain herself as she at last removed her hand from Alex's, but she saw from his half-smile that he had not bought that explanation. He bent to search for another stone to avoid looking at her. Hannah did the same, embarrassed now. She let one rock after another drop from her hand, just as he did. The smoothness of the rocks, tumbled by thousands of years of glacier movement and, more recently, the pounding of river water. The heat of his body beside hers.

In two hands, she held out a flat stone the size of a dinner plate. "Here," she said, joking to ease the uncertainty between them. "Skip this." And Alex did, five times before it belly-flopped into the water. "Impressive," she said.

"Grandpa Dennis taught me to skip stones. He used to bring me down to the lake when things got bad at home. He didn't say a word about Mom and Dad fighting, or about Dad after he left. We just skipped stones together. Somehow that made things better. I knew I would be okay." He skipped the stone he had been holding. "I still come down here when things are rough. I can almost feel Grandpa Dennis skipping stones next to me."

Hannah weighed the rock in her hand. "I hear Mom sometimes, calling me." She glanced at Alex to gauge his reaction before she added, "Other times I feel her in the room with me."

Alex nodded as if this was an everyday occurrence. "The spirits of suicides linger," he said. "They are often confused, clinging to the world they abandoned, and can't walk the spirit trail until they let go." He paused. "Or their families let them go."

Hannah let the stone drop and reached for another. "Mom found a gold ring here one summer, a wedding band. It was stuck over the end of a bullet."

"Seriously?"

Hannah had been standing close to her at the time and would have found the ring if her mother had not. She didn't want to leave the beach after that, and sulked as she followed her mother home for supper. At the age of nine she had caught gold fever, the treasure hunter's sickness.

"At the dinner table that night we tried to figure out how the ring had gotten on that bullet. I mean, did they come together in the river, or did someone stick them together intentionally? Grandpa thought the ring was an omen and maybe he was right. It was only a couple of months later that Mom got sick and Dad started disappearing on us. Then Mom left too." Taking her own life.

Hannah flung her stone across the water and this time it skipped and skipped and skipped, like moments ticking back in time, she thought, watching the circles spread away.

"There, see, you've got it," Alex said.

Hannah grinned at him, the sudden thrill of this small success in her belly, a feeling she had thought she left behind in childhood, but here it was. When Alex held her gaze, she felt a flush rise from her chest to her face, her body revealing the secret she had been keeping from him. She turned away, to pick up another stone, and skipped it.

Beside her, Alex sent his own stone shuddering across the water. "I would never leave like your dad did," he said. "If I loved a woman and she was sick, I would stay." Hannah glanced at him, found him watching her, and looked back to the ripples he had just created. He stooped down to pick up another stone and placed it in Hannah's palm, this one so smooth that it seemed as alive as a hen's egg. He cupped his hand over hers and once again held her gaze so she understood he had also experienced the shift in understanding, in expectation, between them. "The perfect stone," he said, before letting go.

10

Madness from the Walls

WIND PLUCKED LEAVES from the poplar on the front lawn and blew cool air in through the partly open window, bringing with it the sharp, leafy scent of a Shuswap autumn. Just a few more days and they'd be into October. Jesse closed the window but the morning chill remained. The house had never been properly insulated and, with its excessive roof overhang, had rarely been warm, even on summer evenings. This cramped living room was especially cold; Eugene Robertson had designed it that way in the days when a parlour was not only reserved for infrequent guests but for the family dead, who were displayed here until buried. The dead were still here, Jesse thought, present even in this windowsill, where much of the ancient putty had come loose and fallen out. Eugene Robertson had once kneaded linseed oil into this putty to keep it from drying as he worked it, and pressed it into place around the panes. He had left his mark on this window—the whorls of his fingers and thumbs—just as he had left his mark on this land, in the whorls of the ancient stumps of the trees he had felled, which still stood in the fields. Some were so huge it would take another hundred years for them to rot and to return to the soil they had sprung from.

Gina entered the living room with two cups of coffee, handing Jesse his before cradling her own in both hands as she looked out the window with him. He muttered his thanks but kept his eyes on the river. Nevertheless his attention was very much on Gina. She was long and lean and her skinny jeans exaggerated her slim silhouette. Her long black hair held a few wiry strands of grey and smelled of wood smoke, from the two wood stoves that heated the bungalow she shared with Grant. Her face had grown softer, more welcoming, he thought. More forgiving.

"I appreciate all your advice," he told her. "And I can't thank you enough for coming over today. I don't think Hannah will listen to me otherwise."

"Oh, I won't be much help on that front," Gina said. "Even when she asks for my help, she resents me for it."

"She's not still holding a grudge, is she? After all these years."

"Can you blame her?"

Jesse sipped his coffee. "I suppose not."

Gina looked away briefly and Jesse realized he had hurt her. They both watched a flock of Canada geese lift from the field and fly towards the lake, circling as they gained strength for their flight south.

"I hope I can get this place cleaned up before snow hits," Jesse said, to break the silence.

"You do understand you'll need to stay for a while now. You may have to rethink the sale of the farm."

"That's not going to happen."

Gina didn't respond right away. "Got a girlfriend?" she asked him finally. "Is that why you don't want to come back?"

Jesse laughed at the bluntness of her question. "No," he said, meeting her eyes. "No girlfriend."

She smiled a little at him as she sipped her coffee. He was surprised that Gina appraised him with such obvious pleasure. Her attention made him feel awkward; he was all at once the boy in high school, navigating his way into adulthood, that shy, skinny kid who was more comfortable reading books than hanging out at parties. He only found his footing with women in his twenties, after he was married. And then, after Elaine's death, he lost what little confidence he'd had in that regard. He'd spent most nights in recent years eating his supper alone in front of the TV.

"What then?" Gina asked. "Why won't you stay?"

"Work, I guess. I have a business to run."

Gina raised an eyebrow, though she understood all the many reasons he didn't want to return. "Stew is proud of you, you know," she said. "The work you do. He never wastes a chance to brag about how you own your own business."

Jesse grunted. His business was a mobile welding rig mounted on the back of his Chevy pickup. Stew had taught Jesse to weld in the first place, then harangued him to give it up after he earned his ticket, warning him that his chosen occupation would leave him blind if it didn't kill him. Jesse had already experienced his share of welder's flash when he worked at the mill: the painful, watery eyes and sensitivity to light that left him grounded for days, unable to drive or even watch TV. Sparks had set his pants and shirts on fire several times. His hands and arms were covered in burns.

When Jesse didn't volunteer anything more, Gina looked back out the window. "You *will* have to move back," she said. "The kids need you. You have to stay."

"You almost sound like you *want* me back."

Gina kept her eyes on the landscape in front of them, the brilliant yellow leaves of the poplars, the rust and gold leaves of the fruit trees, the deep blue of the river. She didn't reply, but still, a small smile played on her face.

Jesse studied her. "What would Grant think about that? Me moving home?"

Gina's smile faded. "That's all behind us now, isn't it?"

Jesse looked back to the river, the relentless movement of its water, knowing he was stepping into one of those moments he would likely regret. "I think about you all the time," he said, but then Hannah drove her grandfather's truck into the yard.

"Why is she home already?" Jesse said. "She only just left for the hospital." He hadn't been in to see the old man himself again in the days since he arrived. He promised himself he would, tomorrow, or the next day.

As Hannah got out of the truck, Abby ran up to greet her and she bent to pet the dog.

"Are you clear on how you're going to handle this?"
Gina asked.

"I think so."

"Stay calm," Gina said. "Don't let your emotions get
the better of you. She'll undoubtedly fight you."

Hannah had disappeared from view, heading for the
back entrance. As she opened the kitchen door, the wind
picked up again; the glass of the window shuddered and
even the floorboards vibrated as if a giant were attempting to
rip the house from its foundation and expose its wretched,
spider-infested crawl space to the sky.

Hannah entered the living room, apparently intent on
watching some television before making supper, but she
stopped when she saw Jesse and Gina and turned on her heel,
as if she had caught them in an incriminating embrace. Gina
tipped her head at Jesse, nodding him towards the kitchen,
and he followed his daughter. Hannah had put the kettle on
and was placing a round Tetley tea bag in a mug, something
Jesse had seen Elaine do many times.

"How's Dad?" he asked Hannah.

"He was asleep, so I turned around and came home."
When Jesse leaned on the counter next to her, she lowered
her voice to a near whisper. "What's Gina doing here? Fuck,
Dad, she's married to a *cop*."

"I had some questions about Bran, about the drawings
on his bedroom walls. When I talked to him about them, he
seemed confused."

Hannah poured hot water into her cup. "He's into
sketching, that's all. His art teacher thinks he should go to
Emily Carr."

"He's drawing on the walls, for Christ's sake."

From the living room, Gina cleared her throat, reminding him to keep his temper in check, and he lowered his voice. "Do you remember your mother's drawings?" he asked. "The animals? The boy?"

"Of course I remember. When she died you burned them all."

She was right. Jesse had gathered the drawings from every corner of the house and set them alight in the burn barrel. He had watched bits of the burned images lift and drift up from the fire.

"So he's working out some stuff with those drawings," Hannah said. "That's not surprising, is it? He just about lost Grandpa to drowning, the same way he lost Mom."

Gina stepped into the kitchen. "I think we all know there's more going on," she said. "Why don't both of you sit?" Jesse did, but Hannah remained standing. "Hannah, you must be hungry. I'll make you and Jesse a sandwich."

"I'm not hungry," Hannah said, holding up her teacup.

Gina made the sandwiches anyway, moving around the room with the familiarity of family, knowing exactly where the plates, the cutlery, the cheese and bread were kept.

"We had Bran checked out at emergency after he fell in the river," Hannah said. "We were all checked out." Then she looked pointedly at her father. "He's fine."

"The afternoon I got here, Bran walked down to the river in his underwear in broad daylight," Jesse told her.

Hannah looked into the dark surface of her tea. "So he's eccentric. That's not a crime."

"He thought something attacked him in the river," said Gina. "A water mystery. A spirit."

"So he spends too much time with Alex." Hannah held out a hand. "Look, Bran is into Alex's stories in the same way he's into his art. He's playing at it, trying to figure out who he is." She turned to Gina. "And what if he did take some of the old stories seriously? Your own ancestors did. There are paintings all over the cliff face of Little Mountain, what they saw there."

"But those stories aren't from Brandon's culture," Gina said.

"So he has no right to have an interest in them? You go to church. I could say the stories you hear there aren't *your* stories."

Gina placed the sandwiches on the table and sat.

"I think we need to take him to a psychiatrist," Jesse said. "Have him assessed."

"You're not taking him to see a shrink." Hannah looked from Jesse to Gina. "You don't know him. Neither of you know him."

"Hannah, we've already been through all this, with your mother," Gina said, then reached across the table, took Jesse's hand and held it a moment before letting go.

Hannah turned her back on them and braced herself on the counter. "I do remember," she said. "I was here too."

"I know," Jesse said quietly. He saw his daughter's face reflected, distorted, in the electric kettle on the counter in front of her. Jesse had used that same kettle to make cups of tea for Elaine and had asked Hannah to carry them into the living room, where her mother sat drugged and alone in the captain's chair, staring out the window that overlooked the river and the reserve. Elaine took the cups Hannah offered without saying thanks or even acknowledging her daughter. Her eyes remained unblinking on the river or something beyond. Jesse had once watched Hannah bend in front of her mother so Elaine was forced to look into her face. Elaine startled and, for a moment, focused on Hannah. Elaine's eyes were bloodshot and confused as if she had just been woken from a dream. Then she shifted the captain's chair so she could look past Hannah, to the cliff. Hannah had hugged her anyway. Elaine had not hugged her back.

Hannah opened the cupboard under the sink and pulled out a wash bucket and scrubby, before filling the bucket with warm soapy water. "You come waltzing in here like you own the place," she said to Gina, though Jesse knew she was also talking to him. "You act like you're part of this family. You're not. You don't know shit." She lifted the bucket from the sink and headed through the dining room.

"What are you doing?" Jesse asked her. When she didn't answer, he followed her, took her arm and made her turn to him. "I said, what are you doing?"

Hannah yanked her arm from her father's grip, sloshing water on the floor, and carried the bucket through the living room and up to Brandon's room.

"Let her be," Gina told Jesse.

Brandon was huddled in the corner of his bed with his sketchbook on his lap, drawing with frantic strokes. The floor and walls of the room were covered with pictures of animals in various stages of transformation, human into animal, animal into human. Hannah took down one, then another and another, crumpling them and dropping them to the floor, to reveal the drawings he'd sketched right on the wall.

Brandon jumped up. "What are you doing?"

In answer, Hannah pulled the scrubby from the bucket, squeezed the water from it and started washing the wall.

"You can't do that. This is my artwork."

"People don't draw on walls."

"Of course they do. Graffiti, right? And this is my room."

"You're not doing this, Bran." She lowered her voice. "Dad and Gina want to take you to a psychiatrist."

"No fucking way."

"Then quit acting like a nutcase. And stop dressing like a hobo. Put on some shoes when you go outside. For Christ's sake, aren't you wearing underwear? You can see everything."

Brandon looked down at his dirty feet, the outline of his genitals in his sweats. "Underwear don't feel right," he said. "Shoes hurt or something."

"What do you mean they hurt? You outgrew them?"

"No—I don't know."

"I'll get you some new runners."

"I don't need any."

"Boots then. You'll need them for winter."

"I can't feel the ground when I wear shoes. I feel like I'm floating, not attached to myself."

"Floating?"

Brandon picked up a charcoal pencil, wiped the wall with his sleeve and redrew the lines that Hannah had just scrubbed away.

"Stop that." Hannah took the charcoal from his hand and went back to scrubbing the wall. She scrubbed and scrubbed and scrubbed until not only the lines of Brandon's drawing but the paint under it gave way.

Brandon grabbed hold of Hannah by both wrists. "No!" he cried and pushed her to the floor. He redrew the image, the eye of the crow now taking three-dimensional shape within the shallow cavity Hannah had just created in the wall's surface.

Hannah got up and started on another wall, washing away the sketch of a coyote standing as a man.

"Stop it!" Brandon roared, and slammed her against the wall.

Jesse loomed in the doorway. Hannah caught a glimpse of Gina behind him. "Hey, hey, what's going on?" he said.

Hannah shook Brandon off and slopped more soapy water onto the wall. "I'm cleaning up his mess."

"She's destroying my art," Brandon said.

Jesse went to his daughter and took hold of one hand, then the other, to stop her restless scrubbing. But Hannah slipped from his grip and went on cleaning. "That's enough, Hannah. This isn't the time," Jesse said.

"There's nothing wrong with Bran," Hannah cried. "Nothing!"

"Nothing," Brandon echoed. He dropped to the bed and went back to his feverish sketching, mumbling to himself. "Nothing, nothing, no thing, no thing, something, some thing . . ."

Hannah looked at him a long moment, then turned back to her chore. Jesse took her arm to stop her, but she struggled with him, fighting to wipe Brandon's madness from the walls. It was only when Gina said Jesse's name that he finally let go, leaving the red imprint of his thumb on his daughter's arm. It would become a bruise.

"Hannah," Gina said from the door. "You can't wash this away." She stepped forward to put a hand on Hannah's shoulder. "You've done enough. You took care of your grandfather for a long time. We'll let Jesse handle this one, okay?" She eyed Jesse.

After a moment, Jesse nodded. "I'll take care of this."

Gina wrapped her arms around Hannah from behind, to stop her, to comfort her. Hannah dropped the scrubby and hung her head. "I can't do this again," she said.

"We know," Gina said. And she rocked her, even though Hannah remained stiff in her arms.

Hannah looked at her brother as he chanted nonsense in a singsong voice. *Something, nothing, no thing, some thing, thing, thing, thing . . .*

In the few minutes they had been in this room he had completed a drawing that would have taken her hours: the face of a native boy about Brandon's age who glared up at her from the paper with an expression of fury. She looked away, to the animals on the walls—the coyote, the bear, the fox, the crow—and each of them, in turn, stared back at her.

11

Elopement Risk

IN THE HOSPITAL elevator, Hannah eyed the photograph of her grandfather on a poster with a caption that read: *Elopement Risk*. As if her grandfather was at risk of committing this rash act of happiness. Stew was caught hunched over his tray, clearly trying to wrench it off, his face panicked as the flash hit, his eyes red.

Hannah had received a call from the hospital that morning. Her grandfather had left his ward using his canes and was waiting for a taxi outside the building when staff in emergency saw him in his hospital gown and led him back inside.

The elevator door opened.

"Is it really necessary to put my grandfather's photo in the elevator?" Hannah asked the nurse, Annette, as she approached the reception desk. "And how did he get that far without anyone noticing?"

Annette said, "We had no idea he was that mobile. Or that determined."

"Maybe if I'd stayed on Tuesday, waited until he woke up, I could have calmed him down."

Annette held her hand up. "You can't blame yourself. You've got a life to live too. You can't be here every day."

"He should be at home." Hannah strode to her grandfather's room but he wasn't in it. The bed was neatly made and a man in overalls was screwing a shelf back in place above the bed. The man stopped his work and pulled an earplug from his ear. "I'll be done in a minute," he said.

Hannah turned back to the hall. "Where is he?" she asked Annette.

"Stew was restless," she replied. "He yanked the shelf down in the night. We thought it best to give him a change of scene. He's sitting in the visiting area down the hall."

Hannah found her grandfather parked there with several other elderly patients, his head down, his body curled over his tray. She squatted down beside him and took his hand. "Hey, Grandpa. I hear you went for a walk."

Stew searched her face without recognition.

Annette caught up with her. "We have him on morphine for the pain in his hip and knee," she said, maybe to explain his lack of response.

"He shouldn't be left out here," Hannah said. "He hates people looking at him." She turned again. "Grandpa, it's Hannah."

When she touched his arm, Stew startled as if he had just woken. "Where am I?" he asked.

"You're in the hospital," said Hannah.

"My hat?"

"It's at home," said Hannah. "Along with your wallet and keys. They're safe."

"Bran? Where's Brandon?" The worry on his face.

"Bran is okay," Hannah told her grandfather. "Everything is all right."

"No! He's lost! Look. Look!"

Hannah turned to the window, to where her grandfather was pointing.

"He's there. His ghost is by the lake. Don't you see him?"

"His ghost?" Hannah glanced at the nurse. "Grandpa, Bran is alive."

"He may be remembering a dream," said Annette, "or hallucinating from the morphine. Try not to take what he says seriously. They often confuse fantasy with reality."

They, thought Hannah. "Can we just have a moment to ourselves?" she said to the nurse. "I need to talk to Grandpa." She looked around at the other patients in the visiting area. "Privately."

Annette nodded. "Yes, of course."

"I've got to get home," Stew said.

"You can't go home. They won't let you." *Dad won't let you.*

"I've got to go!" Stew pushed at the wheelchair, trying to get it to move. He slapped the tray, then tried to rip it off.

Annette said, "I'll get him another dose of morphine. Take him back to his room and give him a really big bear hug so he feels safe."

"To control him, you mean."

"Yes."

Hannah wheeled Stew back to his room, parked the chair beside the window and hugged her grandfather as Annette had asked, as Stew strained to remove the tray that confined him. "I've got to help Bran," he cried. "I've got to get home!" He slapped the tray with each repetition: "Home! Home! Home!"

"Bran is okay," she said, though of course he wasn't. She knew it, and her father had already booked Bran's appointment with his doctor. Stew fought her until she was nearly in tears. "Bran is okay," she insisted again. "But I need to ask you something." She hesitated before continuing. "Alex told me about Eugene Robertson's wife. His Shuswap wife. He said her name was Libby."

"Libby, yes." Stew stopped struggling.

"Alex said the boy in the grave the construction crew dug up on the benchland was Eugene and Libby's child. Is that possible, Grandpa? Dennis had told Alex a story about how their boy was buried with a nugget of gold in his hand, just like that boy in the grave."

Stew didn't seem surprised. "The boy's name was Samuel."

"Your great-grandfather's name."

"Eugene named him after his first son." To remember him by, perhaps, or, more likely, to make amends.

"I had no idea Eugene and his Shuswap wife had a child together," said Hannah. "You never told me."

"I told you. You weren't listening."

"I don't remember. I must have been very young at the time."

Stew grunted. He wasn't sure now what he had chosen to tell Hannah and Brandon—or Jesse—and what he had withheld from them. There had been a time when he believed some family stories were better left buried with their dead. He had refused to answer Jesse's many questions about his own mother, and Hannah's questions about hers after Elaine died.

"Samuel drowned," he told Hannah. "Eugene never knew his final resting place. The Indians knew it but wouldn't tell him. There was bad blood between Eugene and Libby, in the end."

"From what Alex said it sounds like they had a pretty rocky marriage."

"Oh, she was wild, that woman. The Indians were all wild then. They lived in the ground in burrows like animals until the fur traders came and taught them to build a decent cabin. Even once they lived above ground, any time anything important happened they ran back to the pit house to meet, and they held their winter gatherings there, underground."

There, in the *kekuli*, as the Indians called it, they beat drums, sang and danced like the hooting pagans they were underneath their white women's dresses and white men's cowboy hats. Smoke billowed up from the central fire through the smoke hole that also served as the men's entrance. A ladder—steps chopped into a log—ran down through this hole. The women entered through a doorway in the side of the pit house shored up with poles. These people had made these underground dwellings their homes over the winter for countless generations. Even in Eugene's time, when the Indians spent their winters in a cabin, in summer most of them continued to live as they always had, in tents made from bark or tule mats the women wove themselves, or, if they could afford it, from canvas they bought from the trading post in Kamloops.

"Libby had an affair," Stew told Hannah now, raising one bushy white eyebrow, "with an Indian across the river."

"Alex told me. I expect Eugene left her after that, or kicked her out."

"No, she stayed with Eugene for a time." A short time.

"Eugene let her stay? Would he really allow her to live there after that?"

"They had a son," Stew said. "He was too young to be without his mother. Eugene couldn't work with him underfoot and he wouldn't let Libby raise him across the river. But you're right. Eugene wouldn't put up with much from her after that. He didn't allow Libby's kin to visit at all, and he wouldn't let Libby cross the river."

"He imprisoned her?"

"No!" Stew shook his head. "He tried to keep his wife from wandering off on him, from taking his son."

"Like a man fencing livestock," Hannah said.

"Like a man desperate to save his family."

Libby no longer sat with Eugene in the evenings in the tiny front room of the cabin, reading to him from the Bible. She sat, instead, in the kitchen, looking out the window at the river flowing, now exposed and naked, beyond ragged fields punctuated by the huge stumps of ancient cedars. The roots of windfalls grasped the air like eagle talons. When she turned in for the night, she slept with her son on his straw mattress. She had made her son's room her own, bringing in the pine dresser drawers Eugene had made for her as a gift the previous Christmas, with wood he had cut from the property around the cabin. The scent of pine filled the room, a room she kept closed to her husband. She served Eugene his meals, kept house and watched over their son, but she wouldn't look at her husband and only responded when she had no choice.

"You won't see that Indian again," Eugene had told her.

"I'll do as I wish. You have no interest in me. What does it matter?"

"See him again and you won't live here with me."

"Then Samuel and I will live with my sister."

"If you try to take Samuel from me I'll take him back to my home country, off this continent. You'll never see him again." In that moment, in his anger and hurt at her betrayal, he believed the threat himself.

Hannah let go of her grandfather and sat on the hospital bed beside him. "But you said Eugene brought his wife over from the old country," she said. "His English wife."

"He did, after his son drowned in that frickin' river."

"Is that how it was? His son dies and he abandons Libby? Sends for his other wife?"

"Libby left him first."

Hannah hesitated before asking the question that burned in her gut, not wanting to set her grandfather off again. "After Samuel told Eugene about his mother's affair, after he crossed the river, did he act . . ." She paused. "Strange?" Like Brandon, she meant.

"Oh, yes! The boy spoke nothing but English from the time he was in diapers, then all of a sudden he started speaking Indian. One day he talked to his father in proper English; the next he couldn't understand a word his father said, like all he'd ever known was his mother's tongue. Eugene whipped him each time he talked that gibberish, but he wouldn't stop."

"Libby must have objected."

"No, she understood what was at stake for herself and her son. She spanked him for speaking Indian too. Your mother could have learned a thing or two from her on that front. She spoiled you and Brandon."

Stew had never lifted a hand to her, believing a man shouldn't strike a girl child, but he had spanked Brandon many times after Jesse left, until her brother was too old to be taken over the knee.

"Samuel went strange in other ways too," Stew told her. "Eugene found him standing in the river shallows, naked— naked in October, mind you—staring up at Little Mountain, at those pictures on the cliff, like he was doing one of them

Indian endurance rituals, like how they went off to live in the bush alone when they were just kids. Eugene figured his mother was teaching him things behind his back, getting him ready, even at that young age. When Eugene dragged Samuel out of the water, he just went right back in. Eugene spanked him for that too. When he went in a third time, disobeying his father, Eugene picked up a stick."

Libby stepped from the house to shake out a rug and heard her son's cry. Down by the river her husband held Samuel's thin arm with one hand and hit him with a stick on the back, the backside, the legs, over and again.

Libby dropped the rug and ran down the cattle path in her bare feet. When she reached them, she yanked the boy from Eugene's grasp. He had stopped crying, his face blank in shock, his bare skin lined with bloody whip marks. His eyes looked through her as she lifted him into her arms and held his small, cold, bleeding body against her breast.

Eugene shook with spent rage, the stick clenched in his stinging hand. He looked up at Libby and for the first time in weeks she met his eyes.

"The boy wouldn't leave off the water," Eugene said. "He kept going in. I feared he'd drown."

Samuel whimpered in Shuswap when Eugene spoke and looked to his mother for reassurance, having clearly not understood a word his father said. How could a child so easily lose the language he'd been born into?

"You stop that now," Eugene said. "You speak decent English or I'll give you another licking."

Libby's glance silenced her husband, and she cocked an ear to listen to her son. Her face took on the haunted look of those in the first stunned moments of mourning.

"What's he gibbering on about?" Eugene asked. "Tell me!"

Samuel swam a tiny cupped hand towards the river, mimicking a salmon in flight, and his mother at last translated for her husband. "He says, 'Let me go.' He says, 'Let me go back to the river.'"

"Bran!" Stew cried. He wrenched the tray on his wheelchair and, when he couldn't detach it, pounded it with both fists. Hannah pressed the button for the nurse and almost immediately heard the squeak, squeak, squeak of shoes. A nurse Hannah didn't recognize arrived. "At it again, eh, Stew?" she said. She turned to Hannah. "We'll have to sedate him."

"No!" Stew cried. "I need to get home! I've got to help Brandon!"

"Are the drugs really necessary?" Hannah asked the nurse. "Isn't there some other way to get him to calm down?"

"I'm sorry," said the nurse. "He needs rest, and so do the other patients." She administered the drug and held his hand, murmuring reassurances to him until he calmed. Then she nodded at Hannah and left the room.

Hannah hugged her grandfather, laying her cheek against the old man's prickly stubble. "Don't let Bran out of your sight," Stew said. "That thing will take Bran with it back to the river, like it took Samuel."

"Like it took Mom," Hannah said.

Stew looked up at her. "Yes," he said. His shoulders heaved once in a sigh or a sob, but he didn't say anything more. Hannah felt his body relax and then slump, as he sank into the drug as if into river water.

12

The Dance

GINA WAS DANCING in her kitchen to a collection of '90s tunes on her iPod Shuffle when Alex entered the house without knocking. She saw him but didn't stop. Arms in the air, jangling her bracelets, gyrating her hips, shaking out her long black hair, she felt like *dancing*.

Alex walked around the kitchen island to avoid bumping into her. He helped himself to a Pepsi from the fridge and leaned back against the counter to watch. "What are you *doing*?" he asked, grinning.

"Working off some stress," she said.

"Well, stop it. It's just wrong, like watching your auntie stripping at some bar."

Gina pulled out her earbuds, pocketed them, and raised an eyebrow to Alex. "Now you know how I feel when I see *you* dance, *Coyote*."

Alex lifted his can in a salute, but Gina knew he hated the nickname.

"Does all this dancing have anything to do with Jesse coming home?" he asked.

"Shush." Gina glanced down the hall towards the den, where Grant watched TV, another damn football game.

"Trouble in paradise?"

Gina didn't answer.

"Huh. So Grant is pissed that Jesse's back home. Imagine that."

"He's pissed I'm helping Jesse with Bran and Hannah." Gina ran herself a glass of water and leaned against the kitchen sink to drink it. "There is nothing going on between Jesse and me."

"Not yet," Alex said.

"That kind of talk is only going to cause me trouble."

Alex held a hand out as if to protect himself from her anger. "Okay, okay. I was just joking around. So what's going on? You didn't ask me over to watch you dance."

"No." Gina rubbed her forehead. "Listen, Alex, you've got to tell Bran Dennis's stories are just that—stories. They aren't real."

"You know I can't do that."

Gina studied his face. Did Alex really believe them? "Then stay the hell away from Bran until he gets treatment."

Alex leaned across the kitchen island that stood between them. "Gina, if Grandpa Dennis was right, if his stories about the mystery are true, then Bran's life is at stake. Hannah and Jesse need to understand what's happening. *You* need to let them know the mystery is *real*."

She waved a hand in exasperation. "But it's not!"

"How can you say that? You saw the mystery yourself."
Gina made a face. "I don't know what I saw."

"The boy," he reminded her. "On the water."

That was years earlier, just before Elaine fell ill. She and Jesse had met in the bush along the reserve side, thinking no one would see them there. Their lovemaking was always quick, furtive and electric, so different from the sex she shared with Grant, who, even in their most intimate moments, felt the need to take command. Afterwards, Jesse and Gina walked together to the lake, steps apart, not holding hands, as if they were only neighbours who happened to meet up for a chat. Gina followed in Jesse's footsteps until he turned to take her arm, pressing a kiss on her that she didn't return at first, out of shyness. Yet there was no one to see them except, perhaps, a fisherman out on the lake near the estuary.

But then Gina saw the boy, standing on the river near Dead Man's Bend, presumably on a boulder. Naked. A boy from the reserve, she thought, and then he vanished. He just disappeared. Or perhaps he'd never been there at all. She asked Jesse, "Did you see that?"

"What?"

He looked upriver, then back at her.

"I thought I saw a boy watching us."

"Well if he is, there's nothing much to see, is there?"

Jesse held out his hand and Gina took it, and together they strolled the rest of the way down to the lake. That was one of the few moments of real happiness she remembered from that time. She had thought that with that public display of affection, Jesse was making a commitment, that he could, eventually, leave his wife, that they had a future together. And perhaps with him she would have the children that Grant couldn't give her. She turned back once to see if the boy reappeared. As she faced the sun, the lines of spiderwebs criss-crossing the poplars above their heads suddenly manifested, a network of tangled connections.

Maybe the boy on the water had been nothing more than a shadow, a thought that had escaped the well of her mind, the wish for a son. Still, the memory unsettled her. The thought that she projected her desires onto reality in this way left her feeling unhinged.

She shook her head to dispel the idea. "Alex, Dennis's story about the mystery is just a tall tale."

"You have no respect for the old ways, for our elders."

She grunted. "Our elders?" She leaned so close to Alex she could smell the cigarette smoke on him. "If my elders wanted my respect they should have acted a hell of a lot differently."

"Christ, Gina, that's harsh. I hope you don't talk to the kids you work with like that."

"No, of course not." She pushed back from him. "I'm sorry. Something about this situation with Bran has stirred up old memories, feelings. Anger, I guess. What Hannah is going through—she reminds me of myself at that age."

"You work with kids dealing with that kind of shit every day."

"I know. This just feels . . . different. Personal."

"Because of Jesse."

"Because of *Elaine*."

Alex shook his head. "You weren't responsible for her death."

"She took her life, Alex, while I was having an affair with her husband. The whole community blamed Jesse and me."

"No, they didn't."

"You were too young to notice the way people avoided me. The way they looked at me. The way some still do." She glanced towards the den at the end of the hall, from which the voices of the sports commentators rumbled, unintelligible. The den was Grant's fortress, a room she rarely entered. The garden with its tangled beds and bird feeders was hers. As the weather grew colder, she had no place of her own, nowhere to go when Grant's silence weighed too heavily on her.

"Gina, if you really want to help Bran and Hannah, you need to tell Hannah and Jesse that Grandpa Dennis's stories about that mystery are true. For god's sake, back me up."

Gina snorted and shook her head. "You can't help Bran," she said. "He needs medical care, treatment. Time to recover."

"He's not sick—he's been taken over!"

"No. *You* need to back off. Bran won't get better unless he understands he's sick. You've got to stop supporting his delusions."

"They're not delusions!"

Gina pointed at Alex. "Stay away from him."

Alex stepped back. "What the hell is going on with you?"

Gina stared at him, then put her earbuds back in, turned up the volume on her iPod and twirled away, closing her eyes, lifting her arms. She stomped the rhythm of the music into the kitchen floor, into the earth beneath it.

"You *are* dancing with him, aren't you?" Alex asked. "With Jesse."

She opened her eyes to look past the hummingbird feeder at the Robertson house beyond. "I'm dancing with myself," she said.

Then she felt another rhythm beneath the music: Grant's heavy footfalls pressing the old floorboards that led down the hall into this kitchen. She turned to find him looking directly at her with a closed expression. He had heard Alex, then. Alex cleared his throat, breaking the tension, and Grant turned heel and pushed through the door to the master bedroom that Gina had shared with him until Jesse's return.

— 13 —

A Numinous Truth

HANNAH WOKE WITH a start to the sound of her mother's voice calling her name. She lay in bed confused, thinking her mother was still alive, waking her for breakfast, but it was dark at her bedroom window and her mother had been dead eight years. Still in those waters between dreams and wakefulness, she turned to sit on the edge of her bed, her feet on the floor, and listened, hoping to hear her mother's voice again. The old house cracked as the wood frame contracted in the cold, and in that moment she felt sure that Brandon wasn't in the house with her. This certainty, this *knowing*, held the same charge as when she knew—*knew*—that her mother had drowned, even before her father had found her body.

Hannah listened for the thump of music, the soundtrack of the computer games that Brandon, until recently, had played deep into the night. But the house was quiet. She got up, slid on a T-shirt and a pair of jeans and walked down the hall to stand by her brother's half-opened door. His room was dark. Night air flowed in from the open window, carrying the smell of fallen leaves.

"Bran?" she called. When there was no reply, she pushed the door all the way open. The bed was empty. In the light streaming in from the hallway, the image of the crow with the eyes of a woman stared back at her. She headed for the bathroom. "Bran?" she called again.

"What is it?" Jesse asked.

Hannah was startled to find her father in the doorway of the bedroom he had once shared with her mother, a room she'd kept unused and closed. In her half-awake state she had forgotten he was staying here. He wore the grey boxer shorts and navy T-shirt he slept in. His hair was rumpled and his face was softened by sleep, making him appear younger, the father of her childhood.

"Where's Bran? Isn't he here?"

"I'll deal with it."

"What do you mean you'll deal with it?"

"I'm sure he's okay," she told him. "He probably just went for an early morning walk. He does that sometimes."

Jesse hesitated and then stepped back, almost but not completely closing the door between them. He would go back to bed, she thought, just as he had slept through most of their childhood illnesses. Her mother had been the one to nurse them through the night.

At the bottom of the stairs, she turned into the living room, hoping Brandon was watching TV with the sound low. No one was there, but the window facing the river was wide open and the breeze fluttered the curtains. Hannah went to close it, and there was her brother, staring back at her from outside, naked.

"Fuck." As soon as she spoke, he headed away from the house, into the first haze of dawn.

Hannah slipped barefoot into her rubber boots and threw on a hoodie. The October air was crisp as she opened the door and hurried out onto the front deck. From the doghouse, where she was tied for the night, Abby barked.

"Bran!" Hannah called. "For god's sake, get back in the house." Her brother was a shadow heading for the river. Hannah leapt off the deck and jogged after him. A jay, startled by her presence, flew overhead and cried out. "Bran?"

He ran straight for the boiling pool beneath the narrows. When Hannah was nearly on him, he spread his arms and stepped into the water and the river swallowed him. There was no splash, no outward ripple. The river flowed on as if nothing had disturbed it. Hannah scanned the river, looking for him. On the opposite shore, the street lights were still on along the reserve road. Up on the benchland, a kerosene lantern sat beside the tent over the child's grave— Samuel's grave—as someone kept watch. A fox hightailed it across the path and disappeared into the bush. Then she heard a rustle moving through grass on shore. A coyote, she thought, or a bear. An owl hooted close by and she became aware of someone standing in the shallows by Eugene's Rock, a shadow, her brother.

She jogged down the river path. "Jesus, Bran," she said as she reached him. "You scared the crap out of me.

Didn't you hear me call?" *Or wasn't that you?* she thought. Brandon's hair was dry. This Brandon hadn't jumped in the river. His pale skin seemed even whiter in the early morning light.

Hannah waded into the shallows and touched her brother's shoulder. "What's going on?"

Brandon just stood there with his hands at his sides, staring at the opposite shore.

"What are you looking at?" She saw only the dark outline of the cliff face of Little Mountain against the sky.

The smell of rotting sockeye was strong now that the spawning season was over. Here they were, walking on the precious sockeye eggs. "Come on," Hannah said, taking Brandon's arm. "Out of here."

Brandon wouldn't move. He wavered in the water.

Abby barked and she heard footsteps approaching from the farmhouse. She turned to find her father walking towards them. He had not gone back to bed after all.

"What the hell?" Jesse said as he drew near.

"Dad, he's so cold. I can't get him to leave the river."

Jesse sloshed into the water in his runners and dragged his naked son back to the riverbank. When Brandon stumbled and almost lost his footing on the slippery river rock, Hannah grabbed his other arm and helped him to the cattle path. There, Jesse wrapped his jacket around his son.

A crow flew by and landed on the dead pine above. The feeling Hannah had on waking resurfaced then, the certainty that her brother was not with her. His face held the same bleary-eyed look Hannah saw on him when she tried to rouse him from his dreams on school mornings. He dreamed on but with his eyes open. She said his name and shook his shoulder. "Bran, you hear me?"

His eyes finally focused on her. "Hannah," he said, as if he had been away a long time and this knowledge of her name was a revelation, drawn up from memory.

"What did you take?" she asked.

"Nothing."

"I suppose you're going to tell me you were sleep-walking," Jesse said.

"Sleepwalking," Brandon said, drawing the word out. "No, I was awake. My body walked down to the river and I floated after it."

"Floated?" Jesse asked.

"Like a balloon on a string," Bran said. "I was the balloon, attached to myself."

Hannah glanced at the dark outline of the cliff and thought of the pictographs there: along with the figure rising from the lightning bolt, there were stick figures with oversized heads ballooning as if about to become detached, to float away. These, Dennis Moses had told her, were the paintings signifying spirits.

"Things are so different when I'm outside myself," Brandon said. "Everything is so alive." The animals, the trees, the rocks, even the river itself had soul, he said. He had seen a coyote with the legs and arms of a man walking along the shore on all fours, sniffing salmon carcasses. The Steller's jay Hannah had startled cried, *Help me!* The crow on the branch of the dead pine above them had the eyes of a woman.

"The images in your drawings," Hannah said.

She looked up at the crow, hoping, in that instant, to see what her brother witnessed, but she saw only an ordinary bird—a nuisance that ripped open garbage bags on collection day and strewed soup cans and bread bags across the road.

"This is crazy," Jesse said. He turned to Hannah. "You do understand how crazy this is."

Hannah looked beyond her father, past the crow, to the first ray of sunlight that hit the blue Shuswap hills, and in the way of dreams, what had been a numinous truth for that instant in twilight seemed madness in the wakefulness of day.

— 14 —

Bones of the Salmon

HANNAH HUGGED HERSELF as she walked up to the protestors' encampment on the bridge, still unsure, after all these years, if she was welcome within the reserve village or not. Alex's cousin Zach was on duty, sitting in the cab of the BobCat that partially blocked bridge traffic. She worried he would tell her to piss off, stay off their land, as he had with so many whites, even the befuddled tourists who attempted to enjoy a picnic lunch on reserve lands.

But Zach only nodded at her. The cut of his jaw resembled Alex's, but the likeness ended there. Alex was polished, educated in a way his cousin would never be. Zach was a decade older and had never left the valley.

"Alex home?" she asked.

"Think so."

"Heard you cleaned up at the game last weekend," she said.

"Yeah, I think we got a real shot at winning the tournament this year." The Indian basketball tournament, an event Hannah had gone to with Alex and Dennis when she was still a kid.

"You've got to be excited about that," she said, then felt stupid. She sounded like some patronizing schoolteacher talking to a kid.

"Yeah," he said, "real excited." His voice had gone flat, his face suddenly closed.

A coydog—a coyote and German shepherd cross—trotted onto the bridge, then stopped on seeing Hannah. Behind her, Abby barked at it.

"Yours?" Hannah asked.

Zach said, "I've been feeding him these last few weeks, so I guess that makes him mine. A rez stray. Won't take a crap if anyone is around."

Hannah nodded. Many of the reserve dogs ran loose and unsupervised around the community. Several made a habit of lounging on the gravel road on the reserve side of the bridge. Hannah scratched their ears when she passed them on her way to see Alex, but the dogs didn't respond, as if they could take the scratch or leave it.

Hannah lifted a hand to Zach to signal she was off.

"Say hello to your boyfriend for me," Zach called after her. Hannah felt her face flush. The coydog kept its eyes on her as she passed it, voicing a barely audible growl. She picked up her pace.

There was a skiff of snow on the top of Little Mountain,

so first snow would likely fall on the valley floor well after Halloween. That morning, frost had laced the leaves scattered under the trees and the grass had been crunchy underfoot, frozen. Stew had told her that when he was a child the frost came sooner, any time from mid-September on, and first snow very often fell mid-October. Global warming. Global weirding, more like it.

Hannah left the bridge and turned down the newly expanded road that followed the river through the reserve to the new development. The stop sign at this crossroads wasn't in English, but in Shuswap. It read: ESTÍL. Here, just past the bridge, another sign notified white drivers that they were now on reserve land. Just past that, yet another advertised upcoming events the band organized: *Graveyard clean-up October 21. Lunch provided.* On the lawn closest to the bridge, some asshole had propped up a cardboard sign that read *No white men. Women okay, though.*

Hannah kept her eyes on the road as she walked the rest of the distance to Alex's house. She knocked and waited, glancing behind her to see if anyone was watching. She turned as Alex opened the door. "Hey."

He was dressed in a light blue T-shirt and jeans. His feet were bare. "Well, hey," he said. "What are you doing here?"

"Can I come in?"

Alex stepped aside and she entered the kitchen. "Coffee?" he asked. "I have instant."

"Tea if you've got it."

"Grab a chair."

Hannah sat as Alex filled a kettle and plugged it in. He had inherited this wooden table from Dennis. The surface was cracked and nicked, and the children of the Moses family had scribbled into its edges with pens and dinner knives one generation after the next. During a visit to Dennis's many years before, Hannah had left her own mark, her initials, next to Alex's, carved with the blade he had loaned her. She had been very young at the time and had been in awe that Alex owned a jackknife, a present from his grandfather. Dennis had already taken Alex hunting and they'd spent weekends together in the bush. In a past generation, these hunting trips with his grandfather would have prepared Alex for the time when he would go out into the wild alone, to prove he had the skills to survive, and to find his power—his guardian spirit, the mystery that would protect and guide him.

Dennis said his own grandfather had been one of the last to undergo this ritual. His grandfather's guardian had been a cannibal, a corpse, with entrails dangling that had chased him out of the bush—a shaman's guardian. Dennis had told Hannah and Brandon that his grandfather had continued to see his guardian now and again in the bush around the reserve, keeping an eye on him. The cannibal spirit protected him from disease and injury, and gave him the power to heal, to travel the road the spirits travelled and to bring a lost soul home. That story was why Hannah had come here today, or at least part of the reason.

Alex set down two mugs of tea and sat beside her. "You're looking good," he said.

She glanced down at his long, slender feet, embarrassed, even though she had hoped Alex would notice. She had taken care with her makeup, choosing colours to bring out the green in her hazel eyes, and had left her auburn hair down around her shoulders, instead of bunching her mass of curls haphazardly in a ponytail as she usually did. She had dressed for him.

"So, what's up?"

When Hannah didn't immediately answer him, he took one of her hands in both of his as if he only meant to warm it.

"I heard Brandon has an appointment with his doctor today," he said.

"From Gina, right? Fuck."

"She told me to stay away from him for a while. She says she doesn't want me feeding his fantasies. His 'delusions,' she said."

"I wish Gina would stop sticking her nose in our business."

"She's worried about Brandon." Alex rubbed his thumb in circles around her palm. "She blames herself for your mom's death, for Jesse leaving. She doesn't want you to lose Brandon too."

"Dad doesn't want me seeing you either," Hannah said.

Alex kept his eyes on her hand. "We're seeing each other, are we?"

"You know what I mean."

"I'm not sure I do. Enlighten me."

Hannah pulled her hand away. "Forget it."

"Hey, hey, I was just teasing you." He took her hand again and squeezed. They sat together in silence for a time until Hannah decided to tell him what was on her mind.

"A couple of nights ago, I woke up and Bran was outside naked. He led me to the river and disappeared into the water. I mean, he was just gone, like he was a ghost or something. Then I really did find him there, but downriver. Bran said he had watched his own body walk into the shallows."

"His soul *is* out walking," Alex said. "Brandon led you there, so you could see that for yourself."

"You said that if Bran's spirit is out walking, he could die."

"When a person loses his soul and becomes sick, his spirit eventually travels the streams and rivers south. If he reaches the land of souls, his body dies."

"You really believe in this stuff, don't you?"

"I saw Grandpa's soul out walking, heading down the river, shortly before he passed away."

"When he was in the hospital?"

Alex nodded.

Stew had taken Hannah to visit Dennis Moses in hospital, just days before he died. They had brought the old man mandarin oranges, a favourite treat, but Dennis had already lost consciousness. The cancer had spread to his brain. He had looked so much smaller in that bed, as if part of him had already left them. Stew had put a hand on his old friend's shoulder before leading Hannah from the room.

"Did Samuel's soul go out walking?" Hannah asked. "After that mystery took him?"

"Libby saw his ghost on the river, while he napped inside their house. She knew he was preparing to leave her."

"So she understood what was happening to her son?"

"Libby guessed, but she didn't want to believe at first. Remember she had been living with Eugene from the time she was little more than a child herself. He had attempted to educate her in his ways. A white man's ways."

Nevertheless, Alex went on, Libby came to recognize the mystery within her son. She knew from the way she couldn't draw Samuel up from his daydreams without shaking him that his soul was adrift. She'd wondered at first if her son was deaf, as he wouldn't respond during these times to the sound of his own name. Then there was his habit of taking off on his own. She turned from washing the dishes in the basin on the stump outside the cabin to find Samuel gone and she panicked, searching first the house, then the yard. She most often found him standing ankle-deep in the river, his mouth moving as if in conversation or song. She worried over how he listened to the other who wasn't there. She told herself that he was singing to himself, as she had done when she was a toddler, at play with an imaginary friend.

Then there were the times, at night, when she woke to check he was still with her, and knew the truth of it. When Samuel had stood in the river, he had stared at the painting on the cliff above, the figure emerging from a lightning bolt.

"Let's say I believe you for the moment," Hannah said. "What has possession of Bran? I mean, what *is* it? What does it want?"

"Not *it*," Alex said. "Him. The water mystery has spirit, soul, just like you and me. Everything has a soul: the salmon, the river, the rocks on shore, the trees, the eagles—"

Hannah waved a hand to stop him. "All right, who is *he*? Why is he here? Why did he take Bran?"

Alex released her hand and crossed his arms as he watched her, a small smile playing on his handsome face. He was amused by her, but she wasn't sure why. She had known Alex her whole life and yet now, here, she felt she didn't know him at all.

Alex nodded as if he had come to a decision about her. "All right. I'll tell you the same story Grandpa Dennis told Stew when your mom was sick."

"About Eugene and Libby? About Samuel?"

"No, about the spirit that lived in Samuel, that lived in your mother. The one that now lives in Bran."

Alex had followed his great-grandfather across the bridge to the Robertson side of the river. At fourteen, he was already much taller than the old man. Dennis moved slowly with the aid of his cane and Alex was itching to stride ahead of him, but out of respect he walked behind as they passed through the Robertson gate, with its ridiculous pink flamingos, and made their way to the house. Stew's truck was parked in the yard, but not Jesse's.

"Jesse's not here," said Alex, thinking they should turn back and come another day.

"Good. Then maybe Stew will listen."

Dennis knocked on the back kitchen door with his cane. Then knocked again. Finally Stew opened the door, his breath stinking of rum.

"You sleeping one off this late in the day?" Dennis asked him.

"Kids are at school. Only time I can sleep." He nodded at Alex. "Isn't *he* supposed to be in school?"

"He is," Dennis said. "I've come to see Elaine."

"Elaine? What in god's name for?"

Dennis didn't answer. He pushed past his friend and, with both Stew and Alex following, made his way through the kitchen and dining room and into the living room, where he knew he'd find her. Elaine sat in a captain's chair in front of the window, facing the river and the cliff face beyond. Since Stew and Jesse wouldn't let her near the river, the mystery had to prepare here. Dennis pulled up a chair and sat beside her. Elaine's expression was blank, her eyes focused on the cliff face across the river, the figure painted there.

"She's filled with the mystery, all right," he told Alex, in English so Stew would hear. Then, in *Secwepemctsin*, he said to Elaine, "I see you've begun your work."

Elaine turned her head slowly to look at him, then set her gaze back on the pictograph.

"She doesn't speak any Shuswap," Stew said. "You know that." He paused. "What did you tell her?"

"This isn't Elaine," Dennis said. "Elaine's out walking. I've seen her soul on the river. She's getting ready to take the spirit trail."

"Dennis Moses, what in god's name are you going on about?"

Dennis tucked his chin to his chest as he thought how to explain. "People and animals are separate now," he told Stew, holding up two fingers. "But once, in the time of the old sto-ries, when animal and man were still family, a man's soul could flit away as an owl, or the spirit of a bear could slip under a man's skin. In that time a *Secwepemc* boy could ride the ice floe downstream, downriver, down to the ocean to the land of souls, as the salmon do, and then swim back upstream to his grieving grandfather, reborn within the skin of a sockeye. That time has passed, but sometimes, even now, an animal spirit finds his way back to us, into us, as it has with Elaine."

Stew laughed and Dennis stood slowly, painfully, to put a hand on Stew's shoulder to make it clear that he was seri-ous. "If we don't get this mystery out of her, Elaine will die. Sooner or later, it will take her back to the water. And when that happens, well, it may already be too late for the rest of us as well."

"What do you mean, 'mystery'?"

Dennis turned to his grandson. "Tell me, Alex. What do you remember me telling you about the narrows?"

Alex shrugged. "Only that it's a gateway."

"Gateway?" Stew asked.

"There are gateways all over," Dennis said. "There's a door to bear country in Green Timber. And the entrances to the buffalo and elk lands are out there in Cree territory. You'll find the gateway to the salmon world here, under the rapids at the narrows. The fish wait all winter in their world beneath the river gravel to be reborn, in the way our people once waited for spring within our winter houses. The salmon dance through winter; they sing their songs and tell stories beneath the gravel. In spring they return as their own offspring, to swim downriver to the lake and then, when they've grown, downriver to the sea, following the same path our souls travel after we die. When my time comes I'll swim downriver with the salmon, to the land of souls."

"Dennis, for god's sake. Just tell me what this 'mystery' is."

"There it is again," Dennis said to Alex. "That white man's impatience." Dennis patted the air in front of Stew with a hand knobbed by arthritis. "All in good time." He sat back in the chair next to Elaine. "Now where was I?"

"You were telling us about the gateway, about the salmon," Alex said.

"Yes, the salmon." Dennis laid a hand on Elaine's arm as if to include her, but he spoke to Stew. "Coyote gave us a great gift," he said. "He gave us salmon. He created these spawning grounds. But then, many generations ago, when our people were still as young and uneducated as you folks are now, we waged war on the salmon. There were so many fish our people didn't think they would ever run out, so we went on killing them. We killed even the last salmon buck and took his pregnant wife as a slave.

"When her son was born the people kept him as a slave too. So it was that the last salmon boy grew up with the people. And we mistreated him as people will mistreat a slave, one who is not their own. When he came of age and it was time to find his power, his mother told him the story of his father, and of his lost people." Dennis waved a hand for Stew to take a seat. "Just like I'm telling you now," he said.

The boy, the salmon boy, was angry when his mother told him about the people's senseless destruction of the salmon, of his father's death. He felt a rage that had built during all his years living under these people who would not accept him as one of their own, who had beat him, shunned him, laughed at him and denied him entrance to their gatherings, so that he sat with his mother outside the women's entrance of the *kekuli* as the feasting and dancing went on without them.

Go find your guardian, your power, his mother told him. Go to the mountain. Go. Go!

He hesitated, not wanting to leave her. She had been his only companion through life.

You're here for a reason, she said. You must avenge your father's death, cleanse this place of its sickness and bring your people home.

They'll beat you when they find me gone, he said.

I'll hide until you return. They'll think I've left too.

And when I find my power?

Go, she said.

But he couldn't leave her, not completely. He hung about the edges of the village, hidden within the undergrowth, fearful of entering the mountain forest alone, but also watching over his mother. She did hide as she said she would, within the *kekuli* while the people made their summer camp. But the people soon found her, dragged her from the women's entrance and down to the river. When she wouldn't tell them where her son had gone, they killed her and prepared her body as they would any salmon's, laying her flesh on a drying rack. Afraid for his own life, he watched and did nothing as a storm gathered within him. Then he ran up to the benchland below the cliff, lifted his arms to the sky and, for the first time in his life, howled his rage. The sky responded. Black clouds boiled over his head. Lightning broke the air in two and thunder boomed. He was frightened at first and fell to his knees, his hands over his head, as lightning struck to his left, to his right, as hail pounded his back, as trees cracked and crashed to the ground around him.

He saw the people running to save themselves in the village below. These people who he had feared his whole life were now frightened of the storm he carried inside him. They were as ants, tiny and scuttling. He stood then and unleashed the full fury of the storm on them. Lightning struck again and again, thundering down from the sky, bursting the tents into flames, the grass into flames. The fire licked up the mountains and the trees all around burst into flames. The people ran screaming to the river to escape the fire. Many died before they reached the water, suffocated by smoke or burned to death. Others made it to the river and hid beneath the surface from the fires. So he brought down the rains. Thunderous sheets of water fell, putting out the fires, swelling the river, unleashing a flash flood that drowned the people, washing their last footprints from this earth.

"Then the salmon boy went back to the country of the salmon," Dennis told Stew. "He leapt over the bodies of his people, as a sockeye leaps the rapids to reach home, and in this way brought the salmon back to life. The bones of his mother and father gathered their flesh back onto themselves and their hearts began to beat. This is why we cast the bones of the salmon back into the river, so the salmon will live again, and so we will remember that if the salmon disappear, the river dies, the lake dies, the land dies and we die."

Stew scratched the stubble on his chin. "So you're telling me this salmon boy is the 'mystery.'"

"Yes."

"And it took possession of Elaine." Stew managed a laugh. "Are you *really* trying to make me believe that story is true?"

"Many of our elders believe the old stories really happened," Alex told Stew. "In the same way someone of your generation might read the Bible stories as fact." He glanced towards Dennis, but didn't look him in the eye, out of respect. Dennis believed the Bible stories as literal fact himself, with the same conviction as he believed the stories his grandmother had told him. He saw no contradiction in this. His two faiths sat peacefully side by side, like two family pit houses in the same village. "The story of the last salmon is true in the sense that it's told to help people remember that they shouldn't take too many fish," Alex continued, "so enough can spawn, so the salmon will survive, so we can eat them and live."

"That's your white schoolteachers talking," said Dennis to the boy. His voice held enough anger that Alex sat back, chastised. "Don't presume to speak of things you haven't seen or experienced."

Alex nodded, keeping his eyes on the floor.

"So you didn't believe the story yourself then," Hannah said to Alex now.

"No."

"What changed?"

"What changed for you?" Alex reached over and tugged the sprig of purple aster jutting from the breast pocket of her jean jacket, reminding her of this small habit she'd carried with her from her childhood. When she was a young girl, she had showered her hair and every pocket with wildflowers, imagining herself a woodland sprite. With her reddish curls and heart-shaped face, she had looked the part. She had believed in faeries then, not the pretty figures conjured by Victorian imaginations and sanitized in Disney films, but the dangerous, mercurial creatures of her grandfather's stories, the forest and water spirits her British ancestors had at once worshipped and feared. Stew called them "the old gods."

"I've seen some things I can't explain," she said.

"I've seen that salmon boy on the river."

Hannah scanned Alex's face but he showed no sign that he was joking. "So this boy, the boy on the river that Bran saw, that you saw, is the one in the story Dennis told? You're telling me *he's* got Bran?"

"He's the spirit of the salmon. He'll do whatever is necessary to protect his people."

"People? You mean the sockeye."

"I don't have to tell you the salmon in this river are endangered. He *will* bring on that storm Dennis talked about, like nothing you've ever seen, and wipe this valley clean, so his people can return."

Hannah laughed, but Alex didn't laugh with her. "What am I supposed to make of all this?" she asked him.

"You tell me."

Hannah ran her thumbnail back and forth along a crack in the table's surface. The story Dennis had told had the childlike feel of a Sunday school fable. Still, still. She had seen Brandon's spirit leap into the river. She had followed her brother's doppelgänger to that shore.

"I don't know what to believe," she said finally.

"Good," said Alex. "That's a start."

He held Hannah's hand to stop its restless movement, then turned it over and traced the zigzag of lines on her palm. After a while, he took her thumb into his mouth, his eyes closed and his tongue moving. Hannah's breath caught. Alex pulled her thumb from his mouth and squeezed it as he set her hand back on the table. He sat there, looking down at their joined hands, as if they were still friends in the way they had been only minutes before.

— 15 —

Those Who Saw

AS JESSE DROVE into the yard with Brandon, he noticed that the archaeologist and her team had begun work around the gravesite on the benchland of Little Mountain. "Look," he told his son as they got out of the truck, and together they stood and watched. Several of the field workers were from the Lightning Bay Indian band. Some dug with shovels while others rocked box screens suspended on frames, dust drifting like smoke. One of the men was digging neat steps into the ground, building a stairway that he would follow down into the past.

"How'd it go?" Hannah called out.

Jesse turned to find her waiting outside the kitchen door, hugging herself. He pushed past her into the house and hung his jacket on one of the hooks before he answered. "Maybe we should talk later," he said, and lifted his chin towards Brandon as his son sullenly kicked off the summer sandals he had worn into town on this chilly October day.

"Why? What's going on? What did his doctor say?"

"There's nothing wrong with me," said Brandon. "She just doesn't understand. None of them understand."

"Them?" Hannah asked her father.

"His doctor wanted some tests done. We spent the morning and afternoon at the hospital, dealing with lab technicians. Bran wasn't exactly . . . cooperative."

"What kinds of tests?"

"Blood tests, imaging. She wanted to be sure nothing else was going on, an injury from his fall in the river, something she may have missed before."

"So was there anything?"

"We won't hear back for a week or so. His doctor is setting up an appointment with a psychiatrist."

"I'm fine," said Brandon. "I'm . . ." He hesitated, then said, "I'm awake now."

Hannah crossed her arms. "You're awake?"

"I was asleep before. Everyone is asleep."

Jesse shook his head.

"None of you *see*," said Brandon. "You don't see, or do you?" he asked Hannah. He sounded hopeful, as if he wished for Hannah's company as he walked this strange road.

"What do you want me to see?"

Brandon waved his hands, trying to find a way to explain how he experienced the world now. "Everything is so *beautiful*," he said, his expression a mixture of rapture and confusion. Colours were so much brighter, he said, like those in an old Technicolor movie. He could see the whole spectrum of light. He perceived the last of the fall flowers as a bee would, in ultraviolet, the radiating lines at their centres suddenly visible, landing strips guiding the insect to the pollen. He heard sounds previously unavailable to him, as a dog might. He *felt* sound more than he heard it, the way a butterfly sensed sound with its wings, or as a sockeye responded to vibrations with its whole being.

"The wind sings," he said. "The trees and animals talk to me."

"Bran, trees and animals don't talk. You know that."

"They don't speak in words. But I understand them now."

When Hannah made a face, he said, "Abby tells you things. You understand what she wants, how she feels. She communicates."

"But the *trees*?" Hannah asked.

"I know these experiences seem very real," Jesse interjected. "But they're not, Bran. The psychiatrist will undoubtedly prescribe meds. When the drugs take effect—"

"I'm not taking any pills."

"You'll have to, or you won't get better."

"I'm not sick." He turned to his sister. "Hannah, don't let him do this. He can't take this away from me."

"We don't need to talk about this now," Hannah said. "You've had a long day. How about you chill in your room for a while?"

As soon as his son and daughter left the room, Jesse rolled himself a joint from his stash on top of the kitchen cupboard. Then he stepped outside to the front deck, where he sat on the pile of cedar siding to smoke. The calm spread through his body as he looked up at the navy sky and the deep blue hills that surrounded him. It was only three-thirty, but the light was already failing. Not long now until winter.

When Hannah came outside to sit beside him, he offered her a toke. She took the joint, breathed in deeply and held it before exhaling and handing it back to him. "He's asleep," she said.

"He was so agitated and confused the whole day, Hannah. Did you see how he fought me when I tried to get him into the truck?"

Hannah nodded. "His doctor thinks he's schizophrenic, doesn't she?" she asked.

"I know from what I went through with your mom that the psychiatrist probably won't make a firm diagnosis until Bran has shown the symptoms for a time, but yes, she thinks it's schizophrenia." He held up the joint. "She said weed can trigger the onset of schizophrenia, if the person is predisposed, if they have a family history of mental illness. *Was* he smoking it?"

Hannah took the joint from him before he'd offered it again. "You have to do a better job of hiding your stash," she told him. "I found it the first day you were here."

"If you need someone to blame, point the finger at your friend Alex. Bran really believes the shit that kid has been telling him."

"They're stories Dennis Moses told." She hesitated. "Grandpa believes them too."

Jesse shook his head. "I had no idea Dad was that far gone. I'm so sorry, Hannah. I can't imagine what these last couple of years have been like for you."

"It does seem strange, though, doesn't it?" she asked. "Bran is sick like Mom."

"Schizophrenia runs in families." Along with smarts, Jesse thought. The brilliant and the damned. Those who saw the world in ways others couldn't.

"The animals in Bran's drawings," Hannah said. "The transformers—they're so like what Mom drew. How do you explain that?"

Jesse shrugged. "Schizophrenics often draw strange shit. In any case, Elaine claimed Bran saw those weird animals first."

"Bran did? As a kid?"

"A coyote, standing like a man." Jesse smiled a little. "When he pointed it out to your mother he called it a kangaroo."

Elaine and Brandon were out in the garden at the time, where Elaine was pulling up the tomato plants, and at first Elaine didn't bother to look up from her work. Six-year-old Brandon had all manner of imaginary friends, most of them beasts of one kind or another. He was persistent this time, however; he tugged at his mother's sleeve. "Look! A kangaroo!"

"Kangaroos don't live here," Elaine told Brandon. "Maybe you saw a coyote." The tall pointy ears, the sharp snout, like Roo's in Brandon's illustrated *Winnie-the-Pooh*. Then Elaine stood straight to survey the remaining clean-up work she would have to do before snow fell, and there, past the sunflowers, by the saskatoon bushes, Elaine saw the beast.

The creature did indeed have a coyote's head but stood upright, on two hairy legs; its body was more man than wild dog. She had no name for this creature, no story for it, and so she could not make sense of it. The beast's jaws pulled back in what approximated a smile and it winked at her.

Once Elaine had seen the soul of this one beast, she saw them all, walking the roads or going about their business at the river's edge, the bewildering assortment of ancient spirits that populated the river valley, all of them part animal and part man. The bear that stood on its back legs to eat the last of the apples from her trees had the hands of a man. The fox that stole eggs from her henhouse stood upright with a paw on its hip to eat them; it had the feet of a child. The crow with the eyes of a woman followed Elaine, flying from tree to tree, peering down at her with an obsessive interest.

One morning as Elaine cleaned out the wood stove, she stepped onto the front deck to toss the ashes over her soggy and dormant garden bed and saw someone sitting on the bridge railings, as if about to jump off into the freezing water.

She called out, "No!" But the person only waved her over. Stew was in town, Jesse was in the barn with Hannah, and Brandon was alone inside the house. But the fool on the bridge was endangering his life, so she ran the short distance to the river. When she reached the bridge she saw the person on the railings was already dead. The bones of his ribs were showing through the tattered material of his dated clothing, and his entrails dangled. His bony feet were crossed and swinging over the water. He snacked on the fingers of a human hand as if on a chicken wing. The corpse pointed down and Elaine followed its finger to see the crow with the eyes of a woman hopping in the mud towards her. Beside the bird was a set of bare human footprints that led down to the river, where they stopped. All at once the river seemed terribly inviting, as if the day were hot, a summer's day. The water would cool her, take away this turbulence within her stomach, smooth away the ache that had set its claws into her shoulders and remained since that early September day when she had jumped from those rocks and into this strange new world. She would step into these churning waters and float downriver. She would become water and drift away.

"If you go in there you won't come out again," a woman said, and Elaine turned to find a person standing where the crow had been. An Indian woman. Elaine didn't know her. She knew so few of the Indians on the reserve just across the river. Elaine had lived her adult life on this property and never once stepped foot in the reserve village. The woman wore a dress with an elaborately embroidered bodice, the kind Shuswap girls wore at powwows and occasionally at other events to advertise their Indian pride.

"Don't go in," she told Elaine.

"I wasn't."

"You were. I know you."

"No—we don't know each other."

"Sure we do." The Indian woman looked around at the strange creatures that watched them: the half man, half coyote lying on shore, taking in the late-autumn sun, his paws behind his head; the corpse sitting on the railing of the bridge.

"You see them too?"

"Who are you talking to?" Jesse called. Elaine turned to find her husband walking towards her down the cattle path. When she looked back at the river, the woman was gone. A crow hopped in the mud where the woman had been, but it was just an ordinary crow with the eyes of a bird. The coyote-man was only a coyote slipping into the bush. The corpse on the bridge railing had vanished. An owl perched there instead, watching her with a ghostly intelligence. As soon as she turned to the owl, it flew away.

"There was a woman here," Elaine told Jesse.

"You were talking to air."

"She was here."

"What the hell is going on with you? I come in from the barn to find Brandon crying, and you nowhere in sight. He's still too young to be left alone."

She looked up to see Brandon watching them from the front deck of the house. Hannah held him from behind.

Elaine tried to explain to Jesse about the corpse that had led her here, about the Shuswap woman and the creatures that had manifested everywhere around her.

"There was no one here," Jesse insisted, but there was nothing he could say that would convince her that her visions weren't real. She knew, *knew* what she saw was real with a conviction—with a faith—that Jesse couldn't muster for anything. Not for himself. Not for his marriage, or even the love of his own children.

"Bran sees what I see," Elaine told him. "Ask him."

"He's a child. He'll believe anything you say. And where are your shoes?"

Elaine looked down at her feet to find them bare, sinking into icy river mud. She scanned the river shore, confused. Surely, she would find the footprints of the Indian woman beside her own and she could show them to Jesse? But there were none. Even the footprints she had seen earlier, the ones that led to the river, were gone. Still, this fact did not persuade her that the strange animals were hallucinations. Elaine would never believe she was mad. "What you mistake for madness is but over-acuteness of the senses," Elaine had told him, quoting Poe.

Even after she was so heavily medicated that all she did was spend her days sitting in that damn captain's chair, she would not doubt what she had seen with her own eyes: the eagle that placed an offering of its own wing feather at her feet with its beak. The crow with the eyes of a woman that laughed with her, with a woman's laugh, when a calf got its head stuck in a bucket. The boy from her drawings—the boy she saw in the mirror—who compelled her to climb the railing of the bridge, to stand with arms outstretched to the damp, thunderous wind churned up by the rushing water at the narrows, to take that mystery within her back to the water, back home.

If he had only listened, Jesse told Hannah now, if he had gotten Elaine help sooner, if he had been there for her, rather than turning to other women, she might have been alive today.

"I heard Mom the other day," Hannah said. "She called my name, woke me up. I think to let me know Bran was down at the river. Does that make me crazy too?"

He shook his head. "After your mother died, I saw her many times, in my dreams, even on the street. I ran after her once, when I saw her on this road, but it was some other woman with a similar build, a tourist."

Abby trotted up the steps of the front deck and lay at their feet. "I guess Bran's illness means you'll be staying on," Hannah said.

"Only until I get things cleaned up here and the sale goes through. Gina says there's a group home for kids with mental health issues. She sets kids up there all the time. I'll get Bran on the waiting list for it." He hesitated. "I'll come back regularly, to make sure he's doing okay."

"No, you won't."

Jesse met her eyes. "Yes, I will. I'll have to. I'm his guardian."

Hannah looked away and they sat in silence for a time.

Finally Hannah said, "Alex told me Gina blames herself for Mom's death. Was *that* why Mom took her life, because of your affair with Gina?"

Jesse breathed in a last toke and held the smoke within his lungs. "I think what you're really asking is why would your mom leave you?" he said, exhaling. "Why would any parent abandon their kid? There's never a good answer to that one, is there?" He held her gaze to make it clear he was speaking as much about his own leaving as her mother's.

Captain's Chair

THE CHAIR WAS exactly where the boy had left it, in the living room facing the window. He slid a hand along the armrest, the curve that had wrapped around the woman's hips as they sat together here day after day, staring out this window to the cliff beyond the river. Perhaps, in this woman named Elaine, he had chosen poorly, but opportunities to swim up into this world were rare. The First People living over there, on the other side of the river, had learned long ago not to swim in the mother river. He had taken, instead, to watching these white men who had arrived not long ago. Sometimes they swam. Sometimes they played in that river. Sometimes they jumped into the waters as the woman Elaine had. They didn't know the stories, or him. They didn't fear him. He could navigate these white men, as he would a waterway, into this world.

The white woman named Elaine had seemed promising at first, but she was no good. The medicine that the man named Jesse forced on her made her weak. Tired. Lost. The boy couldn't complete his task through her any more than he could through the toddler named Samuel. Instead he swam with Elaine—always swimming—in the waters between worlds, never surfacing fully. His thoughts were as entwined with hers as the branches of the trees at the log-jam below the bridge. He couldn't always remember what he was here for or who he was. In time he came to realize there was no way he could use Elaine to complete his task.

Finally he had whispered, *Take me back to the river*. He whispered and whispered until the woman rose from this chair and left the house during an unobserved moment. She walked the road to the river slowly, following the footprints he made her see there. She climbed the railing of the bridge. She stood over the rushing river water with her arms spread wide like the wings of a circling eagle. And when he whispered that it was time, she fell as a diving eagle falls, into the water.

In the years that followed, he had waited for another chance to enter this world and complete his task, and here, in Brandon, he had found it. He made a fist and felt the strength in this forearm, the blood coursing through these veins like river water through the narrows. This body was young and strong. This would do.

The boy settled into the chair, feeling the cool wood of the floor beneath his bare feet. Directly in front of him, he saw his reflection in the window, this body he inhabited, this boy Bran. He put his hand to the reflection and saw only one hand now, his own.

"What are you doing?"

The boy turned to the voice and found the girl named Hannah at the door to the living room. She strode towards him so quickly he flinched and put a hand up to protect himself, expecting the blows he had experienced as the boy Samuel. When she didn't strike, he looked up, trying to make sense of her. He was still confused by this world, its shifting light, the reflections from his own that flickered and flitted about this place. Elaine followed Hannah into the room as a shadow, gliding behind her, matching her daughter's movements, mirroring her.

"Get up!" Hannah told him. "You don't sit in that chair. No one sits in the captain's chair. That was Mom's chair."

He understood at least something of what she said. He had been listening in as the other—Bran—went about his days, taking note, learning—or relearning—the language. Still, he was uncertain. Would he give himself away if he spoke? He wouldn't chance it. There was still so much to do.

Instead he stood in front of the chair, as she demanded.

"I'm not going through this again," she said. "You're not doing this!" Hannah took the boy by the arm and pulled him away. Then she picked up the chair and stormed out of the room with it. "No one is ever sitting in this chair again," she said. "It's gone. I'm throwing it on Jesse's dump load."

The boy heard the kitchen door bang shut behind her as she left the house. Then he retrieved a wooden chair from the dining room table and carried it into the living room. He positioned it carefully in front of the window to afford him the best view of the cliff face and then he sat, to look beyond his own reflection.

Brandon was there, walking on the surface of the water, his spirit wandering aimlessly on the river. The tether between his spirit and this body was becoming ever more tenuous. Soon the connection would be lost altogether and Bran would walk the spirit path. Already, without Bran's thoughts interfering with his own, the boy felt more lucid. His purpose was clear. He *must* save his people, and this time, nothing would stop him. Not the weakness of a woman. Not the limitations imposed by a child's undeveloped mind. He looked beyond Bran, beyond the river, to the lightning on the cliff face, settled both hands on the armrests, and began.

17

Inviting the Lightning

THE CATTLE WERE edgy, uncooperative, as they always were before a storm. Hannah had resorted to using her grandfather's yellow plastic herding cane to steer, poke and occasionally hit the cows and calves so they'd follow the fenceline into the holding pen. Abby trotted back and forth, keeping the animals moving. The dog knew her job. Once the cattle were in the pen, Jesse walked them through the funnel entrance into the loading chute and then, one by one, into the stock trailer.

This was livestock day at the small local auction house. Jesse would take this load of cattle today and haul the rest to auction in the weeks that followed. In the pasture nearby, the remaining Herefords lay in a group, huddling together as they usually did before a rain. They eyed the animals in the holding pen and listened, ears cocked, to those moaning within the stock trailer. Hannah was sure they understood they were next. Cows were not the dull beasts they were so often imagined to be. While the heifers were nervous around Jesse, the oldest had trotted towards him with recognition when he first fed them on his return. After all these years they still remembered him.

Jesse handled the animals with a confidence that Hannah lacked. She had rarely helped her grandfather work the cattle and even then only grudgingly. She had her own many household chores, so the task of working with Stew to move the cows had most often fallen on Brandon, and he wasn't in any shape to help. When she had last checked on him he was still sitting in a chair in front of the living-room window, as he had for nearly a week now. She couldn't get him to move, except to sleep. He no longer answered when she spoke to him. He only stared out at the river, the cliff beyond, as her mother had. Hannah had always assumed it was the drugs that had made her mother so unresponsive, and she had blamed her father for forcing the medication on her. But Bran wasn't yet taking anything. His appointment with the psychiatrist wasn't until Friday.

Hannah hung Stew's herding cane on the railing of the holding pen and leaned over it, stunned by the sudden and unexpected grief she felt, at Bran's illness, yes, but also at the loss of these animals. They were only cows after all. They weren't pets—Stew had made sure she understood this early—but they were companions of a sort. She had lived with many of these animals for as long as she could remember and knew their individual personalities, moods and preferences. Abby took up her post at Hannah's feet, as she would have sat beside Stew in the past, looking as if she shared Hannah's sorrow. Perhaps she did. Had the dog recognized that Stew wasn't coming home?

"What about the horses?" Hannah asked her father.

Jesse walked another cow into the loading chute. "Gina said she'd take the strawberry roan," he said. "I imagine I'll sell the rest at auction."

"Her name is Spice," Hannah told him. "Grandpa's mare. Her name is Spice."

Jesse turned to his daughter. "If there's one horse you want, maybe we could find a way. If you're staying in the area, maybe Gina could keep it for you."

Hannah shook her head. She had mucked out the horses' stalls, brushed them down, fed them and talked to them, but she hadn't ridden a horse since the day of her mother's funeral, when she had jumped on the back of her grandfather's mare bareback and, holding her mane, tore across the bridge and through the reserve to the logging road that wound up Little Mountain. She rode past the bald spot above the cliff face, and through the forest beyond, until the horse, spooked by something Hannah couldn't see, or perhaps by her own fresh grief, charged beneath low-hanging cedar boughs, trying to dislodge Hannah from her back. Hannah had held on, whipped and bloodied by branches, until she finally fell, tumbling downhill through snowy boxwood and kinnikinnick, prickly Oregon grape and salal. She had lain there in the slushy snow, winded and bruised, listening as the horse snorted and charged madly through an otherwise silent forest without her. Later, the horse had found her way back on her own, after Hannah had limped home.

Jesse looked up at Little Mountain, at the huge thunderhead that mushroomed above it. "Strange to see a thunderstorm building this time of year," he said.

"Yes," she said. She tasted the bitter, metallic tang of ions and ozone in the air, the taste of lightning, despite the bite of winter cold. "Remember that storm over Little Mountain the Halloween when Mom was sick?" she asked. "The lightning was right on us. Thunder boomed so hard it shook the windows in the house. I crawled into bed with you and Mom because I was so scared."

"Your mom tried to go out into it, but I dragged her back to bed and held her there. I held you both."

Hannah turned to face her father. "That was the last night I can remember feeling like we were a family. Everything fell apart after that."

Jesse kept his eyes on the storm building above Little Mountain but said, "I am sorry I have to sell the place."

"Are you?" she asked.

Before he could answer, his attention was drawn past Hannah. She turned to see several trucks pull to a halt in front of the bridge, kicking up a cloud of dust. Construction workers wearing fluorescent vests and hard hats got out of each of the trucks and marched onto the bridge. Alex was the only protestor there on this weekday morning. He rose from his lawn chair to block the men's passage.

"Are they taking down the blockade?" Jesse asked Hannah. "Trying to enforce that court order on their own?"

"I don't know."

Jesse looked at his watch. "I've got to get to the auction.

Let's get the rest of these cows loaded."

But Hannah was watching Alex and the men who had swarmed around him. "Can you just give me a minute?" Hannah didn't wait for Jesse to answer. She jumped the wooden fence of the holding pen, cut through the pasture and climbed through the barbed-wire fence at the road. As she reached the bridge, a couple of the men from the construction crew threw protest signs over the railings. Another was shouting, jabbing his finger at Alex's chest, which Alex did his best to ignore as he talked into his cell. Hannah realized the angry man was the father of one of her classmates from high school. His last name was Holman. "What's going on?" she asked.

"You shouldn't be here," Alex told her, still holding his cell to his ear. He grabbed her hand, squeezed and let go, urging her to leave.

"You got no right to be here either," Holman told Alex, and ripped down another of the protest signs and threw it over the railing. The sign, which read *O Canada, Your Home on Native Land,* turned circles in the eddies below. "Go home," he told Alex. "We're going back to work."

"I don't think so," Alex said, tapping the screen on his phone to end his call.

"Who's going to stop us?" Holman asked him. "You?" He looked Alex up and down. Hannah suddenly saw Alex as Holman did, still so much the boy.

"I phoned a few friends to join the party," Alex said. He pointed across the river, at the activity his calls had sparked on the reserve. A number of people were leaving their homes to join them on the bridge.

Holman held up his own cell. "Good for you," he said. "I'll phone the cops. There's a court order already in place that says you got no right to be here." As Holman made his call, one of the other men from the construction crew began a chant that all the workers picked up: "Go home, go home, go home . . ."

Holman ended his call and yanked down the remaining protest signs. When Alex attempted to stop him, he pushed Alex back hard.

"Hey!" said Hannah. She stepped between the men. "Leave him alone."

Holman was tall enough to look right over her. "Fucking lazy Indian. Maybe you've got nothing better to do than sit around collecting welfare. But we've got to work—we've got mouths to feed."

"Alex has a degree," Hannah protested. Alex hadn't yet found work in the region, but since his return, he had offered several storytelling and acting workshops in area schools and libraries.

"Hannah, don't," said Alex.

She looked at each of the men in turn. "Any one of you got a degree?"

"Yeah, so what's his degree in?"

Hannah hesitated. "Theatre."

The men burst into laughter. "Hear that, boys? He's an actor." Holman turned back to Alex. "I work on contract. I don't get the work done, I don't get paid. You know how much I've lost because of you? How much my family has lost?"

Hannah put her hand on Holman's arm to get him to look down at her. He smelled of diesel. "Do you understand just how much will be lost if you finish that road and that development?" she asked him. "Do you know what that development could do to the river?"

Holman's glance slid to Hannah's hand on his arm, but then Abby barked from the pasture behind them and Holman looked past her. "What the fuck?" he said.

Hannah turned to see her brother walking towards them. He was naked and barefoot, stepping gingerly on the gravel as if each footfall was painful. In the holding pen behind him, Jesse fought to get the last of the cows into the trailer, oblivious to his son, bare-assed and shivering on the road.

"Jesus," said Hannah. She took off her jean jacket and jogged towards her brother. As she met him, he looked through her rather than at her, to Little Mountain beyond. "What are you doing?" she asked. She attempted to tie her jean jacket around Brandon's waist, but he pushed her away and kept plodding. She got in his way. "Brandon, stop this. You can't walk around naked. Come on, let's go home."

Brandon appraised her dully and then watched as an eagle circled low over their heads and drifted down to land on the dead branches of the pine standing at the footings of the bridge. The bird was a juvenile with rough, unfinished plumage. Brandon tilted his head, as if listening to it, though the bird made no sound, only looked down at him with one yellow eye.

The men from the construction crew laughed nervously at the odd sight of this naked boy. They would soon guess about Brandon's illness. Everyone would know. Hannah saw Gina's dark figure watching from her living-room window. *Shit.* Gina would take over as she always did. She would push for Brandon's hospitalization just as she had for Stew's.

Hannah took her brother by the shoulders. "Brandon! Let's go back to the house." But he shrugged her off and started walking. "Bran," Hannah pleaded, taking his arm again in an attempt to lead him home, but her brother yanked himself from her grip and walked unsteadily towards the bridge. He was stronger than she was now. She couldn't stop him.

The men from the construction crew parted for Brandon, and, one by one, the Shuswap protestors did the same. Brandon ignored them all—the laughing men in their fluorescent work vests, Alex's whispering cousins, aunts and uncles—as he made his way to the rise at the midpoint of the bridge.

Alex grabbed Hannah's hand to stop her from following her brother, then wrapped his arms around her from behind, holding her back. "Just watch," he whispered into her ear. "See what he does."

Brandon stopped at the high point of the bridge, staring up at the pictograph on Little Mountain like some open-mouthed, mentally disabled kid. Hannah strained to get out of Alex's grip, to reach her brother, but Alex wouldn't let her go. "Wait," he said.

Brandon climbed the wooden railing and stood there swaying a little on the top rail, finding his balance. "He's going to jump off!" Hannah cried. "He's trying to kill himself."

Alex breathed into her neck. "I don't think so."

"Someone help him!" Hannah called out to the Shuswap protestors, but none of them moved. She knew these men and women. They would help anyone in the community, on either side of the river, for any reason, but now they seemed unwilling to interfere. No, Hannah thought, scanning their faces. They were afraid.

"I told them Grandpa Dennis's story," Alex explained. "They know what the mystery is capable of, what's coming. Or, if they don't believe me, they're curious to see what he'll do."

Hannah turned within Alex's arms in an attempt to get free, but he wouldn't let her go. She saw Gina striding down the road towards them, in navy skirt and heels. Hannah craned to see her father closing the door on the stock trailer. "Jesse!" Hannah yelled. "Dad!"

From the road, Gina picked up her cry. "Jesse!" And finally he stepped out from behind the trailer to see Brandon standing naked on the top railing of the bridge. He leapt over the holding pen and sprinted towards them with Abby barking at his heels.

"Alex, let me go!"

"Wait for it."

The juvenile eagle left its perch on the dead pine and circled above them, casting a moving shadow like the zig-zag of lightning against the cliff face. Then Brandon raised his arms to the sky and the blue-green clouds immediately coalesced directly overhead, boiling in a circle at an unnatural speed. Almost at once the storm broke on them: lightning flashed over Little Mountain, and thunder boomed in the clouds above.

"Jesus," said Hannah, flinching.

"He's practising," said Alex. "He's building his strength, testing Brandon to see if he's strong enough."

"Strong enough for what?"

"You'll see."

Hannah felt the electricity of the storm suddenly gather around them. Her skin under Alex's hands tingled. The hairs on her arms and on Brandon's head stood on end. She heard a buzzing and turned to see the metal rods on the protestors' tent glowing blue with St. Elmo's fire.

"Shit," said Alex. He let Hannah go, and she immediately scrambled to her brother. Behind her, Alex shouted, "Hannah, no!" And then, "Everyone, get off the bridge! Now! Lightning is going to hit. *Here*." The construction crew scattered back to the relative safety of their trucks. The protestors fled the bridge in the opposite direction, to the reserve beyond.

Lightning cracked the sky directly overhead and a bolt of plasma hit the structure. Hannah felt the thunder vibrate through her bones, the bridge shake beneath her feet. Instinctively, both she and Alex crouched down on the balls of their feet, holding their heads. Brandon remained standing on the railing with his arms high, inviting the lightning to strike again, and it did, hitting the deck only yards away.

The wood burst into flame that spread to the backhoe, setting the wooden deck beneath the vehicle on fire.

"Hannah," Jesse shouted from the road. "Get the hell out of there!" Abby barked and barked beside him but wouldn't step onto the bridge.

"We've got to go," Alex told her, pulling on her arm.

"I'm not leaving Bran." The backhoe was already engulfed by fire and would blow at any moment. "Please," Hannah begged, "help me get Bran down."

Alex nodded and stood, calling out to Brandon, "You've got to stop this now. You're not ready. This isn't the time or the place. Not on this bridge." Brandon kept his arms extended to the sky. Lightning flashed, hitting a dead pine on the reserve side, and the tree burst into flames. "You hear me? It's not time yet."

Brandon turned on the railing to look down at them. Hannah cried out, certain her brother was about to fall backwards into the water, but he found his footing. Alex held out his hand to the boy. "You'll know when the time is right," he said.

At last Brandon leaned down to take Alex's hand, and Hannah and Alex hurried him off the bridge. Behind them the backhoe and bridge deck burned on, throwing up flames as tall as a man. Billows of thick black smoke filled the air with the smell of burning creosote.

Brandon's expression was stunned and his whole body shook. Once off the bridge, Brandon collapsed into his sister, and Hannah knelt with him on the gravel road, cradling him in her arms as Jesse threw his coat over his son.

Rain began to fall, a scattering at first, then a deluge that rattled against the deck of the bridge and pinged against the workers' crew cabs, and sizzled on the burning backhoe. Alex took off his own jacket and held it over both Hannah and Brandon as if this would protect them from the storm's wrath.

"You see now, don't you?" Alex said to Hannah. "Brandon *is* filled with the mystery. He brought down this storm."

Hannah saw Jesse and Gina exchange a look. In the distance, she heard the wail of a police car heading towards them.

"I'll tell you what I see," Jesse told Alex, wiping rain from his face. "I see my son is so fucked up he accepts anything you tell him. I can't figure out if you really believe this shit or not. What's your angle? Do you get some kind of cheap thrill from messing with his mind?"

Alex stood slowly and stepped back. Gina directed Jesse's attention to the men from the construction crew watching from their trucks. "Don't do this," she told him. "Not now."

Just then, the diesel tank in the backhoe blew, throwing a cloud of smoke and flame high into the grey sky. The midsection of the burning bridge collapsed into the river and the blackened husk of the backhoe shifted abruptly, coming to rest on the metal bridge supports beneath. Steam hissed as chunks of burning wood hit the water.

An RCMP cruiser pulled to the side of the road behind the construction trucks, and Gina's husband, Grant, jumped out with a grey blanket and ran through the rain towards them, the yellow band on his RCMP cap bobbing. Grant was so tall, Hannah thought, head and shoulders over the small crowd he pushed through to get to them. She noted how his eyes lingered on Jesse and Gina, on how close they kneeled together. "Is he hurt?" he asked, looking down at Brandon.

"I don't think so," said Gina. She had told her husband about Brandon's illness, Hannah thought. But of course she would.

"You need help getting him to the hospital?" Grant asked Jesse.

Jesse wouldn't look at him. "No, I'll take him in."

"I've got to clear out these vehicles," Grant said. "The fire trucks will be here soon."

He turned first to the men of the construction crew, then to the Shuswap protestors on the far side of the burning bridge. "Do you know what caused the fire?" he asked Gina. "Was anyone here involved?"

"You mean, did one of us start that fire?" Alex said. "Christ, I can't believe you're suggesting that. We would never torch our only way home."

"Grant knows that," said Gina.

"I just need to know what happened," Grant said. "How did the fire start?"

"Lightning struck the bridge, set the deck on fire," Jesse said.

Grant turned to his wife for confirmation. "Lightning," Gina said. "We were lucky no one was killed."

"An act of God," Alex told Gina. "Maybe that's exactly what it was." But Gina wouldn't look at him or respond.

"Okay, better get Bran out of here," Grant said. "I've got to get these men to move their trucks."

Together with Jesse, Hannah wrapped the blanket
around Brandon and helped him up.

"I'll get him dressed and come into town with you,"
Hannah said.

"Maybe it's best if you stay home."

"No, I'm going with you."

"Hannah, I really think you need to sit this one out."

"Dad."

"I don't want you there," Jesse said. "I need to talk to the
doctor without—" He paused. "Without your interference."
He pointed at Alex. "And you stay away from Brandon.
Stay clear of my house."

Jesse glanced at Hannah before ushering Brandon back
to the farm. She stayed where she was and watched him lead
her brother away. They reached the Robertson gate just as
two fire trucks screamed past. A few minutes later Jesse led
Bran, now dressed, out of the house. He got him into the
truck and drove up the hill, past the community hall and out
of sight.

Hannah stood alongside Alex as the firefighters prepped
the trucks and then hosed the bridge deck. Despite the rain
and their efforts, the fire burned on for some time, ash and
debris lifting on the wind and floating back down on them
like feathers.

On the reserve side a crowd had gathered to mourn the
burning bridge. Hannah saw one of her father's old girl-
friends among them, a woman named Fern. She was in her
late twenties now and had put on weight. Hannah understood from what Alex had told her that Fern had a son in

kindergarten who'd been fathered by one of the white mill-workers. A few years earlier, she could just as easily have had Jesse's child, a sister or brother to Hannah. Fern glanced at Hannah and away, as if Hannah were just another white girl across the river.

As the firefighters continued to battle the smouldering blaze, Alex took Hannah by the hand and led her back home, the dog trailing them. She was shivering. They were both wet through.

In the kitchen, Alex put on the kettle, then stripped off his wet shirt and hung it and his jacket to dry on a kitchen chair over the furnace vent. Bare-chested, he turned to Hannah and relieved her of her soaked jean jacket and started to pull up her equally wet T-shirt. Embarrassed, she resisted. He took her face in both his hands. "Let me help you," he said, repeating what Libby's lover had said to her. Hannah complied, holding up her hands as he pulled the shirt from her. He unfastened her bra before slipping it off her shoulders. She covered herself as he hung her wet garments on a chair. Then he took her in his arms and rubbed her back with his warm hands. Here was a moment she had long imagined: Alex's arms around her, the feel of his bare chest against hers. And yet all she could think of was her brother standing on that railing.

"What did I see out there, Alex? Did Bran really bring down that storm?"

"You tell me," he said.

She had seen Brandon raise his arms and witnessed the lightning flash as if in response to his request. She had seen her brother—or this spirit within him—embrace that storm as if it were a part of his nature, his power.

She turned her head to look out at the burning bridge and there, outside the window, Brandon watched them. Hannah startled, withdrawing from Alex, covering herself. "Bran?" But as soon as she said his name, her brother vanished.

"Bran's at the hospital, with your dad."

"He was at the window." Hannah grabbed her wet T-shirt and held it against her breasts as she peered outside, but there was no sign of her brother.

Alex joined her at the window. "You saw his ghost?"

"I don't know." The vision of her brother had been as fleeting as the dark scurry of a mouse half-glimpsed. Had she seen something or not? As with a mouse, chances were she had. Hannah shivered.

"Come here."

Alex pulled her close and kissed her, but Hannah stepped back. "I can't do this right now," she said. She pushed her fingers through her nest of hair. "I feel like I'm going crazy."

"You're not." Alex held both her shoulders and stooped a little so she'd look at him. "You're starting to see, that's all."

"Bran said he was awake now. He had been asleep before—everyone was asleep—but now he was awake."

"Yes, exactly. He sees the world like it really is."

"I'm not Bran," she said.

Alex studied her face. "Hannah, you're not going to end up like your mom."

Hannah hugged herself and Alex let go. "I need you to leave," she said. When he looked hurt, she added, "I just need some time alone, Alex. It's been a bizarre day."

"Yeah, sure."

He slid on his wet jacket, holding his T-shirt balled up in one hand. As he left the house, Hannah called after him. "Alex, I'm sorry."

He paused before he shut the door, but didn't look at her.

18

Blessing of Snow

BRANDON PACED BETWEEN the window and his hospital bed, back and forth, back and forth.

"Like a caged animal," Jesse said. He and Hannah stood with their backs against the wall near the door, away from Brandon, as he clearly didn't want them near. There were no beds available in the small psychiatric ward, so Brandon had been placed in this single room on another floor. The door was locked so he would not escape, and he was under a suicide watch.

Brandon wore only the hospital gown the nurses had inflicted on him, which revealed his bare ass when he turned. He wouldn't put on underwear and had kicked off his slippers. When the nurse had brought him lunch, he had eaten with his hands, smearing the food across his face.

"That's not Bran," Hannah told her father.

"When your mother took sick, I thought some other personality had taken her over too."

Hannah bit her thumbnail and then shook her head. "That's not him. He told us there was something inside him. He warned us. Alex warned us."

Jesse didn't rise to the bait of Alex's name. "There were times your mother dragged me down into her world, when I started to believe the things she told me, to worry about my own sanity."

"You didn't see what I saw on that bridge."

"I saw a naked kid in the thick of a lightning storm, about to jump. Bran could have died, Hannah." Like your mother, Jesse thought but didn't say. Hannah would be thinking the same thing.

"He wasn't trying to kill himself." She hesitated. "He really did bring down that storm."

Jesse turned to face her, resting his shoulder on the wall. "Hannah, schizophrenics often think they can control the weather."

"I know, but I also know what I saw. All this is playing out just like Alex said it would."

"You need to stay away from Alex and his bullshit."

"Fine. Whatever."

They both watched Brandon pace for a time, then Hannah said, "I'm going downstairs to see Grandpa." She knocked for the nurse to open the door.

"I'll meet you there as soon as I've talked to Bran's doctor."

As the nurse opened the door, he said, "Hannah, wait." She stopped, holding the door between them.

"How much do you remember about what your mother went through? You should try. It may help you understand Bran."

"I remember that Mom died and you left us there, with her body."

"Dad was with you."

She shook her head as if he had completely missed the point before closing the door behind her.

She had a right to be angry, of course. He knew it. The day Elaine died, it was snowing just as it was this day. He had stepped outside through those hospital doors into falling snow and raised his hands and face to it as Elaine so often had in the early years of their marriage, before he had begun to leave her. Her small hands catching snowflakes, her shining face, her eyelashes gathering snow; snow melting on her tongue. Before her illness, she was a woman who made a celebration of such simple pleasures. If Elaine had survived that terrible day, he would have bundled her up and carried her into the snow, and everything would have been all right. She would have forgiven him for his many betrayals and forgotten his absences during her illness, the evenings he couldn't bring himself to sit by her side, to hold her. He would have waltzed with her in the snow the way they had in the backyard of the farm in the first winter of their marriage.

Instead Jesse had stood alone in the swirling snow outside the hospital, as his young son and daughter cried in their grandfather's arms by their mother's dead body in that intensive care room. He couldn't hold Hannah; he knew she wouldn't let him, not after his betrayal with a girl named Fern, with Gina, with others she also clearly knew about. So he had walked out into that first flurry of the winter alone, hoping for his wife's forgiveness, her blessing of snow.

Hannah found her grandfather seated at his wheelchair by the window, studying his old, wrinkled hands as if confused by them. Outside, the delicate snowflakes of the first snowfall floated down. "What should I do?" he asked her as she sat on the bed. "I don't know what to do."

When Hannah didn't respond, Stew looked again at his hands. On an arm above Stew's bed, the television Jesse had just rented for him flickered with the volume muted. Hannah stared at it, not taking anything in, as she decided whether to tell Stew about Brandon or not. She knew Jesse wouldn't. Jesse would tell Stew that Brandon was at home, that he was fine.

"Grandpa? Grandpa, look at me."

Stew turned his rheumy blue eyes on her. He seemed so much more vulnerable without his glasses.

"We should talk about Bran."

"Brandon!" Stew cried, suddenly agitated. He started pulling at the tray on his wheelchair.

A woman went by the open door with the book trolley. She stopped to glance in the room and, taking in Stew's confused mental state and Hannah's panic, moved on.

Hannah hugged her grandfather to calm him, to prevent further outbursts. "Bran is all right. He's fine."

Stew shook his head. Even in his drug-induced confusion, he knew she was lying. "He's lost," he said. "We've got to find him."

Hannah rocked her grandfather and shushed him, afraid the nurse would sedate him again if he didn't calm. "Everything's fine," she said, hating that she now sounded like a babysitter comforting a child. She turned up the television volume to distract her grandfather and watched the news with him for a time as she held him, her mind on Brandon in the ward above.

After a time, Stew seemed to relax, and Hannah sat back on the bed beside him.

"You look different," he said.

Hannah smoothed the curls in place around her shoulders. "Just my hair," she said. She had worn it down, rather than in her usual ponytail.

"No, something else." He peered at her. "You in love?"

Hannah shook her head, even as she felt the flush rise to her face.

"Huh," Stew said. "Good. You need something of your own right now. It's that Indian, isn't it? Dennis's grandson. *Coyote*."

Hannah smiled despite herself.

Stew grinned as if that was the funniest thing. Then his expression became serious as he took Hannah's hand. "Maybe he can help us then. He can help Bran."

"Maybe." Hannah said. "He told me a story, a story Dennis told you, about the salmon boy. He thought the mystery had taken possession of Mom, was trying to work through her."

"Yes, yes! That same mystery has Brandon."

"Did Dennis say how to get rid of it?"

"Oh, Dennis tried. He sat with Elaine for hours—while Jesse was on night shift—travelling the 'spirit trail,' as he called it, to find her soul, to bring it back. I thought it was all bullshit, of course. But what the hell? What if Elaine *was* possessed? What if Dennis could bring Elaine home to us? I figured it was worth a shot. And anyway, Dennis brought me over a bottle of Lamb's. The least I could do was indulge him. Jesus, I'd give anything for a glass of rum." He leaned forward as he lowered his voice. "Can you slip in a bottle?"

"I take it Dennis couldn't find Mom."

Stew sat back in his wheelchair. "He found her all right. He said that part was easy. Her ghost was hanging around, stuck here. But he couldn't lead her back inside her body because that thing was already there and it wasn't about to leave. Dennis said he had an idea about how to get it out of Elaine, but by that time I'd had enough of his witch doctor stuff and told him to get the hell out."

"But the mystery did leave. It took Mom back to the river."

"Yes, eventually."

Stew put a hand on her arm. "You've got to find a way to get that thing out of Bran before the same thing happens to him. Bran's soul is hanging around too. I've seen him.

Maybe if that thing is gone, he can find his way back in. You've got to get it to leave."

"How do I do that?"

"Dennis would know," he said. He squeezed Hannah's arm with surprising strength as he pressed his request on her. "Ask Dennis."

"Dennis Moses is gone, Grandpa. He died a long time ago."

"Oh!" Stew cried. "Then what should we do? I don't know what to do."

Hannah realized that her grandfather had been asking the same question she had come to ask of him: he was looking for a way to save Brandon. He was looking for a way out of all this.

19

Ripples in the Air

GINA WATCHED THE hummingbird feeder hanging in front of her kitchen window, a warm mug in hand, waiting for the bird to return. The Anna's hummingbird had stayed on into late fall, hovering around her window daily, as if trying to get in. She kept the feeder full for its sake.

Her garden beyond was dusted in snow, and flakes still drifted down. Early that morning, the curly tips of the kale had been sugared with crystals of frost. Gina wished she had gotten around to planting parsnips, as they grew sweeter after a frost. She would have pulled them from this winter garden, boiled them and fried them in butter, a little salt and pepper, and eaten them for supper with eggs and bacon. The earthy smell of parsnips frying.

This year she had planted a child's garden, really, with fast-growing, showy plants. Cosmos, tomatoes, sunflowers. Now eight-foot sunflowers drooped wet and sad under the weight of slushy November snow. Ragged things. Grant had said he would get around to chopping them down, but both he and Gina knew he wouldn't. They would stand until next spring when Grant tilled the ground for her, offering their seeds throughout the winter to the chickadees and towhees that hung upside down on the flower heads to eat from their faces.

The hummingbird finally zipped up to the feeder, and Gina stepped forward to watch the tiny, shining, vibrating thing.

But almost immediately the hummingbird zagged away, and Gina looked past the feeder to see Jesse entering her drive-way. The hummingbird hovered over him as he approached the house, but he didn't notice it and it left him to resume its haunt of the Robertson house, beating outside Bran's win-dow. She often saw the bird flickering between the house and the river, or perching on the same spot on the electrical wire above the road, on the Robertson side. So tiny she would miss it if she didn't know where to look.

Jesse reached her garden, and Gina opened the door and stepped onto the stoop to greet him.

Jesse didn't climb the stairs to the porch. He didn't want to presume. He stood below Gina, looking up. "Grant home?" he asked.

"He's working night shift this week."

Jesse nodded as he looked back at the farmhouse. "I saw his truck was gone. I was hoping we could talk. I've got a problem, with Hannah. Alex has managed to convince not only Bran but Hannah that the ghost in Dennis's stories is real. She seems to think Bran is possessed by it."

Gina nodded. "Ah."

"It almost sounds funny when I say it, doesn't it? Bran possessed, by a ghost."

"Given the circumstances, and our history together, no, there's nothing funny about it."

"You're not going to tell me you believe this shit too, are you?"

Gina shook her head. "No. I just mean Elaine—the things she believed, that she saw."

Jesse took a step up. "I was wondering if you could have a talk with Alex. Tell him to back off."

"I already have."

"Can you try again?"

"It wouldn't do any good. He believes the stories. You could try talking to him yourself, but I doubt you'd get anywhere."

Jesse looked at the reserve across the river. He had already made an ass of himself at the bridge. He doubted Alex would listen to him or even welcome him into his home.

He turned back to Gina. "Maybe you could talk to Hannah then? Make her understand what Bran is going through?"

"I could try. But you already know what she thinks of me." She paused. "Then there's Grant to consider."

"He's asked you to stay away."

She nodded.

Jesse looked past her into the kitchen. The heat from the open door spilled out into the cold; he could see the ripples in the air beside her. "I've caused problems for you, at home."

"The problems were already here." She sounded tired.

"But my being home doesn't help, does it?" He stepped back down. "You can tell Grant he doesn't have to worry."

"You aren't going to leave, are you? I mean, you're not going back to the coast?"

"Not today."

Gina had once told him she hated his unwillingness to make promises, to tell the lies that were necessary to keep any relationship alive. Hannah had said something similar to him, during one of his rare visits home.

"You don't even pretend to care," she said. "I wish you would at least *pretend*."

Jesse looked back at the old farmhouse. It slumped, elderly, in the snow. "You still love him?" he asked Gina.

Gina didn't answer until he looked back up at her, then she shook her head. "I don't know. I'm not sure I ever did. I loved the idea of him." She shrugged. "Being a cop's wife. The security."

"Did you love me?" Jesse hated the childish whine in his voice. But her face opened to him, like in the old days.

"I loved you," she said. "I might have left Grant, if you'd asked me to. If you hadn't . . ."

If he hadn't fucked around with that girl, Fern. "I was so stupid, about everything," he said.

"We all were."

The hummingbird returned to the feeder by the window, and Jesse glanced at it and then at Gina in wonderment. He climbed the steps to join her for a better view, and the hummingbird lifted from the feeder and circled them, hovering in front of Jesse's face before slipping away.

"I think about you all the time too," Gina said, picking up on the conversation they had had the week of his arrival, the day at the farmhouse when he had faced Hannah with the news of Bran's illness.

"There are so many things I would have done differently," he said.

"Maybe you can, now."

"Maybe."

They waited in silence for the hummingbird to return.

Finally Gina asked, "You want to come in?" She didn't look at him as she spoke, but at her garden beyond. Her tone was hopeful, pleading.

"Is that a good idea?"

"No," she said, but she stepped back, inviting him into the kitchen. After a last glance at the farmhouse to make sure Hannah hadn't seen them, he joined her.

20

The Crow

HANNAH, WRAPPED IN her Cowichan sweater, wiped the damp snow from Eugene's Rock with her sleeve and sat to wait for Alex to arrive. He had volunteered to cross the river to meet her here, so she wouldn't have to walk through the freezing water of the shallows, which was the only expedient way to reach the other side of the river now. To get into town, people from the reserve had to use a logging road that wound through the hills and crossed a rough, temporary bridge upriver past the mill. Many had parked their cars on the Robertson side of the burned bridge and made the daily hike across the river at the shallows so they could get to and from work. Bridge reconstruction wouldn't start until spring.

A wet November snow had fallen again that morning, covering the fields and river shore. Mists rose up from the pastures, obscuring the farmhouse and what was left of the burned bridge. A cloudbank hid the cliff face of

Little Mountain from view and drifts of fog hung low over Samuel's gravesite on the benchland. The countryside was cloaked in white, a dreamscape.

Abby barked from the yard where she was tied, and Hannah looked downriver to see Alex's dark silhouette, shrouded by mist, as he crossed the river at the shallows. As he drew near, Hannah's heartbeat quickened. She had waited a week for Alex to call, uncomfortable with the thought of going to the reserve after all that had transpired on that bridge—and after. When she didn't hear from him, she tried calling a few times but he didn't answer. Finally, two weeks after the bridge burned, he responded with a brief text, suggesting they meet here.

"Hey," he said.

"Hey."

Alex sat on Eugene's Rock next to Hannah, close enough that she could feel his warmth, but not so close as he used to sit. As if accompanying him, a crow flew up and landed on the branch of the dead pine above them.

"What the hell is going on?" she asked him. "Where have you been?"

"I wasn't sure . . ." Alex paused. "I thought of stopping by the house a couple of times, but I saw your dad's truck in the yard. With Brandon in the hospital and you dealing with both him and Stew, I figured I shouldn't—I didn't think this was the right time."

"You could have answered my calls," she said.

"You were the one who pulled away, Hannah."

"The last couple of weeks have been shit. Grandpa picked up pneumonia in that fucking hospital. They've got Bran drugged up so he won't try to leave his room. Anyone would go mental in that place."

"Is Stew okay?"

"No, he's not okay. He's old and he's sick. His doctor told us to prepare ourselves. He likely won't last the winter."

"I'm so sorry, Hannah."

"Why didn't you come see me?" She realized she sounded angry. She *was* angry, but whether it was with Alex or Jesse or Brandon or Stew she wasn't sure.

"Jesus, Hannah," Alex said. "Your dad doesn't want me in your house."

"Maybe you remind him of himself."

"I don't think so."

"Oh, you have way more in common with Jesse than you realize, Coyote."

The crow above them shook itself, its feathers ruffled like an old man's tattered coat. "Don't call me Coyote," Alex said. "I never liked that."

"Hey, if the shoe fits."

"Have you seen me with another girl since I got back?"

No, she hadn't, but she feared it.

"Did you ask to meet me just to guilt me out?" he said.

"No."

"What then?"

"I need to find a way to help Bran." Hannah looked down, running a finger along the fish carved into the rock.

"This thing, this mystery—there must be a way to get rid
of it. You told me Libby tried to save her son. What did she
do?" When Alex didn't immediately respond, she added,
"You did say you would tell me the rest of Libby and
Eugene's story."

"When you were ready."

"I am ready."

Alex studied her face.

She took his hand. "Please."

Alex let go to rub both hands across his knees, but he
nodded. "All right," he said. "A story." From the dead pine
above, the crow peered down at them, as if listening.

Eugene had forbidden Libby from taking Samuel to a winter gathering in her grandfather's *kekuli*. Eugene feared she
would leave him. He feared she and Samuel would catch
the contagion that had spread up the rivers with the returning salmon, as the people moved camp to fish. A terrible
spirit had taken possession of the isolated valley as winter
hit, sickening many of the children and several of the elders.
But Libby stole Samuel away, riding bareback on her mare
across the shallows with the boy, intent on saving her son
from what was, in her mind, a more immediate threat.

To Libby, entering the side door of the *kekuli* was like
entering the warm embrace of her grandmother. Here was
a familiar place of winter gatherings, where her extended
family beat their drums and sang and danced, where the

sacred stories were not only told but relived. But Samuel cried when his mother brought him inside the dark mound. Her grandfather, an old shaman, played peek-a-boo with Samuel from behind his mask to jolly him out of his terror, but the old man only managed to frighten the child further.

Libby had once seen her grandfather put on his mask to find the lost soul of a baby who had become ill. He reeled the child's spirit back on his song as if it were a fish hooked on a line. He had inhaled the child's spirit into his own body, breathing deeply and shuddering as it settled into him. Then he'd leaned over the baby, to push the soul back into the boy with his own breath. Libby had watched the child awaken into himself and cry out, as if in relief. Perhaps her grandfather could do the same for her son.

He inspected the boy's face, pulling up the lid of each eye to peer into the child's pupils. But instead of preparing himself to journey down the spirit trail, he directed her to join the singing and to watch the dancers.

"If I'm here much longer, my husband will look for me," Libby told her grandfather. "Please help my son."

But the old man only pointed again at the three young men who danced in the flickering shadows at the far side of the pit house. "Watch now," he told her.

Two of the men had wrapped a rope around the waist of the third and held the rope taut between them. The man in the centre whirled so that the rope wrapped ever tighter around him. He let out a cry and threw his arms wide, and he was in two, his legs dancing separately at the side of his torso. His legs continued to move away from his body, dancing down the length of the rope as his upper body danced down the rope in the opposite direction. A man cut in two.

Samuel leaned into Libby, terrified at the vision.

"It's all right," she whispered. She had seen the dance before. "He will come back together as one. Watch now."

The man's legs danced back to the centre of the rope, just as the man's body did, turning and turning until his hips and stomach joined back together. The two other men dropped the rope and the dancer was whole again. Her grandfather patted her hand, and Libby understood why he had asked her to watch this dance. This was her son's nature and perhaps her own nature now: like this man, Samuel was not of one spirit, but two, of two worlds.

"The mystery has control of the boy," he told her. "I may have been able to help him if you had brought him to me sooner, but Samuel's spirit is already well down the spirit trail. I can walk that path only so far. And no one can walk to its end and return. We only make that journey after we die."

"Then how do I save Samuel?" she asked. "How do I bring him home?"

"If there is a way," he said finally, "the boy would know. Ask the mystery within him."

"He told us to let him go back to the river."

"Samuel is too young," her grandfather told her. "The mystery can't complete his mission through him. He wants to go home. If you take the boy to the river, the mystery *will* release the boy, in the way your husband lets fish go when he doesn't want them, when they're too old or too small. He'll slip from the boy and swim away into the river."

"And if Samuel's spirit doesn't return to his body?"

"Samuel will drown."

"I won't let my son die."

"Are you willing to walk the spirit trail yourself to lead him back home?"

Libby didn't give him an answer. Her grandfather didn't expect one. He knew the depths of a mother's love.

The old man gently smoothed the hair on Samuel's head. His hand smelled of smoke and cedar. And from the smoke of a darkened corner, Libby's grandmother appeared, dressed as an eagle, holding an eagle feather, to sing and to dance in circles around the fire, swooping, lifting and descending as an eagle would.

"My wife is a powerful shaman," the old man told Samuel. "She gains her power from her guardian, the eagle. The eagle soars so high, she can see the whole river of our lives: what's come before, what's here now, what's ahead for us. She warns us to what's coming, so we can ready ourselves. These are the gifts the eagle gives my wife. These are the gifts my wife brings to our people. She dreams the future. She tells us we're entering a time of terrible change. Watch now."

The old woman raised her arms and downy eagle feathers manifested from the black above their heads to flutter down like snow. The feathers went on falling as long as she danced. Libby looked up through smoke and falling eagle feathers to the ladder that led to the hole at the centre of the ceiling, the men's entrance to the pit house, to see her husband's face looking down.

Hannah looked up to the crow that watched them from the tree above. "So Libby would have to die to save her son. Did she? Did Libby die for him?"

Alex shook his head. "She didn't get the chance. That day Eugene found her at the gathering inside her family's *kekuli*, he dragged Samuel out and told Libby to go live with her sister. He thought she was poisoning Samuel with the old ways."

"But she wouldn't have left her son, would she?"

"No. She set up camp outside the cabin, in the yard. She was afraid her son would find a way to go back to the river when Eugene left him unattended, that he would drown before she could bring his soul home."

Libby fell sick on her bed of balsam within her tent, and Eugene found her there, in the early morning light, delirious in fever. As Samuel slept, and so that Libby would not infect their son, Eugene carried his wife through the ravaged forest. He ferried her across the river in his cottonwood dugout and took her to one of the cabins on the other side. Within the cabin, he placed her on a makeshift bed made of balsam boughs, covered her with wet sheets to bring down the fever and left her in the care of her sister, a woman too ill herself to stand.

The bodies of the smallpox victims were strewn about the encampment, some inside their cabins, some without, some down at river's edge, where they lay half in, half out of water, their bodies dusted with snow. Many had crawled to the river, to drink perhaps, or to feel the cool water on their skin, to relieve the itch and quell the fever consuming them from within. Eugene found a young girl alive there, murmuring in delirium. He carried her to one of the cabins and then went back to check for others. A boy of ten. A woman of perhaps thirty, her face lined by starvation. He helped the few survivors to their homes, made them comfortable, started fires, brought them tea and a few rations from their stores. Even Eugene's heart was moved by what had befallen the people.

In the Robertson cabin, Samuel woke to the cold. The fire had gone out. Above him, he saw the face of a corpse, its flesh white, wet and rotting like that of a dead salmon. A cannibal spirit, but the spectre didn't frighten him. The cannibal's face was familiar from the other place, the place of stories. The cannibal waved a bony hand at him to get out of bed. Samuel left his bed and followed, bare feet padding across the icy floor of the cabin. His father wasn't there. He pushed a chair over to the window and climbed on it to look outside. The cannibal peered outside with him and shook his mangy head. Samuel's mother wasn't in her camp in the yard.

The cannibal waved towards the door, and Samuel opened it and stepped outside. He looked up at the cannibal for direction, and the spirit nodded towards the river. Samuel followed him across the frozen, snow-covered mud of the potato field and on through the rubble of trees his father had felled. His bare feet grew numb from the cold, but still he followed the corpse as it ambled ahead of him.

"Where are we going?" Samuel asked the cannibal.

The creature's teeth and the bones of its jaws gleamed from beneath its receding flesh. "Home," he said.

"Samuel drowned," said Hannah.

Alex nodded. "The mystery went back to the river."

When Eugene returned to his cabin, his son was gone. He searched the yard, the bush, the water, and found his son's body at the bend in the river.

Whatever Eugene had felt in that terrible moment was not part of the story Alex's family had passed on. Alex imagined Eugene would have knelt by Samuel for some time there, on shore, before carrying his son's body home. He would have built a coffin, a tiny coffin made of rough pine boards he had prepared himself. He would have placed the coffin on the kitchen table, lined it with the blanket Libby had made for Samuel out of rabbit pelts and tucked his son into this soft bed. Then Eugene would have sat at that table before his son's body, put his forehead on his hands and cried.

Libby woke late in the day, her fever broken. Around her, the cabin was alive in evening light. A woman keened some distance away, a mourning song. Her son. *Her son.* Libby rose, her legs unsteady, and gathered the sheet around her. She hobbled barefoot through the bodies of the dead and across the shallows at the estuary, where river met lake, and then over the logs and stumps that littered her husband's field, stopping every few minutes to rest, her heart beating in her throat. As she reached the cabin, the sun slid behind the mountain, leaving them all in shadow. The red kitchen door was barred from within, so she thumped her fist upon it. "Eugene," she called.

When she got no response, she limped to the front of the house and cupped her hands against the glass to look in the window. The room glowed with lantern light. An open casket sat on the table and Samuel lay inside. She slapped the window and cried out, but Eugene wouldn't acknowledge her, his shoulders shuddering as he wept. Libby could not reach her child through the window, she could not hold him to say goodbye, and so she pressed a hand to the glass and sang. She cast the song into the air in the way she would have thrown a rope into the water, to rescue her drowning son.

The crow lifted from its perch, and Hannah watched it fly across the river and disappear into the mist.

"I saw Bran's ghost," she told Alex. "That day with you in the kitchen."

Alex nodded. "Then he may not have started his journey south. He could still find his way back to himself."

"But how do I get the mystery to leave?"

Alex echoed what Libby's grandfather had told her. "Ask Brandon," he said. "Ask the mystery."

"And if he doesn't want to go?"

"Then the story will play out."

"Bran will die."

"And this valley will drown. Like it did before."

"You really believe this is true, Alex?"

Alex nodded, and reached out for her hand.

21

Dark Water

THE NURSE OPENED the door to Brandon's hospital room and Hannah stepped in. Brandon sat in a chair by the window, staring out at the bare trees in the snow-covered park and the small lake beyond. His face was puffy and sullen from the medication. His shoulders were hunched, like those of an old man, and Hannah felt chilled by the similarity to her grandfather, and to her mother all those years ago.

Jesse had left to make the hour-long drive into Kamloops for supplies that morning. He had made a point of joining her for each of her visits over the last week, worrying she would fuel Bran's delusions with more of Alex's stories. This was her first chance to see her brother alone since she'd talked to Alex on Eugene's Rock.

"Bran," Hannah said, from the door. He swung his head towards her voice. He didn't look directly at her, but at the ceiling above. She whispered, "Are you in there?" Or was she talking only to this mystery, his illness? She hesitated, then spoke up so he would hear her. "I've come to ask you something," she said. "How do I help you? How do I bring you home?"

Brandon blinked at the fluorescent light above her head. If he had heard her, he didn't seem to understand. "Brandon!" she shouted, but she didn't move any closer. "Tell me what I need to do. How do I fix this?"

Her brother startled at her raised voice and looked directly at her but seemed puzzled and afraid. Then his gaze travelled back to the light above. "Where are you?" she asked him.

When he still didn't answer, Hannah slid down the hospital wall to sit on the floor, her face in her hands. After a time she heard a light thump and looked up to see that a hummingbird had hit the window and was now fluttering against the glass, apparently bent on attacking a reflection of itself. Hannah stood to watch the bird. Snow drifted down over the landscape behind it. Bran had turned towards the movement at the window too. The bird flew off, only to return, to beat against the glass as if it, and not Brandon, was inside a cage. Its shadow quivered frantically on the hospital wall.

She had to get out. *She had to get out!* Hannah tried the door, forgetting that the nurse had to open it from the outside.

"Hannah," Brandon said. She turned to find him looking around the room as if in an attempt to locate her. The hummingbird's wings vibrated on the surface of the glass behind him. "Hannah." His voice sounded hoarse and hollow. Then he found her at the door, her hand on the doorknob. "Hannah, wait."

"Brandon?" she asked. *Is that you?* She crossed the room to put a hand on his arm, but she felt nothing of her brother's presence. He was as absent as her mother had been, though here his body was, sitting in front of her.

"Help me," he said. "Please, help me." His accent was that of a native Shuswap speaker. This was not her brother.

The hummingbird flew off and Hannah pulled her hand away. "What do you want me to do?"

"Take me home."

"They won't let you out."

"Help me get to the river."

"The *river.*"

"Please," he said. "The medicine they give me makes me slow and stupid. I can't do anything here. Let me go back to the river. I'll release the boy. I'll go home."

Let me go back to the river, Samuel had told his mother.

"Will Bran come back when you're gone? Will he be safe?"

"I *will* release the boy."

Hannah studied her brother and then stood, looking towards the door. "Christ," she said with despair and resignation, and wrapped a robe around him. "Let's go."

Hannah knocked, and after a minute or so a nurse's face appeared at the small window and she opened the door for them. "Taking Brandon to the visiting area?" she asked as Hannah helped her brother walk through.

"Yes," she said, but after the nurse left, she steered her brother to the elevator. Hannah guided her brother past the

nurses' station and pushed the elevator button. The attending nurse called, "Taking Brandon for a walk outside?"

Hannah didn't respond.

"You'll need to sign him out."

"Like hell I do," Hannah muttered under her breath.

The nurse stood as Hannah and Brandon entered the
elevator. "How long do you intend to be out with him?" she
called. "You're not checking him out, are you? You'll have to
talk to his doctor."

Hannah pushed the button for ground level.

"Hey, wait!" the nurse shouted, but the elevator doors
closed.

Abby barked from her tether line as Hannah helped
Brandon out of the truck. She wrapped him more tightly
in the robe they'd brought from the hospital and got him
to slip on the Crocs Jesse had left by the back door. As she
walked him to the river, she regretted not grabbing coats for
Brandon and herself as well to protect them from the cold
and light snow.

Once they reached the shore, Brandon kicked off the
shoes and headed straight for the water, but before he reached
it, he stumbled to the ground. Hannah pulled him up by the
arm, but he was so shaky he could barely stand. "Help me,"
he said. "Help me into the water."

It was cold, so terribly cold. Both Hannah and Brandon
flinched as she stepped him in. Once she was up to her
thighs, she would take him no further. Any deeper and the

current would suck them both down. Bran struggled to get out of Hannah's grip and deeper into the water, but she hung on as she fell to her knees with him. Bran turned on his back and Hannah found herself holding him as a preacher might when baptizing a new believer. Bran's billowing hospital robe. The white, freckled skin of his flailing arms. Bran threw back his head, submerging his open eyes and mouth, looking back up at her through river water. He didn't try to right himself. In that moment Hannah understood there was no mystery. Her brother had asked for her help to take his own life.

"Oh, god, no!" Hannah cried. She hauled him to the surface. Brandon coughed and strained for breath as she dragged him back to shore and pulled him partway out of the water. Low overhead, an eagle carried one of Stew's pink flamingos. The plastic ornament was nearly too heavy for the bird; the eagle hit the burnt railing of the bridge with it before landing on the shore nearby to peck at the pink plastic as if it were salmon flesh. A world gone mad, Hannah thought. *She* had gone mad. What the hell had she just done?

"Take me back into the water," Brandon pleaded.

"I won't let you die."

"Dying is better than living like this."

"You're sick. You don't know what you're saying."

"I know more than you know. Let me go home."

"Bran, you are home."

"Hannah, *please*." He was shivering and his voice was faint. "Take me back into the water."

"I can't," she said, and repeated herself as she shook her head. She couldn't sink any further into this madness with him, into that dark water where her mother had gone. Elaine had drowned here. Instead Hannah rocked this stranger, her brother, as they both shivered in the watery winter light.

Brandon stood on the surface of the water, watching his sister rock his body, waiting to see if she would take the boy back into the river. He had waited for weeks near this shore, resisting the river's constant pull on him, both hoping and fearing the boy would find his way back into the water. If he did, Brandon's body would die as the mystery slipped back into the river. Brandon would then be free to awaken within himself, but only if his body was revived. He needed someone there with him. He needed someone to save him.

He had done what he could to alert Hannah to his presence, taking advantage of her few receptive moments to reach out to her, when she rose from sleep, hoping that she saw him and understood. Only minutes ago he believed Hannah was about to offer him the opportunity he had been waiting for, to find his way home. But then, just as the boy was about to release himself into the river, she pulled him back out of the water. Now he saw Gina rushing from her house. Even if Hannah had second thoughts and tried again, Gina would never allow her to take the boy back into the water. But maybe Bran could still return, if Hannah acted quickly.

He moved closer to shore, calling her. *Hannah*. But, in her panic and confusion, she couldn't hear him. The boy looked up, though, and clearly saw him. "Help me," he pleaded.

It was a strange thing to view himself from without, to see his own long torso, his own legs, short for his body, he realized, like his father's. He looked so very much like Jesse, the way he held his head upright—not by intention but by design—his upper body naturally like that of a swimmer's.

Hannah, Brandon called again.

Hannah turned her head towards Gina as her neighbour called her name. "Shit," she said and then pulled the boy further onto shore. Gina reached them and together they pulled him up from the water, even as the boy protested, helped him stumble back to the house and onto the deck. Gina closed the door into the living room behind them.

Brandon stood near the shore a moment longer, looking at the old farmhouse that had been his home. The ragged tarpaper on the outside wall; the stack of siding on the front deck. The windows were dark. He couldn't see inside. The house appeared derelict, abandoned. He felt the realization settle into him: he was already dead. There was nothing left for him here now.

He felt the water flowing under his feet, the pull of the river urging him along. After weeks of resisting the water's call, he finally turned and walked the surface of the river over the spawning grounds, then around Dead Man's Bend.

At the lake, he stopped to take one last look back at the farmhouse and the burned bridge beyond, his home valley. Then he joined the trickle of souls making their slow, winding journey down this watery trail, following the same route the salmon travelled down to the Pacific, south, to the land of the spirits.

— 22 —

At the Threshold

JESSE THUNDERED INTO the house, panicked, angry. He stopped short at the living-room threshold when he saw Grant, dressed in his RCMP uniform, standing in front of the door that led out to the deck with his arms crossed, barring it. Hannah and Bran sat on the tattered red couch, wearing bathrobes and covered in blankets, warming in front of the fire. Gina had made cocoa for them and was drinking hers as she leaned against the wall near the largest window. She wore Jesse's navy bathrobe over her wet T-shirt and jeans.

"Is Bran okay?" Jesse asked.

"I don't think either of them are okay," Gina said.

Jesse's gaze flickered back to Grant.

"I phoned Grant and asked him to stay," Gina explained, "at least until you arrived. I wasn't sure I could handle Bran alone. Once I brought him in from the river, he kept trying to leave the house."

"It's okay. I understand." Then, to Grant, he said, "I appreciate it."

Grant nodded but his face was steely. He looked over Jesse rather than at him.

Jesse went to his children but Hannah wouldn't look at him. Bran tentatively licked the miniature marshmallows floating in his mug as if trying to figure out what they were. He ate one, rolling it around in his mouth, and looked surprised.

"Have you found out what the hell happened?" Jesse asked Gina.

"I figured I should wait for you. Hannah hasn't been . . . communicative."

Hannah glared at Gina briefly, then drank from her mug, ignoring them both.

Jesse squatted next to her, forcing her to look at him. "The nurse who called said you kidnapped Bran from the hospital," he said. "Then Gina phones to tell me you took him into the river."

"I can't kidnap my own brother."

"You can't just take him out of the hospital."

"That's bullshit." But Hannah glanced at Grant, as if she feared arrest.

"No, that's for Bran's protection," Jesse told her. "I shouldn't have to point that out to you, especially now. Gina said he could have drowned."

Hannah pulled her robe closed at the neck. "Bran wanted to go to the river, that's all. So I took him. Then he slipped. No big deal."

Gina put her cup on the window ledge and sat on the chair opposite Hannah. Jesse felt the heat of her body next to his and, aware Grant was watching, shifted away from her. Gina leaned towards the girl as she said, "Hannah, I saw you help Bran into the river."

"Jesus," Jesse said. "What were you thinking?"

Hannah looked away from her father. "You wouldn't understand."

"You're damn right I don't understand."

Gina put her hand on Hannah's briefly to give her words weight. "Bran really could have died, Hannah. Do you understand that? He could have drowned, or died from exposure."

"Well, he didn't."

Bran slurped up the last of his cocoa and Hannah took the mug from his hand. Then she tucked the blanket around him. When Bran looked up at her, apparently confused by her actions, Jesse noticed that his son was weeping and yet seemed unaware of his own tears. Jesse ran a thumb over his son's cheek to remove a tear and Bran wiped his face. He looked down at the wet on his palm, perplexed.

"We should get him back to the hospital," Jesse said. "He's clearly out of it."

Grant took off his cap and stepped forward. "I can drive him." He nodded at the side window, at his police car parked in his own driveway across the road.

"He won't hurt anyone," Hannah said. She looked pointedly at Gina. "We don't need your help. And he's not going back to the hospital."

"Hannah, it's the best place for him right now," Jesse said.

"You stuck him in that ward because you don't want to take care of him, just like you don't want to take care of Grandpa. You just want to sell this place and leave."

Jesse clenched and unclenched his teeth but didn't respond.

Gina sat back. "Hannah, that's hardly fair."

"Why are you still here?" Hannah asked her. She turned her back on Gina as she helped Bran stand and led him up the stairs to his room.

Jesse stood. "Are you getting him dressed?" he called after her.

"He should rest," Hannah said. "He's exhausted."

"But I'm taking him in." Jesse turned to Gina for confirmation. "They'll want him back immediately, right?"

"Let her be for a while," Gina said. "He'll be easier to manage after a nap in any case."

Grant took Gina's elbow, to urge her up. "We should go," he said. "Allow them some privacy."

"You go," she told him as she stood. "I'll head home in a few minutes."

"I think Jesse and Hannah have this under control."

"You know your job," she told him. "I know mine."

Grant lowered his voice. "Is that really why you're here? Your job?"

"Yes." But she was the first to look away. "I'm here for Hannah," she said.

Grant held up both hands. "Fine." He turned back to Jesse. "If you do need help taking Bran in, give me a shout. But next time something like this happens, you find another social worker. Understand?"

Jesse nodded but didn't make eye contact.

"That's not your call," Gina told Grant.

"Isn't it? I'm your husband." He put his cap back on and left by the deck entrance, closing the door a little too hard.

Gina stood at the window, watching him stride up the driveway and across the road. Jesse joined her there, aware of her shoulder against his.

"He knows," said Jesse.

"He suspects."

"So you haven't told him about us."

"No."

"Will you?"

"You almost sound like you want me to."

Jesse didn't say anything, just held her gaze as he waited on her response.

Hannah came back downstairs and paused as she pointedly took in how close together her father and Gina stood. Then she headed for the kitchen.

"Hannah, wait," Gina pleaded. "Sit. We've got to talk about this."

Hannah wavered for a moment, then flopped on the couch, crossing her arms. She looked like a woman now, Jesse thought, but she was still so much the teen.

Gina resumed her perch on the chair opposite Hannah. "What really happened out there?" Gina asked. "Did Bran talk you into taking him down to the river?"

"No." Hannah paused. "Not exactly."

"Did Alex?"

"No!"

"But he's been telling you stories, hasn't he? Dennis Moses's stories, about the mystery in the river."

Hannah stared past her, out the window, at the river.

"Bran believed his stories, and maybe you came to as well?" Gina asked. When Hannah still didn't respond, she said, "Brandon believes what he's experiencing is real. He *knows* it's real, with a level of conviction, of faith, that the rest of us will likely never understand. That can make him very convincing. I've dealt with kids with similar psychosis over the years, kids thinking they can control the weather or talk to spirits. I can see how you might be drawn into his world."

"I didn't say I believed him."

"Then why did you take him into the river?" Jesse paused. "You weren't helping him to commit suicide."

"No! God, no. I was trying to save him. At least I thought I was." Hannah held her head in her hands. "For a while it all made sense. Now nothing does. I think I'm losing my mind."

Gina came to sit beside her, reached out and smoothed her hair. "Anyone would feel unsettled in your situation."

Hannah didn't pull away. "I want so much to help him, for everything to be okay." Hannah looked up at her father. "I don't know what I'm supposed to do for Bran. I don't know how to fix this."

"There's nothing you can do," Gina said. "He needs medical care, medication, time to heal. All you can do is be there. Just be there for him."

"How can I do that when he's locked in that hospital room? He's all by himself in there. And they increased his dosage to control him, just like they drug Grandpa."

"They medicate Brandon so he isn't a danger to himself or others," Gina said. "He needs his medication to recover. You have to help him understand that." She paused. "He'll likely be in and out of the hospital many times." She took Hannah's hand in both hers as if Hannah were family, a daughter. "But that's not the worst of it, is it? You feel like you have no control over what's going on."

Hannah's cell buzzed and she leaned away from Gina to read a text. She responded to it before pocketing the phone. Then she stood and opened the front door. "Dad won't sign Bran out of that fucking hospital," she said to Gina. "Once Grandpa dies . . ."

Gina glanced up at Jesse as she spoke. "You're afraid your dad will leave."

Hannah turned to her father. "I know he will."

Jesse held a hand out. "Hannah, you've got to understand—"

But Hannah didn't let him finish. She stepped outside and banged the door shut behind her.

"You should follow her, talk to her," Gina said.

Jesse shook his head, feeling the anger hot on his face. "I don't think so."

"Listen, Jesse, you've got to pay much more attention to Hannah. She needs to know she still has a family. Bran isn't the only one suffering here."

"She acts like she doesn't want me around."

"She's hurt. You left her, remember? You'll have to work to regain her trust."

"Are we talking about Hannah or you?"

Gina stood back, crossed her arms and stared at him.

Jesse nodded. "Okay, you're right. But how long will this go on for? When will Bran get better?"

"You mean how long will you have to stay? I don't know. There's no way to tell."

"It could be years, right, before he recovers? Or never."

"There's a very good chance Bran will recover. But yes, it could take years. Before Bran is released, you'll have to have a conversation with Bran's doctor, to come up with a care plan for him at home."

Jesse rubbed his chin. "Are you willing to help out?" he asked.

"I think you need to handle this on your own." She glanced out the window. Hannah was striding towards the river. "And Hannah has made it clear she would rather not have me involved." She squeezed his hand. "Go talk to her." Then she turned to leave.

"Can we meet up later?"

Gina looked back at him from the doorway. "We got a reality check today, Jesse."

"You're breaking things off?"

"I'm cooling things down. Grant sees us. I'm not sure I'm ready to give up everything when I don't know what's waiting for me."

Jesse stepped towards her. "Please, Gina, meet me later so we can talk this out."

Gina shook her head. "Your focus should be here right now, with your kids, not with me."

"I don't think I can do this again."

"Yes, you can. You have to." She hesitated, then kissed him on the lips, lingering a moment before pulling away.

The eagle had abandoned the plastic pink flamingo on shore. Hannah kicked it, sending it spinning into the water. It bobbed on the current, sliding downriver ahead of her as she strode to meet Alex. He marched up the path towards her, the ankles of his jeans wet from wading across the shallows. As he reached her, he shouted, "Jesus, Hannah. What the hell? I get a text from Gina saying you took Bran into the river, that he nearly drowned. She's holding *me* responsible."

"Aren't you? You were the one who said that was the only way to save him."

"I said you needed to talk to the mystery."

"Well, I did. At least I thought I did. For a while I actually believed Bran was the mystery. He asked me to take him back home, to the river. He said he would release Bran."

"So you let him try to drown himself?"

"No! I only took him to the river to let that thing go."

"Hannah, we've got to make sure Bran's spirit is still here first, that he can get back, that we can revive him. You can't do this alone."

"*Revive* him. Do you hear yourself? You *are* asking me to drown my own brother."

"I'm not asking you to do anything. You came to me looking for help, remember? All I did was tell you what I know." He looked away as he rubbed his neck. "In many ways it would be better to let things run their course, allow the mystery to bring down the storm. He's here for a reason."

"All that is bullshit. Everything you told me, the story is bullshit. If you hadn't told Bran about the 'mystery' and all that other crap, he wouldn't be sick like this."

"You know that's not true."

Hannah waved a hand at the water in exasperation. "He thinks he's some kind of spirit, for god's sake, and that he lives in the river."

"He is, and he does! Hannah, that boy in your house isn't your brother. Bran's soul is out here somewhere, if he hasn't already left."

"If he isn't already dead, you mean."

Alex nodded.

"My brother is very much alive. He's sick, that's all. And he *will* get better. I won't let him end up like Mom."

"He will unless we help him. And it may already be too late to do anything."

"Fuck," Hannah said, under her breath. Then she told Alex, "Dad is right. You need to stay away from our house, from Bran." She pointed a finger at him. "And you need to stay the hell away from me."

"You don't mean that."

"Yes, I do." She turned heel and strode back upriver.

When she reached the pasture path that led to the house, Hannah looked back. Alex was still standing where she left him. She held his gaze a moment before she continued on her way.

— 23 —

Cut No Trees

JESSE WALKED AHEAD of Hannah, carrying an axe, pushing a trail through the snow. They were both bundled up in snow boots and winter jackets. Jesse's wool hat and mittens were a vibrant, unexpected red, so at odds with the white and deep green of the reserve bush around them. Hannah had chosen less festive attire, her grey wool toque, grey gloves.

Jesse had suggested a hunt to find the perfect Christmas tree on this patch of reserve land, and Hannah had gone along grudgingly. Stew had taken Jesse to find a tree here every year when he was a kid, and Jesse had carried on the tradition when Hannah and Bran were young. That first Christmas after Hannah's mother died and Jesse had gone, Stew had tried to lift Hannah's and Bran's spirits by taking them out on this annual hunt, but that had been the last one. The family ritual had lost its magic and was only a reminder of their parent's absence.

Stew was clearly failing in the hospital, and Bran had spent the last couple of weeks back in a ward there as well. Hannah had visited her grandfather only twice in that time, and Bran only once. Her brother wouldn't talk to her. She felt as if he were dead, and her grief was nearly as deep as what she'd endured following her mother's death.

And here Jesse wanted her to find a Christmas tree.

Jesse shook the snow from a small balsam, releasing its sweet scent. "How about this one?" he asked. "Too small?"

"We should wait until Bran comes home. Choose one then. He loved picking out a tree when he was a kid."

"You know he won't be up to it, Hannah." He looked back at the tree, holding the thin trunk in one hand. "This one's got a nice shape to it. What do you think? We'll get this decorated and have the lights on when we walk Bran into the house tomorrow. Make a celebration out of him coming home."

"The band doesn't want us cutting trees here anymore. Remember the sign?" It was posted near the recreational site: *Cut no trees*. "There's so little bush left along the river. The last thing we want to do is take out another tree."

"It's one frickin' Christmas tree."

"They'll hear you chopping," said Hannah. "They'll see us carrying it across the shallows. They'll know we stole it off reserve land."

"Jesus, Hannah, you're killing me. I'm making an effort here. Can't you see that?"

Hannah nodded but avoided looking him in the eye.

"I know the situation isn't the best, but I wanted to make this a good Christmas." Jesse pulled out a joint and patted his pocket for a lighter.

"Do you have to smoke that?" She disliked her father when he was high. His bloodshot eyes, his clumsy affection. He talked too much.

Jesse eyed her a moment, then pocketed it and took out gum instead, offering Hannah a piece before unwrapping his. "Can I ask you something?" he said.

"I guess."

"We used to have pictures on the walls, family photos of you and Bran with your mom and me. There were others, too, of Dad and me with my mom before she died. I looked for them as I cleaned out Dad's stuff in the outbuildings, but I didn't come across them. You know what happened to them?"

Hannah hugged herself. "I tossed them."

"You threw them out?"

"I was thirteen. I was pissed. You didn't come home that Christmas or visit at all after." She turned away from her father to look at the river. "Anyway, I didn't want reminders."

"Reminders?"

"Of the family we had, how I messed things up."

"What are you talking about?"

"Mom killed herself. You left. I drove you both away."

"Oh, Jesus, Hannah. Is that what you think?"

Hannah turned back to Jesse. "Isn't that what happened?"

"It's not your fault; you didn't drive me away."

"But I said all those things, about you and those women. About Gina, Fern. I was so angry at you."

"You had every right to be."

"But I pushed you away." Hannah glanced at the reserve village, at Alex's small house. "Just like I push everyone away."

"That wasn't why I left. You can't blame yourself for that."

"You blame yourself for Mom."

"That's different."

"Is it?"

Jesse gave the tree another shake. "Are we taking this damn tree or not?" he asked. "Or do you want to look for another?"

She shook her head. "This tree is as good as any. Let's just get it over with."

Jesse lifted the axe and Hannah stepped back to watch the blade bite into the trunk, throwing out shards of wood and releasing another wave of balsam scent into the air. In motion, Jesse was the younger man, the father she had known before her mother died. He had driven her around the valley in her car seat until she fell asleep each night. He had hammered together a wooden dollhouse for her one Christmas, a gift she'd kept. It sat in her closet, hidden beneath a bag of unused clothes and forgotten until this moment.

Hannah.

She turned to the sound of her name ringing between the axe strikes.

Hannah.

A woman's voice, her mother's voice, calling to her from across the river. She searched the far shore.

Hannah!

Hannah stepped out of the bush and walked to the river's edge, expecting, *willing* her mother to be there, on the other side. But where she would have found her mother, there was only a crow hopping in the muddy gravel along the shore, cawing. The bird cocked its head to look at her, across the water, and cawed again. But now it sounded like any other crow.

After a time Jesse came up to Hannah, carrying the axe and smelling of balsam. "The tree's down. I'll need your help carrying it out." When she kept her eyes on the far shore, he asked, "What are you looking at?"

"Nothing." She paused. "A crow."

Jesse looked at the crow for a moment with her, then turned back to the fallen tree. Hannah watched the bird a little longer as it raked the snowy gravel with its beak, turning over pebble after pebble, as if looking for the perfect stone, then she went to help her dad.

— 24 —

Ghosts

HANNAH LED BRAN from the kitchen, where they had all just eaten Christmas Eve dinner, to the living room, hoping to park him in front of the television. The TV was one way to keep Bran from attempting to escape the house. After Jesse brought him home from the hospital this time, Bran had kneeled right in front of the TV to run his fingers over the flickering screen. Evidence of the influence of the drug he was on, Hannah hoped, something that might pass with time. This evening, though, when she clicked to the Space channel, Brandon's favourite, he hid his face and cowered from the laser fight there, two spaceships gunning it out. He appeared genuinely afraid. So Hannah switched channels and found *MythBusters*. Brandon had rarely missed an episode: the roll and boom of slow-motion explosions, the nearly invisible energy wave spreading outwards from the ignition point in all directions. But now, when a car was blown to bits on the screen, Brandon stood in alarm and called out.

"Okay, okay!" Hannah held out a hand to get her brother to sit down as she switched to *The Simpsons*, Marge and Homer at the dinner table. Brandon settled into the couch and calmed, apparently engaged by the simple lines and colours. He watched beside Hannah for a few minutes, then stood and made his shambling way to the living-room door that led to the deck. When Hannah rushed to get in front of him, Brandon swept an arm out to push her back, nearly knocking her into the Christmas tree. Exhausted, frustrated, Hannah grabbed him by the shoulders and pulled him back to the couch. She wrestled with her brother until he finally tired and slid sideways to lie down.

"Jesus," she said, sighing.

The Simpsons ended and the news came on. Brandon blinked as if the glare of the television, or its content, bothered him. He covered his head with his arms and made animal noises of fear or confusion. Hannah turned off the TV, and when Brandon squinted at the light above them, she flicked the switch on that too and sat with him in the glow of the white LED Christmas tree lights.

After a few minutes, he fell asleep. His body was so still—his arms over his head in an odd, unnatural position—that Hannah touched him on the shoulder to satisfy herself that he was still alive.

The snap of static on her fingertips sparked her fatigue and she broke down and sobbed. Hannah had been sleeping on this couch since Brandon came home, so she could hear her brother coming down the stairs and stop him from

reaching an outside door. She hadn't had much sleep since
he'd been home.

Jesse came into the room, flicking on the light. As soon
as he saw Bran sleeping on the couch beside her, he flicked
it off again and came to sit on the couch armrest. "Hey," he
said. "What's going on?" He didn't lay a hand on her shoulder or rub her back. She knew that he was being respectful of
their strained relationship. Still, in that moment, she wished
he would try to comfort her.

Hannah wiped her face with her sleeve. "Just tired, I
guess."

"Let's get him into bed."

Together they helped Bran, still half-asleep, up the
stairs and to his room. Jesse stood at the doorway, watching
as Hannah tucked him in. Then he stepped out of the way
as she closed the door.

"You sleep in your room tonight," he said. "I'll take a
shift on the couch."

"No," she said. "It's okay. I don't want you to get tired."
She waved a hand. "I mean, I don't want you to get fed up
with all this."

"Hannah, I'm not going anywhere."

"For now."

He didn't respond to that. He had always told her he
wouldn't make promises he couldn't keep. Instead he said,
"You need a break. I'll keep watch tonight."

"If he leaves the house—"

"I won't let him."

She looked down at her father's scarred hand, the way he smoothed his thumb over his fingertips, one by one and back again. She had forgotten the restlessness of her father's hands. They were constantly moving, rubbing the fabric at the bottom of his shirt or, on a summer night, smoothing the bare skin on her mother's shoulder as they sat together watching TV, as if he wished to make sure Elaine was still there. When she wasn't there any longer, his fingers had worried the corner of the armrest of the couch. He had slept on that couch in those final weeks of her mother's illness, just as Hannah did now.

"I *will* keep him safe," he said.

"Okay."

Jesse stared at the empty screen of the television, which reflected the Christmas tree lights he had left on for the night. He couldn't sleep. Who *could* sleep on this couch? This ancient, filthy couch that his mother had chosen almost forty years earlier. The clock on the wall read 2:25 a.m. The tick, tick, tick in the night. He had read in some Sunday newspaper that before the invention of the light bulb, before the industrial era with all its glittering lights, people were accustomed to this period of wakefulness in the night, in which the mind was at once alert and scattered with the remnants of dreams. He wondered if there was some natural purpose to this altered state. Perhaps here was a meeting place where the living met the dead, as in those Victorian stories of hauntings, where the deceased visited the living in the small hours.

As a child, Jesse had hungrily researched the subject of ghosts and the various methods of contacting spirits. He had read that seeing the dead within a reflected surface in a darkened room was a feat anyone could accomplish, a trick of the human mind that would project memories of a beloved into a mirror or window of a darkened room. He had tried to find his mother in this way, within his bedroom window, but without success.

Jesse called his mother now, into the ancient, warped window of the living room. Perhaps if he looked long enough into that dark, shining surface he would see his mother, and not just his own reflected face. But eventually it was Stew's face he saw superimposed over his own. The old man seemed to be on the outside of the glass at first, looking in, but then he stepped forward and Jesse turned to find his father standing behind him.

"What the hell?" Jesse stood up from the couch to face him. "Dad?"

Stew turned and walked towards the stairwell, slowly, methodically, taking his time, as if expecting Jesse would follow, though he didn't look back. Jesse trailed him up the stairs and into Brandon's room, but when he stepped into his son's space, his father was gone and Brandon kicked in seizure on the braided oval rug by his bed like a fish landed in the bottom of a boat. Then his thrashing stopped and he was suddenly awake, looking up at Jesse, wild-eyed. He let out an animal howl and repeatedly hit his own head against the floor.

"Jesus, Bran. Stop! Stop it!" Jesse grappled with his son until he got him sitting upright, holding him firmly in a bear hug, so he couldn't hurt himself further. "It's okay," Jesse whispered in his ear. "It's okay."

Hannah appeared at the door in her jammie bottoms and T-shirt. "What's going on?"

Jesse lay Brandon gently on the floor. "A seizure, I think," he said. He stood and took Hannah's hand so she would listen to him. "We've got to get him to the hospital, have him checked out. No arguments."

She released his hand and crossed her arms, but nodded. "Okay."

"Help me get him dressed."

Hannah handed him a pair of sweats and Jesse slid them on his son. "I just saw your grandfather," he said, without looking at her.

"Here, in the house?"

In the kitchen downstairs, the phone rang, and Hannah and Jesse exchanged a look. There would be no other reason for anyone to ring at this hour. The phone stopped and then started up again. Hannah hurried from the room to answer it. Jesse heard her muffled voice through the heat grate in the floor as he slid shoes on his son's feet.

When Hannah came back, she held the door frame on either side of her as if to stop from falling. Jesse stood to face his daughter. "It's Dad," he said.

"The nurse said he won't last the night," she said. "Everyone leaves—everyone leaves me."

Jesse studied his daughter's face in the half-light, searching for some remnant of the girl he'd known, the child he had lifted into his arms every night on his return from work.

At Jesse's feet, Brandon arched and stiffened. His eyelids fluttered and his eyes rolled back in his head, the whites staring up at him.

"He frightens me, Dad."

"I know. I'm scared too." He held her gaze, hoping she would understand that he had felt as helpless facing her mother's illness. Jesse went to his daughter and pulled her close. For the first time since her mother's death, she let him hold her.

25

A Blue Scarf Floating

JESSE AND HANNAH stood on either side of Stew's bed. The old man's heart was failing and fluids had filled his lungs. For a brief, terrible moment, time shifted beneath Jesse's feet: He was standing on one side of his wife's bed as Hannah, his young daughter, stood on the other. Elaine's chest rose and fell with the assistance of a machine, but she was already gone—she had died in the river—her body small beneath the hospital sheet. Her essence, that weighted thing that was her, was gone. Hannah had taken her mother's hand but Jesse couldn't stay in that room. He escaped outside, into the snow. Even as a ten-year-old, Hannah was brave, braver than him.

Stew suddenly roused. "Bran!" he cried.

Jesse squeezed his father's hand. "You don't need to worry about Bran. That's my job."

"I've got to find him, bring him home."

"Bran is okay," said Hannah.

"No, I looked for him, but I couldn't find him. I looked everywhere for him." Stew scanned the room as if seeing beyond its walls. "Is he dead?"

"Bran is fine. He wanted to be here, but we thought it was best if . . ." Jesse stopped, uncertain what to tell his father. Brandon was in the ward upstairs, recovering from his seizure. He was anything but fine.

"Where's Elaine?" Stew looked past Jesse, at the door beyond.

"Mom?" Hannah turned, as if she might see her mother too.

"She was here just a minute ago. I saw her in the kitchen."

So, Jesse thought, Elaine was as present for his father as she was for him. But then the past was never far away, just a step through a red kitchen door, a short walk through a dormant garden covered in snow, past an upturned bucket in the wet sand of a sandbox, down the thin path through brown, snow-laden pasture grasses. Jesse made his way through this memory, across the road to the woman casting ashes over her own winter garden.

"Gina," he said as he reached her. She set the ash bucket on the ground and stood as he took her hand. "Come on."

She let go of his hand and looked across the road to see who was watching, to the children, Hannah and Brandon, bundled up and playing in the pile of snow-covered sand Jesse had dumped in the yard for them. "Where's Elaine? Is Stew home?"

"She's sleeping," he said. "Dad's in town."

"You can't leave the kids alone." She glanced at the dark window of the farmhouse. "You know you can't leave Elaine alone."

"The kids are fine. Hannah is just about old enough to babysit. Please, I need this. I need you." When she still looked doubtful he said, "We can see them from the window in the woodshed." He had never made love to Gina in her home or his. Instead they found their love like teenagers, in the back of Jesse's minivan down a grassy side road; in the bush on the reserve within the drift of autumn leaves; in Gina's woodshed.

Jesse called to his son and daughter, "I'll be right back. Don't go near the river."

Hannah ignored her father as if she hadn't heard, but Brandon lifted his bucket to reveal the next perfect turret of his castle. He called out, "All right." His high child voice.

Gina ran ahead of Jesse, in the gumboots she'd slipped on under her skirt. Jesse overtook her and grabbed her about the waist, and they danced their way to the shed. The smell of lodgepole pine. The axe in the corner. Jesse was already erect as he pushed her against the wall and lifted her skirt. He came quickly and, after rearranging his clothing, they both leaned against the wall near the window as he brought Gina to her own release. A Mustang drove across the bridge carrying an Indian girl dressed in a white ski suit on the hood. The girl waved at the houses as if she was a snow queen in a Christmas parade. Her boyfriend drove the car too fast for such a dangerous game. The risk, the ecstasy of early love.

Jesse heard his daughter call, "Mom!" Then louder, "Mom, stop!" Then he saw Elaine running down the road to the river.

Jesse let go of Gina and bolted from the woodshed, following his wife's wet, bare footprints through snow and onto the bridge. The footprints stopped at the railing. There were two footprints on the top rail.

"Mom!" Hannah called, terror in her voice now. Jesse saw the ribbon of blue scarf floating downstream. Hannah had tied the scarf around her mother's hair that morning, as her mother stared into the middle distance.

Hannah ran downriver, following the scarf as it was carried towards the lake, hoping to see her mother. But Jesse kicked off his boots and jumped into the frigid, roaring water at the narrows, thinking her body may have been caught by the clutching branches of the logjam. The current swirled him first upstream, then down into the water's depth. He opened his eyes to see his wife below him, her clothes tangled in the many sticks that surrounded her. Her head was down, and her arms floated in the current; was she already dead? He pulled her from the debris and fought to bring her to the surface. In the struggle, his wedding band, already loose on his finger, slipped off and cartwheeled away from his reach.

Stew tried to sit up in his hospital bed, but his chest hurt and he felt weak. "Did you talk to Dennis?" he asked Hannah. "Did you ask him what we should do?"

Hannah paused, glancing at Jesse. "He told me a story," she said to her grandfather. "He said Libby would have to travel the spirit trail to find Samuel and bring him home. But she could never come home herself."

Stew fell back onto his pillow as he understood. "Yes, of course." There was only one way to save Bran now. It was a relief, in its way, to step off this shore, to fall back into the water, arms outstretched, to feel everything drifting away from him as he was carried downriver on the current. He sank into his bed and drifted.

"Dad," Jesse said. "Dad!"

Stew reached back into the hospital room, and held his son's hand as he had when Jesse was a boy. "We had a good time," he said, to make sure his son fully understood that despite everything, he loved him. Then he settled back into the waters and the current swept him further from this place. The room lost shape, became a white haze around him. He turned circles within it until he found himself on the river shore.

He knew what he had to do. He would find his grandson's lost soul within the countless others making their way downstream. He would lead Bran back home, though he could never return himself.

"Grandpa?" Hannah said. "Grandpa!"

He heard his granddaughter's voice calling, from a distance, "Nurse! We need help!" But he was already walking the river shore near Eugene's Rock. It was snow-covered and the river was rimmed with ice. He took a tentative step onto the open water and found it held his weight.

He took another step and another, in awe of the water moving beneath his bare feet. Then he looked forward, to the curve of the river at Dead Man's Bend, to the lake beyond, and started his long journey south.

26

The Wooden Horse

HANNAH WATCHED FROM the living-room window as Alex made his way up the river path to the house. The Christmas tree was still up in the corner, though its branches were now brown and needles littered the floor. She should have taken the damn thing down two weeks ago, or asked Jesse to do it, but she couldn't find the will. She hadn't left the house since Stew's memorial service at the community hall. She and her dad had both been eating frozen leftovers from the reception that followed, until there was nothing left. Jesse had finally taken a trip into town that morning to buy groceries.

As Alex reached the yard, Hannah looked at herself in the mirror at the foot of the stairwell and attempted to tame her hair. She wore no makeup and looked ragged, raw. She pinched her cheeks, trying to draw colour into them, as she made her way through the dining room to the kitchen door. She opened it before Alex knocked.

He looked up, surprised, and she felt foolish, too eager.
"I saw you . . ." she started, then stopped. He was dressed
beautifully in a long wool coat. A red scarf was tucked
around his neck, playing up his dark colouring. Hannah felt
grubby in her sweats.

"Jesse's not home? I saw his truck was gone."

"He's in town."

"Good." Alex glanced away, as if uncertain how to
proceed.

"I saw you up at the community hall, at Grandpa's service," Hannah said. "I tried to find you after."

"I took off as soon as the service ended. You were busy.
I didn't feel comfortable—"

"Surrounded by all those old white guys?" Mostly
retired farmers and ranchers and their wives who had
known Stew.

Alex grinned that sideways grin of his. "Maybe." He
looked to his feet, kicking snow. "I was sorry to hear about
Stew, and about Bran. I hear Bran's back home."

"He's sleeping." She stepped to the side, making room
for him to enter. "Come in."

He shook his head. "I can't stay. I just came to give you
this." He pulled a small parcel from the inside pocket of his
coat, wrapped in what appeared to be very old rabbit hide.
"I was going to give you this as a Christmas present, but
then Stew passed away."

Hannah opened it to find the fur inside still intact. A
tiny carved horse was nestled within it, carefully rendered
from wood and worn shiny from use. A child's toy.

"It's beautiful."

"It belonged to Samuel. Eugene made it for him. Libby must have kept it to remember Samuel by. It was passed down through my family. Dennis gave it to me when he first told me the story about Eugene and Libby and Samuel. Given the circumstances, I think Dennis would have wanted you to have it."

Hannah ran her thumb across the smooth, curved surface of the horse's back. "I don't know what to say."

"These people really lived and died, Hannah. The story I told you *is* true."

When Hannah didn't respond, Alex said, "Well, that's all I came to say." He turned to leave.

"Alex, wait." Hannah looked down at the horse in her hands as she thought of some way to make him stay. "What happened to Libby after Samuel died? She didn't go back to Eugene."

"No. She lived for a time with her sister, my ancestor. She lost everyone else—her parents, her grandparents, her brothers and other sisters—in that smallpox epidemic."

Hannah looked up at Alex. "Did she get back together with her lover?"

"He died, too, along with so many others. Whole communities, whole villages died."

"But Libby survived."

"Yes. And her sister lived, or I would have never been born."

Hannah offered him the horse. "Then you should keep this. You have more right to it than I do."

"No, I want you to have it. It's important that you understand the story I told you was real." He paused. "The danger
is real."

Hannah looked back down at the horse in her hands as
she chose her words carefully. "I know Libby and Eugene
had a son, that he died. The rest—"

Alex didn't allow her to finish. "Have you seen Bran
around, I mean . . ."

She knew what he meant: Bran's doppelgänger, his ghost.
"No, not since that day . . ."

That day hung there between them for an uncomfortable moment, the day they had kissed in the Robertson
kitchen.

"Then there's no turning back," Alex said. "Bran is
gone. The mystery will bring down that storm. The valley
will be wiped clean."

"Jesus—you almost sound like you want that to happen."

"No, of course not. But I think now that it may be necessary. This river has to heal itself."

Hannah slowly wrapped the horse back in the rabbit skin.
She handed it back to him. "My brother is sick. He needs
medication and care. There is no mystery."

Alex weighed the gift in his hand. "Then how do you
explain what you saw?"

"Bran's ghost? A hallucination. I was tired, upset."

"And the storm he brought down, the one that burned
the bridge?" They both looked to its remains, the broken
deck that jutted out over the rapids. The burned BobCat still
perched on the bridge supports beneath, where it had fallen.

"I'm not sure what I saw anymore," Hannah said.

Alex nodded. "Okay." He sighed as if there was nothing more he could accomplish here. "I should get going."

Hannah followed. "Alex—"

He turned back.

"I'm sorry," she said. "I wish—I sometimes wish I saw the world like you do. It seems . . ." She hesitated. "Magical."

Alex flushed and Hannah realized he thought she'd accused him of magical thinking, a child's thinking. So many before her had made the same assumption about his culture. But then he said, "It *is* magical."

"Can I call you?" she asked. She paused. "Maybe we could hang out?"

Alex glanced towards the reserve village. "I don't think that's a good idea."

Hannah followed his gaze. "You're seeing someone."

He didn't answer.

"Is it serious?" she asked.

"I don't know yet."

"We used to be friends."

Alex pocketed Samuel's wooden horse. "Yes, we did," he said, turning, and this time he was the one who walked away.

27

A Bucket of Ashes

JESSE REMOVED HIS helmet and gloves and turned off the MIG welder. Lunchtime. He had skipped breakfast and was starting to feel it. He undid the buttons on the leather shirt he wore for protection and stepped out of the round, open entrance to the machine shed, to stretch and look at the winter landscape. Fog hung low over the snowy fields and obscured the hills on the other side of the river. A crow lifted from the roof and flew off, fading as it entered the low cloud.

He'd moved his equipment into his father's old shed and set up shop here, taking on work as he could find it from the mill and local farmers, something to keep him busy in the weeks following his father's death. He needed to keep busy. The familiar restlessness he'd experienced in bouts for most of his life had hit hard. In the evenings, he couldn't sit still long enough to watch a television show with Hannah and had to get up to smoke a joint outside, or to make a sandwich. He'd put on ten pounds.

Now he fidgeted with the buttons on his leather shirt, wishing for a smoke, but he had promised himself he'd cut down after Hannah started giving him the evil eye. So, a sandwich then. He'd bought himself some rye and smoked meat. A good mustard. A few cans of beer.

Jesse hung up the shirt and headed towards the house without his jacket, feeling the bite of January cold on his bare arms. It was refreshing after the heat of welding. He stopped outside the kitchen door. Gina's car was in her driveway, and Grant's truck was gone. He thought briefly of going over to see her, as he had many times these last few weeks. But she was a married woman and she had made her wishes clear. He would only make a fool of himself. Still, she had held his hand a little too long at Stew's memorial. She had looked into his face a little too long.

There was a smash, the sound of a dish breaking against the floor inside the house, and Jesse pushed into the kitchen to find Brandon poised to throw his mug too. A broken plate and disassembled egg sandwich was strewn across the floor.

"Whoa. What's going on?"

Brandon turned to Jesse with the cup still in hand and pointed in his sister's direction. "She poisons me!"

"He wouldn't take his meds this morning."

"She put poison in my food!"

Jesse held out both hands and walked to his son slowly, hoping to calm him. "Hannah would never poison you."

"Actually, I ground up his pills and put them in his sandwich."

"Shit, Hannah."

"Well, he refused to take them."

Jesse ran a hand through his hair. "Look, Bran, you *do* need to take the pills. If you don't, you won't get better."

Bran gestured with the mug still in hand, sloshing coffee to the floor. "These pills make me fat and stupid. I can't think. I don't know myself. I don't know what I'm doing. I sleep all the time."

Jesse nodded. "Side effects. Just give it some time. If these don't work, then we'll talk to the doctor about switching meds." Jesse took another wary step forward, thinking of Elaine when she got like this. She had been like a wild animal, impossible to reason with. She had hit him once. "You've got to be patient. The pills will make you feel better, over time."

Bran's eyes shifted back and forth as if he were trying to follow Jesse's words and failing. Then he dropped his mug and held his head. "You imprison me! You keep me in this house. I go nowhere. I need to get out."

He turned and strode towards the kitchen door, and when Jesse blocked that exit, he turned heel and headed for the dining room, intent on leaving the house by the front door. Hannah stepped in front of him. "Let me go!" he cried.

"You can't leave the house," she said.

"Let me out!"

He pushed Hannah and, when she wouldn't budge, he swept the dishes drying on the rack to the floor. Jesse attempted to stop him, but Brandon pulled free again and again, grabbing and flinging whatever he could reach: the salt and pepper shakers, the box of baking soda Stew had always had at the ready on the stove to put out grease fires. Hannah jumped to the side as Bran overturned the old table and chairs and sent her lunch flying. Ceramic shards and food spun across the floor in all directions. Jesse finally got a grip on his son from behind, wrapping him in a hug as Brandon tired. "Let me go!" Bran cried. "Let me go!"

Bran struggled in Jesse's arms, then suddenly became shaky, too weak to stand. Jesse leaned him against the wall and let him go, and the boy slid down and sat on the floor. Bran rolled his head back and forth, anguished. "Let me go!"

Jesse squatted beside his son. "Bran, look at me." He held his son's shoulders but Bran yanked himself away.

"Don't touch me!"

Jesse held up both hands. "Fine, but you need to listen to me." He tried looking Bran in the eye, but Bran wouldn't meet his gaze. "You feel this way because you haven't taken your pills. Either you take the meds willingly, or I will take you back to that hospital, where the staff will force you to take them. You understand me? That means injections, needles."

"I hate these needles," Bran said. "I hate this hospital."

"Then take the damn pills."

Bran finally stopped rolling his head back and forth and nodded. Hannah offered him the pills and a glass of water and Bran took them. Both Jesse and Hannah watched him swallow.

"Open your mouth," Jesse told him.

Bran glared past Jesse, at the upturned table behind him, but opened his mouth. Jesse pulled back Bran's lip with his finger to make sure the pills were gone and Bran bit him.

"Fuck!" Jesse jumped up, nursing the finger. The imprint of Bran's teeth on his skin. His son had drawn blood.

Hannah stepped forward, putting herself between Jesse and Bran. "Can you stand?" she asked her brother.

He nodded, glancing at Jesse as if he now feared him. Hannah helped him up. "I'll tuck him into bed," she said to Jesse.

Hannah spoke to Bran in a low, soothing voice as she guided him upstairs to his bedroom, taking control from her father as Gina once had when Elaine first fell ill. Jesse felt the same mix of gratitude and annoyance towards his daughter now as he had felt then towards Gina.

Jesse cradled his finger as he surveyed the damage. He turned the table upright and set the chairs back in place, but left the rest of the chaos scattered across the floor. Hannah could damn well deal with it.

He pulled down his stash from the top of the kitchen cupboard and rolled a joint at the kitchen table. He lit it and breathed in deeply as he heard Hannah thump downstairs. "He's already asleep," she said as she entered the kitchen. "Do you hear how he talks?"

Jesse nodded. The distinctive, clipped accent of those who had grown up on the reserve. "So he spent too much time around Alex."

"Alex doesn't talk like that. Bran sounds like he's learning English all over again."

"Schizophrenics often struggle to communicate. Or don't talk at all." Later in her illness, Elaine had sat in that captain's chair for hours, days, weeks, never saying anything at all, even in response to a direct question. "At least he *is* talking now. He hasn't in weeks."

Hannah sat at the table with him and stared out the window for a time, her eyes clearly fixed on the reserve village, on Alex's house. She looked so tired. Beyond tired.

Shattered. Jesse elbowed her, offering the joint, but she shook her head. He shrugged and inhaled.

"We're not doing this anymore," he said. "Bran's going back to the hospital until I can find some decent care for him."

"You promised if he took the pills he wouldn't go back."

"You're exhausted. It's obvious we're getting nowhere with him. If anything, he's getting worse. He's becoming violent. He could hurt you."

"We'll talk to his doctor about changing up the meds, like you said. She told us it would take time to work that out. She said we'd have to experiment with different drugs."

Jesse shook his head. "I've had enough."

"What are you saying?"

"There's nothing to stop the sale of the farm now. I can't put it off any longer."

"You're leaving?"

"Hannah, there isn't anything here for me now. And you need to go back to college. I'll make sure Bran gets the care he needs."

"You need to stay here and be his dad."

Jesse shook his head as he blew out a stream of smoke. "Today was the first time he talked to me in weeks. Some days I'm not even sure he knows who I am."

"You're really just going to walk away?"

"I have a life, Hannah."

"Just not here, with us."

Jesse pinched out his joint and stood. "I can't do this right now."

"You're running away, like you always do."

"Whatever."

"I hate you!"

Jesse turned and pointed at her, the joint still in hand. "I'm sick of you blaming me, judging me. I came back here. I paid the bills. I took care of things with Dad. I made sure he got good medical care. And I took care of things with Bran too. You think you can do better, then go ahead and try."

"Maybe I will."

"Fine. Go to it. I'm out of here."

Jesse slammed the door and stood on the kitchen steps. Then he kicked the side of the old house, putting a hole in the tarpaper. "Fuck." He took out his lighter and relit the joint and smoked as he walked to the orchard.

The landscape before him was a grey wash, the cloud and low-hanging fog indistinguishable from the snow beneath. The churning river was the only horizon. Winters in this narrow valley were heavy and dark. He felt he would suffocate under the weight of this one.

Across the road Gina stepped outside with a bucket of ash after cleaning her wood stove. Her sweep of black hair covered her face as she bent to toss the ash over her garden plot. Embers in the ash, catching oxygen, lit up, showering the air with light before they hit snow.

When Gina straightened, she saw Jesse watching her. Jesse waited for some gesture, some invitation from her, but she only stood there. Finally she turned and carried her ash bucket back into the house.

28

Family Services

AS HANNAH CROSSED the slushy road to Gina's yard, Spice, Stew's mare—Gina's mare now—whinnied in recognition and trotted through snow to the gate of her enclosure. Hannah scratched her forehead and rested her face on the mare's neck, taking in the familiar smell of her. Other than Abby, Spice was the last of her grandfather's animals left in the valley. Jesse had trucked the rest to auction.

Hannah turned as she heard the crunch of Gina's boots.

"You know you can take her out for a ride any time," Gina said.

"I don't ride anymore."

"You should. It would be good for you."

Hannah gave Spice a last scratch and stepped away from the horse. "She's yours now." She glanced at Grant watching them from the window. "I wouldn't want to impose."

Gina paused as she registered the emotion on Hannah's face. "How you holding up?"

Hannah shrugged but felt on the verge of tears. "Okay, I guess."

"And Brandon?"

Hannah looked away, to her home where Bran slept in his bedroom. She had chosen his naptime to talk to Gina, but she still had to watch from here. Bran took any opportunity to run away. "Not so good. That's why I'm here. I wonder—shit." Hannah wiped her eyes with the heel of her hand, crushing her tears. Then she looked directly at Gina. "Am I the reason you stopped coming around, to help us out? I mean, I know I was rude a lot of the time."

"Oh, no. Hannah, it wasn't you." When Hannah looked back at the house, her lip trembling, Gina asked her, "Hey, hey, what's going on?"

Hannah shook her head, and rubbed her face with both hands, trying to pull herself together. "Jesse's leaving," she said.

"Did he say when?"

"He wants to put Bran back in the hospital. He says he'll leave as soon as that's set up. He has a doctor's appointment tomorrow."

"I'm not sure what you want me to do."

Hannah hugged herself tighter. "This is so hard for me, you know, asking." Begging. "Could you come over again, give us a hand with Brandon? Maybe if Jesse didn't have to help out so much he'd stay. Or if he does leave, maybe I could keep Brandon at home, if I had help. When the farm sells, Bran and I can find a place."

"That would be a decision you'd have to make with your dad," Gina told her. "He has custody."

"Jesse just wants to leave. Could you talk to him for me? I could take care of Bran myself, if I had help."

Gina looked back at the bungalow, where Grant still watched from the living-room window. She fiddled with her engagement and wedding bands. "Spending time at the farmhouse would cause certain issues for me at home."

"So you aren't going to help."

"I didn't say that."

Hannah turned from Gina, feeling sick to her stomach. She scanned the blackened supports of the old bridge, the dark windows of the reserve houses that dotted the thin strip of lowland on the opposite shore, and found Alex keeping watch at the tent over Samuel's grave up on the benchland. He had fished the protest signs out of the water at Dead Man's Bend and set them up around the tent: *O Canada, Your Home on Native Land.* The gesture was senseless now, Hannah thought. The crew couldn't cross the river until the new bridge was built, and construction on that wouldn't start until spring. Yet Alex kept vigil over the grave.

"You're in love with Alex, aren't you?" Gina asked, following her gaze. When Hannah looked away, Gina added, "It would be hard, you know, to be with him, hard to fit in. I tried to go back as soon as I was old enough to leave my foster home. I felt like I didn't belong in their tidy, sterile world. But it took only days to realize I no longer belonged on the reserve either."

"Alex and I aren't seeing each other. I managed to fuck that up."

"But you do love him."

Hannah didn't answer. The question made her angry. She glared at Grant watching them from the window until he moved away into the shadows. She turned to Gina as the pieces fell into place. "You were seeing Dad again, weren't you?" Hannah asked. "Grant figured it out and you broke things off with Dad. That's why you haven't been around."

Gina paused before answering. "It's not that simple. Jesse needed to step up, to take care of you and Bran on his own. If I was there, he wouldn't. You know he wouldn't."

"Dad had other affairs back then, you know. There were other women before you, and one while you were together."

Gina breathed out slowly, purposefully. "I know," she said. "I was married too. Jesse and I both had our reasons for hooking up." She paused. "I wanted a child."

"But you never had kids."

"No."

"Dad wasn't just screwing around on Mom. He betrayed Bran and me too. He broke up our family." *You* broke up our family, she thought.

Gina shook her head. "He wasn't trying to leave *you* then, Hannah, any more than he is now. Taking care of someone so sick—losing someone you love to madness—that can destroy you. Maybe he made the wrong choices then, just like he is now, but he did need something—someone—to help him through your mother's illness. I shouldn't have to explain that to you, especially now."

"But after she died, Dad should have stayed. He should stay now."

"Of course he should have stayed, and I agree, he should stay now. But not all of us can cope. Jesse is a brilliant man. He could have done anything he wanted. When we were all still at school, everyone thought he'd end up at university, rather than in a trade. In my experience, the really smart people often have the most trouble coping with the terrible realities of the world. You must have felt like running away many times over this last year. I imagine you feel that way now."

Hannah straightened her back. "I can cope. I had to, with Grandpa. I have to now."

A crow landed on the tin roof of the house and clattered to the edge to peer down at them, ducking a cluster of electrical wires. Hannah had once seen a crow land on an electrical transformer in town and get zapped with the pop of an explosion, like a gun going off. The crow had dropped dead, smoking, to the street. Black feathers fluttered down after it. Terrible. Darkly funny.

"Did she love me?" Hannah asked Gina, still looking up at the crow.

"Your mom? Oh, Hannah, of course she loved you."

"Just not enough." Not enough to stay. Jesse didn't love her enough to stay.

"I know how hard all this is for you. Losing your mom, your dad. Now Stew and Brandon. You must feel abandoned. Orphaned."

Hannah swung around to look directly at her. "Don't throw your counsellor bullshit at me. You have no idea how I feel."

"Stew drank," Gina said. She didn't ask. She stated it as a fact.

Hannah paused. "Yes."

"He drank when Jesse was a kid too. My own mother drank and later turned to crack. That's how she lost custody of me. Neglect. Neglect of herself, mostly. My older brother lived on his own and would have taken me in, but family services put me in a foster home up the valley, with a white family. The Tomlinsons. Remember them? Janet and Phil?"

"I didn't know about your mom," Hannah said. A flood of embarrassment rose up from her chest to her face.

"Well, gossip rarely crosses that bridge." Gina lifted her chin to the burned remains of the old wooden structure. "After the Tomlinsons took me in, my mom phoned, wanting to see me. She was usually stoned when she called. She turned up at the door once, stinking of booze, and Phil turned her away. The Tomlinsons were good people, naïve in their way. I was embarrassed, for myself, for my mother, for the Tomlinsons, that they had to see her like that. Then Mom died of an overdose."

"I'm so sorry."

"So I do know something of what you've been living with. I should have come to help you much, much sooner. Maybe I should have continued to help after Jesse and I—" She stopped short. "I should have talked to you before stepping back. But you didn't want me there."

"It wasn't your problem."

"I should have made it my problem."

Hannah looked back across the river, to Alex and the pictograph on the cliff face above him. "You and Dad never got back together, after Mom's death, I mean?"

"Oh, no. How could we after that?"

"Do you regret . . ." Hannah hesitated as she thought how best to ask. Did Gina regret ending her relationship with her father? If Gina wanted children, had she ever wished to take Hannah and Bran on, as her own?

She glanced up to meet Gina's keen hazel eyes, a hand-me-down from some white ancestor. This woman who might have been like a mother to her if circumstances, if Gina's choices and her father's, had been different. Gina said, at last, "You look so very much like your mother, like Elaine did when we were all young." She put a hand to Hannah's cheek as if she knew how Hannah might have finished her question, as if her past was visiting her on this late winter day.

— 29 —

Welder's Flash

GINA LIFTED THE hummingbird feeder from its hook in front
of the kitchen window and carried it down the stepladder.
The feeder was covered in snow. The Anna's hummingbird hadn't been around for weeks. She had watched for
it, kept the feeder thawed and fresh, available during the
bird's usual feeding times, but now she had to admit it was
gone. Dead. Likely frozen within some tree in the night
when temperatures dipped. It would have died alone, huddled under the branches. The thought made Gina weep.
She wiped the tears from her face as she carried the feeder
to the kitchen door. She had been too emotional in recent
weeks, and sleep was hard won. The change coming on, she
thought. It had hit her mother early too.

As she reached for the kitchen doorknob, she heard the
front door close and saw Grant jog down the deck stairs and
cross the snow-covered lawn as he left for work. Avoiding
her. He had kept his distance since Hannah's visit the day

before. She assumed Grant had taken Hannah's appearance as a sign that she had continued to visit the Robertson
house either for Jesse or for the kids. She hadn't bothered
to correct him, if that was in fact what was bothering him.
He was a man who resorted to cold silences rather than
outward rage. His unwillingness to talk things through, to
argue, used to bother her. She had once peppered him with
questions until he finally opened up to her, revealing the
source of the wound he nursed, but in the last few months
she had lost energy for it. She realized she no longer cared.
Nevertheless she raised a hand to Grant when he glanced
back at her as he got in his truck. But he didn't say goodbye.

Gina crossed the road to the Robertson driveway in the
dark, the yard light by the old farmhouse guiding her way.
The snow squeaked underfoot and flakes continued to fall,
as they had for most of the evening. She loved these winter
nights, snowflakes drifting, collecting in the shaft of light
from the farmhouse.

Hannah was in the living room. Gina could see her
through the window, sitting on that old red couch. Brandon
was in the room with her, perched, as she so often saw him
now, in a chair in front of the main window. He sat where
Elaine had sat, leaning forward, eyes staring straight ahead
with a similar intensity, though what he was looking at was
anyone's guess. The river beyond was dark. Only the street
lights of the reserve offered light.

As Gina reached the outbuildings, Abby barked once from the machine shed, but then only wagged her tail. The dog knew her. From her house across the road Gina had seen the spray of sparks leap from the shed and out into falling snow. So she knew Jesse was out here working late, as he had since Stew's death, keeping his distance from the house, from Hannah, from Bran.

Gina waited outside the round metal shed as Jesse finished up his weld. She shielded her eyes to watch the blue and white sparks, and not the brilliant glow at the heart of the weld, fearing welder's flash. She had nursed Jesse through an episode during Elaine's illness. He had groaned with the pain and had been all but blind for a day after he'd stupidly worked without his mask. Jesse lifted the shield on his helmet to inspect his work and startled a little when he saw Gina there, waiting in the snow outside the shop. "Gina," he said.

She stepped inside, brushing the snowflakes from her hair. "I didn't want to interrupt," she said.

He took off his helmet and welding gloves, placing them on the workbench beside him. "I was just finishing up for the night."

"You've been working late a lot. A rush job?"

"No, just a bit of fabrication. Stairs and railings for the mill. I've been picking up work from them now and again." He turned off the MIG welder.

"I bet they would hire you back."

"I suppose. If I wanted the job." He unbuttoned his leather shirt and turned off the valve on the tank. "So, what brings you here?"

Gina noted the distance in his voice. She had talked to him only once in the last couple of months, for a few minutes stolen at Stew's funeral, when she had offered her hand in condolence. There had been others waiting to talk with Jesse, his father's old friends, farmers from the valley, and she'd had to move on.

"Hannah came by yesterday."

Jesse shrugged off the leather shirt and hung it on a hook by the door, then took down his coat. "Does Grant know you're here?"

"She tells me you're leaving, heading back to the coast."

"Once I get Bran set up."

"He'll need ongoing care. You can't just house him in some ward or group home and leave."

"I have a life I left behind, Gina. A business. A house."

"You have a life you left behind here. Your kids."

"Hannah is a grown woman. I said I would help her pay for a place while she's in school. Brandon needs more care than I can give him." He put on his jacket. "Look, we gave it a shot. Keeping Bran at home is just too much for us. It's not fair to Hannah either. She should be in college, making a life for herself, not playing nurse to Bran."

"You're right, of course." Gina looked out into the snow. The flakes shining in the shop light like sparks from a welder. Then she turned back to him. "Would it make a difference if I stepped in to help?"

"You made it clear that wasn't going to happen. Grant made it clear."

"Would you stay if I did?"

"I don't know."

Gina took his hand. "You're burned," she said, circling her thumb around the edge of the fresh wound on his finger. There was a bandage on the palm of his hand where he'd suffered another burn, evidently that evening.

"I got lazy," he said. "Welded without my gloves."

She kept holding his hand, inspecting, and rubbing a thumb over the many recent and healed burns that covered it. "I've missed you," she said.

He pulled his hand away. "You made your choice."

"I said we needed to cool it. Things were moving too fast. And you had other things to think about. I haven't made a choice, Jesse."

"You're still in that house, aren't you? You're still with him."

"We've slept in separate bedrooms for months." Gina felt a twinge at this half-truth. They did sleep in separate rooms, but she and Grant had come together a handful of times on the couch, out of need, familiarity, grief.

"You said you weren't ready to give everything up. Him. The house. Your place here."

"I said I wouldn't give it up if I had nothing to go to."

"So, what? You want to live *here*? With me and the kids?"

"No." Gina raked both hands through her hair. "I don't know."

"You tell me you want me to make a commitment, and yet you won't make one yourself."

"Can't we just take some time to figure it out? Together, I mean?"

"But you'll live in that house, with him."

"For now."

"And we sneak around, behind his back."

Gina crossed her arms and stared out into the night. "Or I move out," she said finally, without looking at him. "So I have a place you could come to, when you can. So we can see how this goes."

"You would do that? Move out?"

"If you stayed." She nodded slowly as she worked things through. "I could get an apartment right away, but it would take me a while to unwind everything here. Grant won't want to sell the house. He'll want to come to some kind of settlement. I'll have to figure out what to do with the animals. They'll have to stay on the place for now." She looked at Jesse. "I would have to stop in daily to care for them. I know Grant won't."

"Am I just an excuse for you to leave him?" Jesse asked.

She took his hand again, touching the many scars there. "Maybe. I don't know. I'm not sure of anything at this point, except I don't want you to leave."

They stood there together saying nothing for a time. Then Jesse turned her hand and shook it firmly as if they were making a deal. "Okay, but no guarantees," he said.

She smiled. "No guarantees."

Jesse pulled her close to study her face, and she felt him growing against her. He smelled of heated metal and sweat. His face appeared sunburnt, and flushed. Sometime that night he had welded without his mask. Stupid, stupid man, she thought, and, perversely, loved him for it. He would risk injury, blindness, but not love. Well, maybe he was risking it now.

He kissed her and his lips were hot, as if he were feverish. She felt feverish herself. She had come to convince Jesse to stay with his children and yet, in this machine shed, she had chosen to leave her husband. But then, she had left him months ago. Perhaps Jesse was right; that was the reason she had come here all along. She was surprised to find that this time she experienced no guilt, no remorse. It was done.

Abby shifted and whined from her spot under the overhead heater. Somewhere close, a coyote cried and another took up its call, echoing off the hills, filling the narrow valley with a chorus of yips and howls.

— 30 —

Restless

THE BOY SAT in the chair and looked out the living-room window to the river and cliff above. There was still a skiff of snow on Little Mountain, but on the valley floor the fields were brown and leaf buds had appeared on the trees. The sockeye young, the alevin, had hatched from their eggs over the winter and now waited for spring within their gravel beds, restless after their long sleep. In a month they would burst up into the river as fry. Not long after, they would be ready for their journey to the lake. He had so little time to prepare.

The boy placed his hands on his thighs, breathed in deeply and began. But then the girl, Hannah, entered the room with pills and a glass of water. "Here," she said.

He glanced up at her but didn't answer. He never answered now. Nor did he fight her. He simply placed the pills in his mouth and swallowed.

Hannah watched him carefully as he did so, then turned and left the room, carrying the glass. As soon as she was gone, the boy fished the pills from the side of his mouth and slipped them into the pocket of his jeans. He spit the bitter taste of the medicine into the lone wilting plant in the corner. Later, when he was alone in his room, he would hide the pills with the others in a pair of shoes beneath his bed, as he had for over a month now. His mind had almost recovered. He felt clearer, stronger. He was ready.

He listened to be sure Hannah was occupied in the kitchen, attending to her chores, and he wouldn't be disturbed. Then he sat in his chair, focused on the image on the cliff face and, once again, began.

Spring

THE SALMON FRY had escaped their gravel nests and now darted in the shallows of Lightning River, waiting for the spring freshets that would wash them to the lake. They scattered from Hannah's path as she sloshed through the water. She had seen Alex heading back to the reserve and had raced down the path after him.

"Alex," she called. "Wait!" He stopped on the other side of the river, as if deciding whether to acknowledge her or not, then turned and walked back to her. They met in the shallows.

"Brandon is missing," Hannah told him. "He left without a coat or shoes sometime in the night. I checked on him at about three. He was in bed, asleep. Dad and I walked the river at five-thirty, as soon as we realized he was gone." Hunting for Brandon's body in the early morning light. She couldn't say it out loud, but she knew Alex understood. "We searched all the outbuildings. Dad just left with Gina to drive the roads. I don't know where else to look."

"Have you phoned the cops?"

"Gina called Grant before they left. Grant said he would get out here as soon as he could."

"Okay." Alex took out his cell as he led her to the shore near the development site. "I'll get the word out." Hannah watched him make call after call to relatives and friends on the reserve. She could think of no one to phone herself. Alex ended his last call and shook his head. "No one has seen him. As soon as your dad gets back, we'll put together a search party and comb Little Mountain. Brandon has got to be hiding here somewhere."

"Or he's in the river." Tangled in the branches on the river bottom. Hannah covered her mouth. "Oh, Jesus."

"Hey, hey. Come here."

Alex took her into his arms and she buried her face in his chest. He smelled of cigarette smoke and oranges, and as he rocked her back and forth, she calmed somewhat.

"I found a stash of pills in one of Brandon's shoes under his bed," she said. "He's been making like he's swallowing them, but when I'm gone he spits them out."

Alex released her. "For how long?"

"I don't know. A few weeks."

"The mystery has gained strength then. Listen, Hannah, it's no coincidence Brandon has gone missing right now."

"What do you mean?"

"The salmon fry. They're ready to head to the lake, and the mystery is free to bring down the power of that storm. I think he may have already started." He pointed at the thunderhead above them, which had taken on an eerie green cast. The clouds had begun to circle at a frightening speed. Alex gauged her reaction, then said, "You still don't believe me."

Hannah was uncertain what to say. Despite her father's reassurance and everything she had read about her brother's illness, she still felt Bran was no longer with them, that someone, some*thing* had taken his place. She looked down to avoid Alex's gaze, to the shoreline at her feet. There in the mud were the directionless tracks of dogs, so easy to differentiate from the footprints of the coyotes, which didn't meander but ran with purpose. Amid the coyote tracks, she spotted one set of bare human footprints that she had managed to miss on her earlier search. As she stared, another set of footprints appeared in the mud as if someone had just stepped down in front of her. She looked up but there was no one close.

"What is it?" Alex asked.

"I'm not sure." Another set of footprints appeared, then another and another, heading upriver. "Don't you see that?" she asked, pointing.

"What?"

She followed the prints and they led her to the band's recreation site near the bush. As Alex caught up with her, she turned to him. Behind her the footprints were gone; only Alex's and her own wet boot prints remained.

"What the hell is going on?" he asked.

"I think someone is trying to tell me something," she said. She searched the trees ahead of her and there was Brandon, running through bush. "He's there!" she cried.

"Where?"

Hannah sprinted after her brother. "Bran, wait. Stop!" The blur of bare skin through bush. "Bran, wait!" Her brother didn't slow or turn and his dark figure receded into the bush, following the path up Little Mountain.

Alex overtook Hannah and she followed him up the path until it opened onto a logging road on crown land. Alex stopped and looked both ways. Hannah caught up to him, out of breath. "Which way?" she said.

"I don't know. Are you sure you saw him?"

She stood there, baffled, searching. Then she saw her brother again, far up the road that wound around Little Mountain. "There." She sped ahead but lost him, and began to doubt what she had seen until she once again spotted him up ahead, at the lookout near cliff's edge. "Brandon!" she called, but as she reached the turnaround, her brother wasn't there.

Hannah wiped the sweat from her face with the edge of her T-shirt. Her legs felt weak, not in her control. They vibrated from exhaustion, beat with the blood pumping through her. But there was something more, a buzz from the fireweed brushing against her leg. Hannah reached down and pressed the stalk between her fingers and felt the vibration between her hands, like the electrical hum she experienced when she ran her hand over the back of her laptop as she closed it.

Alex reached her and bent over with both hands on his knees to catch his breath. "You see him?"

"He *was* here. He just disappeared."

"We can't stay up here to look for him. We've got to leave."

"Why?"

Alex glanced at the clouds swirling immediately over-head. They rumbled as lightning flashed across the sky. "You feel that electrical hum around us?"

"I felt the buzz running through the fireweed."

Alex pointed up, at the hydro towers that loomed high above her and receded one after the other back through the cut block down the next slope. The lines hung low over their heads. "The electricity is bleeding from the lines to us on the ground. Standing out here, we're just asking that lightning to hit us."

He held out his hand and Hannah touched it tenta-tively, with just the pads of her fingers. She startled as a jolt of electricity zapped between them. She tried again, taking his hand, and felt a tingling that electrified every nerve.

Hannah glanced up at Alex in wonder. He grinned at her. "This isn't the first time I've felt that with you," he said.

Hannah released his hand, uncertain how to respond. "We can't leave Bran up here," she said.

"You sure he went this way? I didn't see him, not even once."

"How could you miss him? He was naked."

Alex shrugged.

Hannah put her hands to her face and turned circles as she called her brother. "Bran! Brandon!" Lightning arched to the left and then to the right of Little Mountain and thunder immediately boomed.

Alex said, "He could have taken another path down. We should head back to the river. Watch for him there."

Hannah stepped forward, to cliff's edge, to look out over the valley, hoping to see her brother on the trails below. An eagle, perched on a pine that clutched the cliff face, took flight, circling over the benchland, and Hannah did see Brandon there, standing on the cliff side of Samuel's grave. The tent hid him from anyone standing on the opposite shore. "Look!" she cried. "There's Bran!"

"If he was up here, how did he get down there so fast?"

"I don't know." Hannah grabbed her phone and pressed 'Jesse' on her contact list. "But I saw him." She waited for her father to pick up.

"Then his soul is still here." Alex paused. "Or has returned."

Hannah shook her head, bewildered. The Brandon she saw by the tent below was only dressed in underwear and a T-shirt, but at least he wasn't naked.

Jesse picked up. "Dad, Bran's at the grave."

"Oh, thank god. We're at the turnoff to the highway. I can be back in twenty minutes."

"Hurry."

Hannah hung up and pocketed her phone.

"I was right," said Alex. "He *is* calling down the storm. Look."

Below, Bran faced the cliff on which they stood, staring up at the pictograph, his arms outstretched. Then he roared, his voice ringing against the rock face, and the clouds burst. Rain at first sprinkled them, then poured down. Lightning flashed and flashed again, followed immediately by booms that shook the ground beneath their feet. All at once, Hannah saw Brandon standing at cliff's edge right in front of her, even as she also saw him below, at Samuel's grave.

"What the fuck?" she said.

"What?" asked Alex.

"Don't you see him?" *This* Brandon was naked. He opened his arms and fell backwards off the cliff edge and into the thunderous rain as if into river water. Instinctively, Hannah reached out, crying, "No!" But her brother didn't fall to the benchland below. He simply disappeared. Hannah understood. She *knew* with that same powerful certainty she had experienced when her mother had died, the knowing of schizophrenics and mystics. Brandon had just asked her to do the necessary thing, to submerge herself with him in these dark waters, to dive into his madness, to save him.

— 32 —

A Leap of Faith

THE BOY PRESSED into the wind and sheets of rain as he made his way downhill from the benchland, reaching and then passing the reserve houses. He walked slowly, but with clear intent, towards the remains of the burned bridge. Alex and Hannah raced towards him down the mountain road, cold rain cascading down the back of their necks. Furious winds pushed and pulled the trees, bending them nearly in half. Thunder boomed, and lightning flashed and flashed again, striking the hillside above, the fields on the other side of the river, the lightning rod on Stew's barn. Lightning hit a dead pine on the opposite shore, setting it alight despite the heavy rain. Hannah's hair, T-shirt and jeans were soaked through, and the shoulder of the road was giving way under her feet. Rainwater ran in streams down the reserve road towards the river, up to her ankles in places.

"Brandon! Stop!" Hannah cried. Then, to Alex, she said, "We're not going to reach him in time." Brandon was already stumbling onto the burned deck of the bridge. He lost his footing and fell, lying there as if stunned before righting himself. Beyond the bridge, Hannah saw Jesse drive into the yard and park the truck by the gate. He and Gina jumped out, holding their coats over their heads.

The eagle Hannah had seen perched on the cliff circled low overhead, watching them all, she thought. The bird landed on the railing and appeared to wait for Brandon there, eyeing him as he approached. As soon as Brandon reached him, the bird flew off. Brandon held the railing where the bird had perched and looked down into the rushing water. Rain pounded the blackened wood of the bridge all around him. The scorched deck hung suspended, and dangerous, over the rapids, the metal ribs of the supports beneath exposed. As Alex and Hannah ran onto the bridge, the deck bounced and swayed. Hannah wasn't sure the remaining deck would hold.

Brandon climbed the railing of the bridge and stood looking down into the water. Hannah saw Jesse and Gina racing towards the river shore through the field.

Alex held both hands out. "Wait," he called to Brandon. "Just wait. You don't have to do this. We can find another way to get you home."

Brandon turned to face him, slipping on the railing's slick surface. Hannah thought he would fall, but then Brandon righted himself, leaning into the thunderous wind to look down at them. "There's no other way," he said.

Above them the eagle cried. Brandon turned his face upward and closed his eyes as the rain cascaded over his face.

Then he spread his arms and stepped back into the water. The river swallowed him.

"Brandon!" Hannah cried. Her brother resurfaced a few yards downriver at the pool. He thrashed in the water, gulping for air, his body reacting on instinct. Then he sank again, pulled under by the rolling currents of the swollen river.

Hannah kicked off her boots and as she did so, Alex grabbed her arm. "You can't. For god's sake, Hannah, you'll drown."

She shook him off and jumped too.

Hannah floundered, gulping cold water instead of air as the river carried her downstream. Jesse and Gina ran down the river path on one side, Alex on the other. She saw Brandon beneath her, his clothes tangled within the branches of the many fallen trees. Hannah kicked against the current with the desperation of a salmon. Her hands found a branch, then another jutting from the trees trapped in rock, damming the narrows, and she pulled herself along this underwater forest until she reached her brother. She took hold of his shirt and turned him in an attempt to release him from the clutch that entangled him. As she did so, bubbles escaped his open mouth and with them a presence, a trailing shape in the water that swirled away from him like a cloud of breath on a cold night.

The energy, the mystery, circled around them as if holding them both safe, then it dispersed into the water. Freed now, Brandon drifted upward. Hannah wrapped her arms around him and allowed herself to be pulled downriver by the current to Dead Man's Bend, where she knew they would be tossed onto shore. Perhaps she could still save them both if she could make it to the surface to take in breath.

A darkness lay between the rocks, and within that dark there was a deeper black. The current pulled Hannah down towards it and the dark took shape. A hand. An arm. A leg. A boy. A toddler. *Samuel.* The child's body hung in the water, the foot caught between logs submerged beneath the rush at the narrows. The current shifted the boy's hair from his face and he looked up, directly at her. His dark brown eyes held hers. Then he was gone.

Hannah realized she must be drowning, her mind conjuring visions as it suffocated. Yet she was aware of the flow of the rapids above, the river stones below. The cold. The *cold.* Hannah felt her body turn in the water, pushed upward and carried along by eddies. *I'm dying,* she thought. *I'm already dead.* Above her the choppy water was a broken mirror, each shard reflecting her image back to her: a thousand, a hundred thousand selves. Hannah was each of these incarnations, and yet she was separate from them also. She was both a series of individuals caught, static, within time, and a continuum. Hannah chose a moment and rose up, her soul expanding, to become that reflection, to become the rough, troubled water, the electric air and the grieving, weeping sky.

On the far shore, at Dead Man's Bend, Brandon lay on a bed of glistening river-rounded stone as Gina kneeled beside him and attempted to bring him back to life. Jesse stood behind them both, hugging himself, a look of panic and sorrow on his face. All around them raindrops, thick as fingertips, were suspended in the air, caught in the instant of their fall. Hanging directly above, like a chandelier, a lightning bolt was frozen in place. Thick, black-blue and green clouds draped low, heavy in electrical charge and moisture. Only the eagle, in flight, was in motion, circling and circling, crying *eye-EYE!*

Hannah watched the eagle spiral down, then looked back to Dead Man's Bend. There was Stew, standing behind Jesse, with his hand on his son's shoulder. He nodded at Hannah and pointed upriver to the shore on the Robertson side, by the spawning grounds.

Hannah. It was her mother's voice, reverberating as if in a chamber.

Hannah.

"Mom?"

Hannah searched the shore, but all she saw at first was shadow, a hazy dark figure. She blinked and squinted and the figure became the silhouette of a woman. Then the woman took on colour, dimension, and became her mother. Elaine was bent over the sandy rocks on shore, searching through them, dressed in the sloppy sweatpants and T-shirt she had worn day in and day out in her final weeks, the clothes she had drowned in.

Hannah took a step forward, realized she was walking on water and faltered. She looked down to find a child's body, her own from childhood. These ten-year-old hands, these small, clumsy feet slapping the surface of the water as if in play.

She took another step, then another, and, gaining confidence, she strode to shore. When she reached her mother, Elaine didn't acknowledge her. "It's got to be here," she said to herself.

Hannah looked down at the sand where Elaine turned over stones. "What are you looking for?"

Her mother mumbled to herself, as if Hannah was another figment of her imagination.

"Mom, it's me." Hannah touched her shoulder and her mother shrugged as if dispelling a horsefly.

"It's got to be here," Elaine said.

"I missed you," Hannah told her. "I've missed you so much."

Elaine lifted another stone, oblivious to Hannah's presence.

"There are so many things I want to tell you," Hannah said. "So many things I want to ask."

"Ask," Elaine whispered, echoing her.

"Yes!" Hannah stepped in front of her mother, but Elaine looked through her. She bent and turned another stone.

"You used to play with Brandon and me. Do you remember? You used to chase us through the laundry hanging on the line. You sprayed us with the hose when you watered the garden. Then you didn't play with us anymore."

Hannah took her mother's hand to stop her searching and Elaine looked down at their joined fingers.

"I thought it was me. I thought Brandon and I were too much for you. Grandpa told us that. He told us to go play outside, to leave you alone."

Elaine half-turned to her.

"But it wasn't me, was it? Your leaving had nothing to do with me."

Elaine's attention focused downriver, and Hannah turned to Stew, to Jesse and Gina with Bran's body at Dead Man's Bend. On the opposite shore, on the reserve side, she saw herself, a young woman, her body lying half out of the water, floodwaters rising to her waist. Alex was there in the mud with her, dragging Hannah's body away from the river. He had jumped into the water for Hannah. He had risked his life to save her. All around her the suspended raindrops were so thick they appeared to be a transparent curtain, a waterfall, obscuring the view.

"I wanted to save you," Hannah told her mother. "I wanted to fix you, make you better, bring you home, but I couldn't." I *couldn't*, she thought, realizing the truth of what she was telling herself. She couldn't bring her mother home then, any more than she could bring Brandon home now. It was his journey to make. She had her own.

Hannah saw the flash of gold at her mother's feet and reached down to pluck it from the wet sand and gravel. A ring, a gold wedding band. She offered it to her mother. "Is this it? Is this what you're looking for?"

Elaine looked at Hannah as if seeing her there for the first time. The confusion lifted from her face. "The ring," she said. "We found it here."

"You found it here." The ring had been slipped over a bullet and had been fixed there by grit and time. This was the same ring—Hannah recognized the jeweller's marks— though it no longer held the bullet.

Elaine took the ring from her and slipped it on her finger. She looked directly at Hannah. "I've been looking for this for so long." She held out her hand to admire the ring and turned it on her finger. "Now I can go."

Elaine stepped onto the river and then headed downstream, walking on the surface of the water.

"Mom, wait!"

Hannah tried to follow, but the river swallowed her and pulled her down, even as her mother walked on. "Mom!" She struggled to keep her head above water. "Mom! Wait!" Her mother reached Dead Man's Bend, where Stew waited for her. They both looked back once before rounding the bend. Then they were gone. The eagle circled and cried, *eye-EYE!* and time moved on. The storm broke overhead. The raindrops, suspended the moment before, fell in a torrent. Hannah sank below the surface of river water.

"Hannah." A man's voice, familiar, shouting to make himself heard over the thunder of rain and river water. His voice was desperate. "Hannah, come back to me."

Hannah panicked, struggling towards the surface of consciousness as she would from a nightmare. She felt pressure on her chest, then again, and again, and then a kiss, lips on her mouth. No, he was breathing his own air into her. He was forcing life back into her. It hurt. Surfacing, she coughed up river water and woke into herself, into an aching chest, into stinging lungs, into biting cold.

Alex removed his hands from Hannah's chest and turned her on her side, to drain the fluid from her lungs. "Jesus, Hannah," he said. "I thought I lost you."

He lay beside her, spooning her as she coughed the water from her lungs, both half in, half out of the water. Rain pelted down on them, as the floodwaters rose. The air felt liquid, as if she was still submerged.

"Can you understand me?" he asked. "Do you know who I am?"

"Yes. An asshole."

She felt him laugh a little against her. "Do you know who you are?"

"An idiot."

"Good. You're okay then." He rubbed a cheek into her wet hair. "Hannah, I thought you were gone." He squeezed her and spoke into her ear, his breath the only warmth against her body. "I don't want to lose you again."

"I'm so cold."

He shifted her so that she was in his arms. "The river's rising fast. We've got to get out of here. Can you stand?"

"I think so." Then she remembered. Gina and Jesse and Bran at Dead Man's Bend. "Bran."

"He's across the river. The floodwaters are so high I'm not sure we can cross." He paused. "Hannah, I don't think he made it."

Together they looked through the curtain of rain at Gina and Jesse both huddled over Bran's body lying prone in the mud. Jesse's shoulders shuddered and his head was in his hands. He was sobbing.

"I've got to get across." She dragged herself on hands and knees up the slick bank and coughed up more of the water from her lungs. With Alex's help, she struggled to her feet, slipping before she finally gained ground.

Alex raised his voice to be heard over the torrent of rain and rush of river water. "We'll need a stick if we're going to try it." He rummaged in the nearby bush as Hannah shivered, waiting for him. He came back with two makeshift walking sticks. "Let's go," he said.

They kept their heads down as they pushed through the wind and stinging rain on their way to the shallows. Alex stepped into the river first, the water up to his thighs. "Come on," he shouted, holding out his hand. She took it and, hand in hand, they pushed their way through the water. At the centre point of the shallows, the rush of water was too much. Hannah slid and fell, gulping water. Alex pulled her back up and wrapped an arm around her. "Hold on to me," he shouted. She wrapped her arms around his neck and, with one hand around her waist and the other on the stick, Alex dragged them both through the floodwaters to the opposite shore.

The water had risen nearly to the top of the eroded bank that rimmed the pasture. Hannah scrambled up out of the water and onto the muddy bank. Alex followed, splashing through the muck and rain. Rain fell so thick Hannah felt she was swimming through it, breathing it, drowning in it.

Gina stood as Hannah and Alex sloshed through muddy water to reach them. "Thank god you're all right," she said. She took Hannah's arm and, together with Alex, led her to Jesse and her brother. Beneath the barbed-wire fence that hung over the bend, Jesse held Brandon and rocked him. Hannah was sure her brother was dead. She understood why Jesse rocked him, why Brandon had rocked himself within his blue room. She rocked herself now. "Oh, Brandon," she said.

But then her brother's face turned to the sound of her voice. "Hannah," he said.

She put both hands to her mouth. "You're okay!"

Bran pointed past her. "Look!" This time Hannah saw the boy when he did. A Shuswap kid about Brandon's age, naked, standing in the middle of the swollen river, standing on the rough, muddied water, as if it were uneven ground.

Dead Man's Bend

AS JESSE DROVE Hannah and Brandon home from emergency, the rain still fell so hard the wipers couldn't keep up, and he had to peer out the truck window to see the road in front of him. A passing car threw a wash of water over them. Lightning hit the fields on either side, and static crashed into the music on the Chevy's radio with each strike. Jesse clicked off the radio. "Christ," he said. "When is this going to let up?"

"Not until it's done," said Brandon.

Jesse laughed, thinking he had stated the obvious.

"Until what is done?" Hannah asked him.

The set of Brandon's mouth was grim. "We shouldn't go back home," he said. "Not yet."

"Where do you suggest we go?" Jesse asked him. Brandon didn't answer. He looked straight ahead, at the wash of water pouring down the windshield, obscuring the landscape around them.

They drove on. Trees along the side of the road thrashed back and forth. Jesse dodged one that fell in front of them, then struggled to control the truck in the raging wind. The driver of an approaching truck flashed his lights and honked as they met, apparently trying to tell him something, but Jesse kept going, driving through the stream of water that covered the road. The rain fell faster than it could drain.

Alex was standing at the red kitchen door under the roof overhang when they finally arrived in the farmyard. He held his jacket over his head as he sloshed towards them through the pool that covered the lane. Large drops pelted the water around him as if he was under fire. Hannah opened the truck door.

"We've got to go now," he said.

"What are you doing here?"

"I couldn't get back across—the river was too swollen. I waited inside. Hope you don't mind." He looked at Jesse.

Jesse leaned over Bran to talk to Alex. "Thank you for helping to find Brandon—and for saving my daughter's life." He paused. "I'm sorry about the things I said to you in the past."

"We can worry about all that later," said Alex. "Right now we've got to go."

"Go where?" Hannah asked.

"Doesn't matter. Anywhere on higher ground. The hall." He pointed at the community hall on the hillside above them. "Grant's going from house to house, warning people in the valley to leave. The logjam at the narrows has started to collapse. It isn't going to hold much longer."

Above the remains of the burned bridge, muddied stormwater had broken the banks and threatened to burst the log dam completely. Water already churned muddy and thick with debris into Gina's pasture and had begun to flow into Stew's fields as well. "Shit," said Hannah. "Spice." The mare was struggling to maintain her footing in the rushing water within her small pasture at river's edge. "We've got to get that horse out of there."

"Where's Gina?" Alex asked. "Can't she take care of it?"

Jesse said, "After she followed us into emergency, she headed back to her apartment."

"I've got to get Spice," Hannah said. She got out of the truck and ran through rain to the gate. Across the road, Spice had fallen and was now sliding backwards along the fenceline as the current tugged her along.

"Hannah," Alex called. "It's too dangerous."

"She'll die if I don't help her," Hannah called back.

Alex splashed through the water behind Hannah for a few yards, then stopped. "Hannah, don't. There's no time. Look." The torrent had undercut the bank at the entrance to the burned bridge and a chunk of gravel road slid into the water. The river was about to overwhelm the logjam at the narrows, threatening to flood the valley.

Hannah turned back to Alex. "Go!" she shouted. She nodded at the yard of the farmhouse. "Get Abby into the truck and head up to the hall with Jesse and Brandon. I'll ride Spice there."

"I'll give you a hand."

"No. Spice doesn't know you. There's nothing you can do." When she saw Alex hesitate, she called out again. "Go!"

Hannah climbed through the fence and waded to the horse. The mare was still down, backed into the corner of the fence where the ground had given way. Her back legs were stuck. She was without a halter and Hannah had no rope. She looked around in desperation. By the time she got to the barn and back, the horse would be swept into the river.

Hannah slid her belt from her jeans and looped it around the horse's neck, fastening it. Then she pulled with all her strength. "Come on, Spice, you can do this. Let's go!" At Hannah's urging, the horse struggled to her feet but then slid and fell again. The water was rising so quickly, Hannah thought Spice was lost, but then the horse hurtled forward onto more stable ground.

Hannah waited a moment as the horse recovered, patting her neck, then jogged with her through the water-filled pasture. As they reached the gate, Hannah heard a boom like that of an explosion and turned to the river. The thundering water had pushed through the dam, lifting the logs from the narrows. Water rushed out in all directions, surging into the pastures, flooding the reserve road, and pulling a soup of logs and debris in its wake that travelled downriver as a mass. On the far shore, trees toppled and power poles fell one after the other, the lines sparking and sizzling as they hit water. Cars were lifted and turned by the current. One flipped on its side, exposing its undercarriage. The people from the reserve had already scrambled to higher ground. Many of them now stood in front of the grave tent, staring down on the chaos below. The water was rolling across the orchard towards the Robertson farmhouse.

"Jesus, come on, Spice, let's go." Hannah jumped on the horse, grabbing her mane, and slapped the mare's rump. "Go!" she shouted. "Git!" The horse galloped up the road with Hannah struggling to stay astride. She hadn't ridden since the day of her mother's funeral. Jesse had waited with Brandon, Alex and Abby in the truck at the gate to make sure Hannah was okay. As Hannah charged past on the horse, Jesse revved out of the yard, fishtailing in a spray of water onto the road. Following Hannah, they raced the floodwaters up the hill to the hall. As Jesse parked the truck, Hannah remained on the horse as Spice cooled down, and she saw the swollen river swallow the valley floor. The development at the mouth of the river was completely destroyed. Only the cabs of the machinery were visible on the construction site. A pickup truck slid sideways towards the lake, dragged along by the rush of water. A half-finished house had been torn from its foundation and floated on the current.

Soon her grandfather's outbuildings, the ancient granaries, the machine shed and, finally, the barn were engulfed. One by one, the buildings slid sideways before collapsing into the waters. "Not the house," Hannah said under her breath. "Please not the house." But the river ate the farmhouse, too, lifting and then shifting the old building from its foundation. The rush of water dragged the building forward, and the house that Eugene Robertson had built floated like a boat over the drowned pasturelands, then downriver and around Dead Man's Bend.

— 34 —

River Restoration

JESSE RUMBLED IN the loader through the pasture towards the riverbank. Grasshoppers flew from his path, their wings shimmering in the heat of the summer day. On the opposite shore, logs and trees—deposited there by the flash flood that had burst the dam at the narrows that spring—lay in a row like dead awaiting burial. The development at the mouth of Lightning River was a tangled mess of upturned boards, trusses and two-by-fours. The reserve houses closest to the river had been torn apart, too, and his own farmhouse now sat on shore near the shallows, half in and half out of the river, sagging on one side.

For now, Jesse, Hannah and Brandon lived in a mobile home they'd parked near the crumbling foundation of the old house. Jesse planned to rebuild—the insurance would cover the cost—though all that would take time.

He stopped by the river and paused to take in the work ahead of him. The back of his elderly Chevy pickup, parked in the pasture closest to the river, was filled with bundles of willow and cottonwood saplings. A pile of logs and a second pile of boulders, unloaded there by dump trucks a few days before, sat ready. Jesse would move these down to the riverbank at Dead Man's Bend. He would lay the logs in rows along the shore to reinforce the bank and anchor them in place with rocks. Then Hannah and Alex would plant the young trees. The cuttings would spring to life and grow; their roots would hold the banks in place. Bush would once again line this river, as it had before Eugene Robertson and the other farmers and loggers had deforested the banks. Eventually the roots of those trees would take over as the logs beneath them rotted. Silt would no longer choke the spawning grounds and the estuary. The foliage would cool the river. Perhaps, over time, as the river healed itself, the sockeye would return.

Just as Brandon had, Jesse thought. His son sat on the pile of boulders now, watching the river's flow with keen interest, as if waiting for someone who was late. His doctor said he was making good progress. Brandon now spoke of his future, of going to art college, to Emily Carr. He took his medication voluntarily, and the new drug he was on appeared to be working, though Brandon didn't see his recovery that way. He claimed that after his grandfather had died, Stew searched for him on the spirit trail and helped him find his way back home. Brandon continued to maintain that his visions—of the transforming animals, the boy on the river—were real and not hallucinations. Jesse supposed it didn't much matter now, as Brandon also said he no longer saw these spirits. They were lost to him.

And Jesse no longer worried about Brandon leaving the house in the night or taking his own life as Elaine had, but still he was watchful.

Brandon looked up and waved at Jesse, then leapt down off the rocks, out of the way, thinking his father was waiting for him. Before starting to move the logs, Jesse glanced out the side window of the cab, to make sure Hannah wasn't in his blind spot. When he didn't see her, he scanned the landscape and spotted her walking hand in hand with Alex on the far shore, approaching the footings of the new bridge that was still under construction. As Hannah stooped to pluck a sprig of wild rose, her curls covered her face. Then she stood to face Alex, handing him the thorny stem heavy in rosehips. He bent the stem and tucked it into her hair as if it was a crown and she was a dark faery queen. She raised herself on the balls of her feet and kissed him, holding his face with both her hands.

In that moment Hannah made Jesse think kindly of himself. He was not his damaged father, nor his absent mother, not if he'd played any part in creating this beautiful woman, one capable now of such open affection and trust. Perhaps, this late in the game, he could still be a father to Hannah. He would, at the very least, help support her through university. He *must* be the father to Brandon, who would require his help for the unforeseeable future. Jesse could not leave this place, nor did he want to now. The thought was a revelation, and a relief.

Hannah and Alex linked hands again to hike towards the grave, and Jesse turned in his loader seat, back to the boulders, the logs, the river and his son.

Hannah rearranged her makeshift crown of rosehips and walked ahead of Alex, up the rise towards Samuel's grave. Here, at the edge of the bush above the river, ripe saskatoon berries hung on thickets of scruffy shrubs, their pomes laced with white spiderwebs that were nearly impossible to remove from the small fruit. Many of the berries not picked or eaten by birds would dry on the bush, shrivel like tiny prunes and stay on the stems throughout the fall and winter, feeding overwintering birds. Hannah pulled a lanky arm of the shrub down and pinched off several berries, rubbing off what she could of the spider's web, before popping them in her mouth. Seedy, not terribly sweet.

Red ants scurried on the path in such numbers that Hannah couldn't help but step on them, but she tried to avoid them nonetheless, walking at times on tiptoes. She felt Alex watching her as she walked. She felt the pleasure of her own hips.

Once they reached the grave, Alex held the tent flap open for Hannah, and the smell of earth rose up to greet her. "Careful," he told her. Her eyes took a moment to adjust to the dim light, and then she found herself right at the edge of the grave, looking down at the tiny backbone of the child curled like a sleeping infant.

The band council would hold a burial ceremony here in the coming week and the grave would be filled in shortly after. The band had come to an agreement with the developer to leave the remains of the child in place, by the side of the road, where they had been found. A concrete slab and monument would both mark and protect the grave from vandals or unscrupulous collectors who might seek to make an artefact of this poor child's bones. Construction crews would begin work on the development all over again at the mouth of the river once the bridge was rebuilt, and once the rezoning changes went through. Development almost always won out over other concerns. At least, she thought, this developer would not have the Robertson land, Jesse's land, her land.

Hannah had wanted to see Samuel before the grave was closed, before the monument was built, before development finally took over this place. She felt compelled to come here, to make some kind of connection with this child, her distant relative, and to the story that had led her to this peace, to Alex. She unzipped the tent window to cast more light into the grave, and the nugget of gold cupped within the child's finger bones shone. All at once Hannah was struck by this proof of Alex's and Stew's stories—Dennis's stories. Samuel *had* found that gold in the river. He had carried it to his mother. She had buried it with him in this grave. Perhaps the rest of the story was true as well.

"Did I really see that mystery the day I drowned?" Hannah asked Alex. "Or was that just a hallucination?"

"You tell me."

She pressed her lips together and shook her head. *Don't presume to speak of what you haven't seen or experienced,* Dennis had said. She supposed she could presume to speak of what she herself had seen. But what would she say? The only thing she knew with any certainty was what Alex had been telling her all along: the history of his people and hers wasn't back there, in the past; they lived it every day. The proof was here, in this tent. Dig away just a few shovelfuls of soil and here was their story, at her feet.

Libby had dug this grave for her child in a hurry: the evidence was in its shallowness, the misplaced bones. Very likely, Libby feared capture. She would have dug up this child's body from the reserve cemetery upriver and wouldn't have wanted to alert anyone to her labours, so she would have picked a moonless night. She would have dug in the dark, without a lantern, with that white picket fence of the grave around her. She had removed the cross before digging, propped it against the picket fence. Her child's grave was like every other here, and there were so many others. Only her son's name, chiselled into the cross, set it apart: *Samuel Robertson*. She had stolen the shovel she used from the bridge construction crew. The wooden bucket she had brought with her was the one she used to haul water from the river; she had woven the large basket from cedar.

Libby was in her early forties now, and drunk, drunk on a bottle of whisky she had bought from a white bridge worker with her body. The man's name escaped her at the moment, though he visited her cabin often. A regular. He liked her, too, and said he was thinking of staying in the region once the bridge was complete later that fall. Ernest, that was it. Ernie. Another damn Englishman. She stopped to take a drink from the bottle before returning to her digging.

In the river below her, many of the sockeye from that year's run were already dead, floating belly up in the water. But the smell of their rotting carcasses did not overwhelm the place as it had when Libby was a child, as so few salmon now returned.

After a time, she felt her shovel hit wood; she had reached the plain pine box Eugene had built for their son. She scraped away the remaining soil and used the shovel to pry the lid open. Water had seeped into the grave, rotted the bottom of the coffin and allowed the worms and insects to eat Samuel's garments and flesh. All that remained were his muddied bones.

Libby gathered her child's bones in the bucket and basket, feeling for them in the dark of the grave; the skull first, then the leg bones, the arm bones. Finally, she found the tiny, fragile bones of the fingers. These she tucked within the pocket of her apron. She left the hole of the grave open, left the empty bottle of whisky, too, and carried her son's bones to the river to wash them, bone by bone, beside the carcasses of dead sockeye.

Light had already hit the tops of the blue Shuswap hills that surrounded her; she would have to hurry. She carried her child's remains up to the benchland that overlooked the narrows, beneath the mystery painted on the cliff. She dug a shallow grave and arranged her son's bones within the earth as he would have slept within her as a foetus. She draped his bones with a new robe she had sewn from her own dress, a dress she had made from fabric Eugene Robertson had bought for her many years before, and placed within the delicate bones of her son's fingers the nugget of gold he had once brought her as a gift, the gold she had first given back to the river, and later retrieved, as a memory of him. Then she buried her child once again and swept his grave with the branches of rose bushes to keep Samuel's spirit from roaming this earth.

Eugene Robertson crossed the new bridge to reach Libby's cabin after dark, as she knew he would. He wouldn't venture across the river in daylight hours and risk being seen by his English wife. Libby had watched from across the river as this white woman named Mary had tended her garden, brought flowers into the cabin Robertson had built for Libby, as she produced and then raised Robertson's children. A girl. A girl. And finally a boy. His legacy. Libby watched the cabin grow into a house as Eugene added a front parlour and then a second floor, with bedrooms for himself and Mary and their children. Eugene wouldn't have told Mary he had another wife across the river, but then Eugene and Libby had never had a ceremony or piece of paper between them. Only history and the bones of a dead child.

Robertson, her husband, limped as he made his way to her door. His body had clearly grown tired of him and his habits.

"Where have you put my son?" he demanded, as she opened the door, holding a candle.

"You're so old now," she said. His hair was white, not the ginger it had once been. But he was still freckled. He was as spotted as a trout.

"And you've become fat," he said.

The flame of the candle flickered in the wind and almost went out. She cupped her hand to it to keep it alight. She wasn't fat. She had only grown womanly. The boyish figure of her girlhood marriage had blossomed into one that the men of the bridge crew had found comely enough to pay for.

"Where is my boy?" Eugene asked again.

Libby didn't answer. Eugene looked away from her, at the silhouettes of the ragged garden in the dark. These people hadn't learned to work the soil, he thought. Farming wasn't in their blood. Even so, they made their attempts, now that homesteaders increasingly fenced the land that had once fed them, now that they were forced to live on these tiny tracts of land, these reserves.

"You've taken up whoring," he said. He had seen the men from the bridge crew make their way to this cabin. Libby had never been worth his effort, the time he had taken to teach her to read, so she would be able to teach their children; the money he had spent on fabric so she could fashion herself a decent dress.

"My husband won't support me," she said. "My sister can't feed her own children, much less me."

"I could have you arrested," he said. "Desecrating a grave is a crime."

"Does Mary know you're here? Does she know about me? Should I introduce myself?"

"You've been drinking. I can smell the whisky on you."

"So have you."

The wind blew up, snuffing the candle, and the two of them stood at the threshold in darkness.

"I could come in," Robertson said finally. "I sold a mare and her colt this week. I have a little money."

He couldn't see her face and she said nothing, but after a time she stepped back into the cabin and allowed him to enter.

— 35 —

The Spawning Grounds

HANNAH AWOKE IN Alex's arms, in his bed, to find they had been engaged in lovemaking while still submerged in dreams, her body and his swimming together of their own accord. Alex was still deep within those dark waters, she could tell. His half-opened eyes looked through her, rather than at her, as a man does when he is about to come, though she could tell he wasn't there yet. His small room hugged the used double bed they nested within, and a string of tiny, solar-powered lights lit the ceiling above them; Alex had hung them there for Hannah, and arranged them, she realized only now, to resemble the Milky Way. The wooden horse that Eugene had carved for Samuel sat on the dresser. It belonged to them both now.

"You awake?" she whispered. When he didn't answer, she asked, "Where are you?"

He went on touching her as if she hadn't spoken, and she opened to him, pulled him deep inside, wrapped herself

around him, and he came. Then, finally waking, Alex kissed
Hannah's cheeks, her hair, her collarbone. He ran his hand
down her torso and strummed her as he would his gui-
tar, leisurely, taking his time, the melody going nowhere
in particular.

She drifted, floating on the perimeter of sleep as if on
water lapping the shore, dreaming of Leviathan, an enor-
mous fish swimming in the water at her feet. Within her the
possibility of a child swam upriver, navigating the underground crevices of her body as salmon fry chart tiny water-
ways under rock, until it reached her redd. Her single egg
drew this potential towards itself, pulled this possibility in,
and the bloom of life began, here in this riverbed inside her.

On the opposite shore, a boy watched her. He nodded
when she saw him and waved her over before going back to
his task, reinforcing the shoreline with rocks and fallen trees,
planting saplings that would eventually shade and protect
the river. Hannah picked her way across the water at the
shallowest point and joined him, to shovel out small holes
and step willow and cottonwood saplings into the ground.
When they had completed this chore, Hannah and the boy
brushed the dirt from their hands and stooped to gather the
sun-bleached bones of the sockeye from the river-rounded
stones on shore.

Some skeletons were complete, the eyeholes of their
skulls staring up at the sky. Others were scattered by scav-
engers, and Hannah had to pick up the bones one by one,
placing them within a cedar basket the boy had provided
for her. When their baskets were full, Hannah and the boy

tossed the bones into the water. Beneath the water's surface, the bones coalesced, took form and grew flesh. The tails of the salmon beat as the fish leapt back to life. The salmon transformed further, from the blue and silver of the open sea to the red of a sockeye returning to the river. One by one, the mature salmon gathered at the spawning grounds, to hover over their stone nests in shallow water—this blessed place of both endings and beginnings—to spawn and die, to spawn and die, to spawn and die, and live.

Acknowledgements

THERE ARE HUNDREDS of salmon spawning streams and rivers in British Columbia. I've set this work of fiction in my home country, the Thompson–Shuswap region, one of the largest salmon spawning areas in North America. The Lightning River and surrounding community in this novel do not exist, however, and are intended as a mythic representation of our interactions with all our salmon-bearing rivers, both in the past and present. I offer my thanks to the volunteers—including my husband, Mitch Krupp—who worked on river restoration projects throughout British Columbia and in Ontario and showed me their work and answered my questions over the last decade.

A great many books on the history, cultures and rivers of British Columbia offered inspiration for this novel—too many to list here. The following publications were of particular use: *The Shuswap* by James Teit, edited by Franz Boas (E.J. Brill, 1909); *Shuswap Stories, Collected 1971–1975*, edited by Randy Bouchard and Dorothy I. D. Kennedy (CommCept, 1979); and Mark Hume's *The Run of the River: Portraits of Eleven British Columbia Rivers* (New Star, 1992). *Shuswap History: A Century of Change* by Annabel Cropped Eared Wolf (1996); and *Shuswap History: The First 100 Years of Contact* (1990) by John Coffey et al. were both produced by the Secwepemc Cultural Education Society in Kamloops. I found inspiration for parts of this novel in the "Story of the TsôlenU'et's Son" which appears on pages 669 and 670 of Teit's *The Shuswap*. Dennis's story in Chapter 14, "Bones of the Salmon," is based on this story. The dances in Chapter 20, "The Crow," are a recounting of dances described in *Shuswap Stories*, pages 130 and 131.

The epigraph for *The Spawning Grounds* is by Alan Haig-Brown, from his introduction to Mark Hume's *Adam's River: The Mystery of the Adams River Sockeye* (New Star, 1994). The first chapter of this novel was inspired in part by an account written by David Salmond Mitchell in his unpublished manuscript, "A Story of the Fraser River's Great Sockeye Run and Their Loss" (1925).

"The Raggedy Man" is by James Whitcomb Riley from *The Golden Book of Poetry* edited by Jane Werner (Golden Press, New York: 1966). The quote from Edgar Allan Poe is from "The Tell-Tale Heart." The signs of protest as well as other signs throughout the novel were inspired by or taken wholesale from real signs posted along actual rivers throughout British Columbia and Ontario.

My deepest appreciation goes to Anne Collins, who helped me to sculpt my initial draft into the story you see here, and to my agent, Jackie Kaiser, for her invaluable advice and encouragement over the years it took to write this novel.

Lastly, I'm grateful to the Canada Council for the Arts for financial support as I wrote the first draft of this novel.

GAIL ANDERSON-DARGATZ has been published worldwide in English and in many other languages in more than fifteen territories. *A Recipe for Bees* and *The Cure for Death by Lightning* were international bestsellers, and were both finalists for the Giller Prize. *The Cure for Death by Lightning* won the UK's Betty Trask Prize, the BC Book Prize, the VanCity Prize, and was shortlisted for the Chapters/*Books in Canada* First Novel Award. Both *Turtle Valley* and *A Rhinestone Button* were national bestsellers in Canada. Her first book, *The Miss Hereford Stories*, was shortlisted for the Leacock Award for humour. She currently teaches fiction privately through online forums and lives in the Shuswap in south-central BC, the landscape found in so much of her writing.

For more, visit Gail's website, gailandersondargatz.ca, and follow her on Twitter @AndersonDargatz.